I0527605

PURSUIT OF THE WEAPON FROM HELL

by

William Hallstead

The contents of this book regarding the accuracy of events, people and places depicted; permissions to use all previously published materials; all are the sole responsibility of the author, who assumes all liabiliaty for the contents of this book.

© 2015 William Hallstead

All rights reserved. Except for fair use educational purposes and short excerpts for editorial reviews in journals, magazines, or web sites, no part of this book shall be reproduced, stored in a retrieval system, or transmitted by any means without the written permission of the publisher.

International Standard Book Number 13: 978-1-60452-066-8
International Standard Book Number 10: 1-60452-066-3
Library of Congress Control Number: 2015945088

BluewaterPress LLC
52 Tuscan Way Ste 202-309
Saint Augustine FL 32092

http://bluewaterpress.com

This book may be purchased online at -

http://www.bluewaterpress.com/pursuit

Also by the author

Hard Days in Paradise
Raging Skies
River of Madness

Writing as "William Beechcroft"

Position of Ultimate Trust
Image of Evil
The Rebuilt Man
Chain of Vengeance
Secret Kils
Pursuit of Fear

In the late 1950s and early 1960s, U.S. scientists at California's Ernest O. Lawrence Radiation Laboratory (now the Lawrence Livermore National Laboratory) were developing a nuclear-powered, multi-warhead cruise missile. Shortly after they successfully tested the missile's engine, the entire project was determined to have such an unacceptably huge mass-destruction potential, it was canceled.

1.

Though their faces were ebony in the Arizona desert night, the skinny driver and the big man beside him in the truck's cab were not African-Americans. They weren't Americans at all. They were Iranian, and they had come here in a sacred mission: to steal.

For this, the bony little driver thought, I've been waiting so long. An impatient "sleeper" in the Great Satan's big city of Chicago. Driving a garbage truck awaiting ultimate glory.

The other man in the truck's cab, his arms bulging the sleeves of his rumpled shirt, snapped on his pencil of a flashlight to consult his Texaco road map for the third time since they had rumbled south out of Tucson on Interstate I-19.

"Turn here," he said.

The small man's native tongue was Farsi. The big man was from Southeastern Iran, and his language was Arabic. So they both spoke Arabic, which put the small man at an even further disadvantage.

The bony little driver swung their flatbed truck into the deceleration lane and braked cautiously down its slope. They had rented the truck in Phoenix, shortly after they met as planned at Sky Harbor International Airport. Now ten miles south of Tucson, he still wasn't certain he had mastered this cumbersome vehicle, its turns affected by the weight of the hydraulic crane and a crate of nylon strapping mounted on the flatbed's planking.

Ten minutes later, they neared an intersection with a crossroad. The big man in the passenger seat of the jouncing cab jabbed his thumb leftward. The driver pulled off the interstate and turned westward on the macadam crossroad. The engine roared back up to speed. They rumbled in the warm darkness, deeper into the desert. Minutes later, as they neared a T-intersection with another, narrower macadam road winding off to the right, the big Iranian leaned forward. He checked the roadway ahead and behind them. Not another vehicle's lights in sight.

"Slow. Turn in there, then all lights out," he ordered. And he flicked on a penlight.

Navigating the dark macadam with only the dim glow of the damned penlight was misery. But the driver's night vision turned out to be acute. He ran off the roadway only once, fortunately into nothing worse than low cactus jutting from flat hardpan. His passenger only grunted as the driver clashed gears and eased the rig back onto the lane to resume picking their way through the scrub. A few minutes later, they reached their destination, a place that even in broad daylight no average tourist would consider visiting. "Stop here," the big man growled.

Here? The driver squealed the big flatbed and its crane to a stop along a chainlink fence. What kind of destination is this aircraft junkyard?

In the post-midnight silence, he heard only the ticks of the cooling engine. To the north, a faint glow just above the starlit horizon marked the locations of downtown Tucson and Davis-Monthan Air Force Base near the city's southern outskirts. Miles into the desert scrub, not a single light was visible. Nothing lives here, the driver thought, but ghosts.

Within the eight-foot-high chainlink fence that enclosed a huge compound, the aerial relics of three wars moldered. Their corroding wings, rotors and tail assemblies formed a jumble of eerie silhouettes against the distant city's faint glow. This was a massive graveyard for surplus military aircraft. In this desert limbo, they awaited the scrap merchant, or the museum curator, or desert rot. In the cool night air, the driver smelled traces of stale oil, gasoline and oxidizing metal.

"So what now?" he wondered.

"Now we drive a tenth of a mile from this corner," his passenger told him..

Ghostly himself in a white shirt and light-colored slacks ill-chosen for clandestine night work, the driver peered at the fence. A tenth of a…mile.

He silently cursed this arrogant country's refusal to convert to the easily understood metric system.

He shifted into low, and they crawled along the compound's fencing.

The big man from the Baluchistan mountain town of Khash "superior to your Shiraz, the 'City of Poets,'" he had grunted during their drive south, had immediately taken charge and treated the driver as an inferior. Perhaps that was justified to a degree by the fact that the man from Khash knew what their assignment was. But once they were headed down 19, he told the driver nothing.

Now, more than two hours into their trip and some miles south of Tucson, the driver still had no idea what they were looking for, and finally said so.

"Three crates. Marked with orange. Stored along the fence."

"Convenient," the driver dared mutter.

"*Filoos*. Money. It talks with a loud voice."

The arrogant man played his tiny beam through the fence. They passed the towering vertical fin of a military transport... a bomber's crumpled tail assembly...the shattered greenhouse nose of disintegrating helicopter...

Just beyond the helicopter, they spotted spray-painted orange blotches on each of three crates. The smallest of the slat-reinforced containers looked more than two meters long. Seven "feet," the driver thought disdainfully, and less than two meters in width and height. The other two marked crates were impressively larger, each perhaps eight meters long and well over two meters in height and width. No wonder he had been instructed to arrange for a flatbed equipped with a power crane.

In the penlight's narrow beam, the driver noticed a small bush had been flattened outwards beneath the near edge of the smaller crate. So they had been placed here recently, parallel to the fence on eight-by-eight-inch timber runners. A good thing, he thought. Otherwise there would be no way to slip our heavy nylon straps beneath the boxes to form lifting cradles.

"Turn the truck around," the man from Khash ordered. That made sense. Better to turn around empty, the driver realized. But he needed all his skill to manhandle the big truck around to face the way they would go out loaded. When he finally shut off the engine and dropped down from the cab: another order.

"You can climb easier than I. Go up and over. I will throw you the straps and lifting rings."

The driver clawed up the chainlink and dropped inside to stand in weeds beside one of the two large crates. Did desert rattlesnakes prowl at night? Despite the big man's assurance, might this facility be patrolled? Now that they were in the very act of stealing U.S. Government property, the driver felt far less secure than he'd felt back on the highway, perched high in the cab of their rented flatbed.

A clump of strapping and steel lifting rings thudded into the weeds beside him. Rigging the first of the two big containers with a makeshift hoisting cradle was more difficult than he expected. The skids had been set far enough from the ends of the huge box so he was not forced to worm his way through the narrow air space beneath. Yet nearly ten minutes were needed to double-strap the crate, then rig the strapping to the lifting rings. Uncertain of the weight in the container, he used three of the steel rings.

When he again stood outside the fence, he was filthy, sweating, and silently furious at the big man from the "superior" town of Khash; he who had done no more than toss the strapping over the fence.

"I will operate the crane," the driver said, trying to harden his tone. "You guide the hook through the rings."

"I prefer that you do that, yourself."

"Do you know how to operate the crane?"

In the penlight's dim glow, the big man scowled at him.

"Then you will have to climb the fence." The driver was glad darkness concealed his self-satisfaction. The man from superior Khash had an air of cold purpose that made the driver's gut crawl.

The first container, for all its bulk, was not impressively heavy. The crane handled it well. Two more times the driver scuttled over the fence to rig the second and third crates. He was not accustomed to this kind of activity. On his last scramble, his hands slipped. The sharp ends of the twisted wire at the top of the fencing snagged his shirt pocket.

"*Damn!*" he muttered in English. He dropped outside and bent down. "*Noor, noor!* The light."

The big man grunted in irritation and grudgingly swung the penlight beam toward the driver, now on his knees outside the fence.

"My dark glasses and pen." He fanned his hands across the weedy sand. "Ah, here are the glasses."

"*Yalla!* Let's go!"

"The pen..."

"Forget the cursed pen. *Yalla!*" The big man clicked out the light, lumbered up the chainlink fence and thudded down inside to guide the hook to its cable rings. Deftly handling the flatbed's crane, the driver eased the final, smaller crate well forward, across the pair of much larger, longer crates. When the big man grunted back over the fence, they lashed all three big boxes securely in place with the lifting straps.

When they had finished, the man from superior Khash growled, "Hold the light."

From the cab, the big man took a small carton. The stuff I was told to buy in Chicago, the driver noted, then mail to myself at General Delivery in Phoenix.

From the carton, the man from Khash pulled out a can of spray paint and a roll of stiff paper secured by a rubber band. He snapped off the band and unrolled the paper, a stencil. Together they worked for another fifteen minutes to paint the exposed sides of the crates in black letters: REFRIGERATION UNITS.

The big man returned to silence as they rolled away from the aircraft graveyard and retraced their route along the access lane, again using only the penlight to pick their way. When they turned onto the wider macadam stretch, the driver switched on the running lights. The headlight beams cut into the pre-dawn blackness as the driver and his unpleasant passenger settled back for the thirty-mile pull to the Mexican border.

***

As the horizon paled in false dawn's dim wash, the driver's head throbbed. His muscles ached. This was not the glamorous kind of adventure he had expected when he agreed to travel from Iran to America and become what had they called it? A Chicago-based "sleeper" for Khomeini's purposes. He would be glad to return to Chicago.

They rumbled past an isolated all-night gas stop and diner. The driver wiped his face with a grimy handkerchief. "We could have stopped at that place for breakfast."

"We do not stop until we are there."

"Until we are where?"

"I will tell you when you need to know."

The scarred man didn't tell the driver for the next twenty miles. Not until they suddenly roared into Nogales. The driver braked heavily. Ahead, shadowed by a steep hill from the just-risen sun, stood a rampart of gates.

"What?" the driver asked, stupefied by the all-night drive and the bone-grinding labor at the aircraft graveyard.

"The Mexican border. Tell them we are American citizens delivering to Mexico City. A load of refrigeration parts."

In this dead hour of the morning at the Nogales entry plaza, everyone was half-awake. That worked well. But even if the official had wanted to check, would he have known what the items in the big crates really were? The driver himself did not know.

The uniformed Customs man waved them through. So easy? The driver had heard bribery at the border was not unusual. He shrugged to himself, shifted up through the gears to put them back in their steady, kilometer-eating pace, now into the hilly Sonoran desert.

For the next 160 miles, the man from Khash dozed while the driver fought to stay awake. The highway rolled on and on through seemingly endless wasteland until they passed a sign announcing a town ahead.

"Hermosillo," the driver said.

His passenger grunted awake. *"Eyh?* What?"

"The city of Hermosillo. Ahead."

"Take second turn left."

It came up so fast, the driver almost missed it. They screeched hard left, then resumed their deadening pace from Hermosillo's outskirts back into the desert.

Thirty minutes later, on a long, straight stretch of the narrow pavement, the big man checked the empty highway ahead and to the rear, then pointed at an approaching dirt lane.

"Turn there."

The driver swung the cumbersome truck leftward off the pavement, and they rumbled into a dirt lane through desert scrub. What seemed like endless, gritty, rock-strewn kilometers later, they passed through a cut in a high ridge. The driver was stunned by the sudden appearance of a broad valley. In its center sprawled a sizable construction site.

The scarred man pointed. "Left, around the construction trailer. Pull up behind it."

As he swung the flatbed around the office trailer, the driver glanced across the cab through the passenger window at a tall wooden structure rising from the valley floor. Living quarters for workers? Among the scatter of shacks between here and the central building lay stacks of building materials.

"Stop here at the foot of the ridge," the arrogant passenger told him. He squealed the truck to a halt. The man from Khash clambered out. "Wait here." He strode off and the driver watched him requisition a crew of laborers from the construction site The fast way that was done told the driver the big man was in authority here.

Some of the workmen appeared to be Iranian, but not all of them. To the driver's surprise, they were ordered to enshroud the truck and its cargo with sand-colored camouflage netting. Then the big man told all but two of the crew to return to the work site.

The two who remained stood behind him with folded arms. As if they awaited word to do something more. The driver, the man who had guided him here, and the two laborers were now hidden from everyone else by the truck and its concealing nets. In the morning's growing heat, the little driver from Chicago suddenly felt ice rush through his veins.

Something was very wrong. He could not believe the big man from superior Khash had just pulled a fat-nosed pistol from his waistband beneath his baggy shirt. Nor could he believe what was happening when the 9mm slug exploded his skull.

***

As the sun rose above the valley's western ridge the big man from Khash, Sayyid Zul-Junnah, set down his cardboard cup of thick, Mideastern-style coffee. This construction trailer was an oven. At present, the project's generators serviced only the camp's canteen, but would, of course, also cool the big central building, now close to completion.

He rose from the metal chair to peer through the trailer's single front window. Three hundred meters distant, the raw board siding of that two-story "barracks" building was now the most prominent feature of this remote broad valley ringed with its sandstone ridges.

Zul-Junnah had expected unrest with the mixed labor crew, but through the past two weeks the non-believers seemed happy with the money and the "oil field" cover story. Three drilling rigs would be set in place and go into action shortly. Each of the Iranians and like-minded believers had been individually sworn to secrecy by Zul-Junnah himself, and each had been assured swift and appropriate punishment would be administered to anyone who broke his sworn word. The offending tongue would be removed.

Zul-Junnah doubted that any of his true believers could have conversed with the project's several dozen infidel workers, even if they wanted to. They had trouble enough conversing among themselves in Farsi, Arabic, Syriac, and only Allah knew what else. But all were united in the determination that the new softness toward the West by the officialdom of Iran was a deplorable error. In his heart, Zul-Junnah was certain the old way was the best way, that only a spectacular terror action against the Great Satan could restore sanity to the wavering governments of Islam.

He found the coffee cup back in his hand. Was he that nervous? He had taken care to shoot the miserable son of a dog from Shiraz on the side of the truck away from the worksite. The pop of his small, Egyptian-made Helwan pistol surely had been swallowed by the around-the-clock construction noise. Before daybreak the body had been concealed and buried a distance from the work site by the two laborers who had witnessed the execution, both of them trusted former members of Hisballah.

No, there was no way the Mexican non-believers out in the construction area could have seen the shooting and burial. He was concerned only slightly with them. They would be sent back to their villages before this work site would be converted to its true purpose. Convinced this was yet another drilling site to be operated by prospecting Saudis, they would remain ignorant of its true purpose.

The truck driver was to return to Chicago at Zul-Junnah's discretion, but from the moment they had met in Phoenix, Zul-Junnah distrusted the scrawny little man. Two years of Western softness had made him unworthy of trust, but his skill with the truck and crane was temporarily needed. Back at the aircraft storage yard, Zul-Junnah closely observed the crane's operation. Now he was confident he himself could handle its next use.

Sayyid Zul-Junnah was proud of his work. He had come a long way from his first crude revolutionary efforts, the brutal street beatings he had enjoyed administering to the Shah's loyalists during the Iranian riots in 1978. He had been Sayyid Bakhtiar then, only eighteen; big-shouldered, hard-muscled, in the prime of youthful revolt against Pahlavi's hated SAVAK. They had arrested him, beaten him purple with fists, then with truncheons, one of those butchers cutting his cheek open with the backhanded blow of a fist armed with a jagged finger ring.

They had dumped him back in the street, bloody, with every joint aching. A worse shock was to come when he stumbled home to find that SAVAK had not been satisfied to arrest and beat him. Just inside the door, he found his father, face down, shot four times in the back. In the bedroom lay his mother, naked, her legs spread wide from bloody violation. She had been shot in both breasts.

His shoe rolled on the ejected cartridge cases that littered the floor. He picked one up. American-made, with U.S. stamped on its base.

His smoldering detestation of the Shah burst into a searing flame of hatred, not only for everything the Pahlavi rule stood for; now it extended to the Great Satan. That infidel nation had supplied the bullets that slaughtered his father and mother. When Khomeini so cleverly seized power, Sayyid Bakhtiar rejoiced.

He eagerly joined jihad-dedicated Hizballah, though it was essentially Lebanese. Iranian-backed, the organization was intent on establishing a Shiite Islamic state in Lebanon and was actively anti-America. In 1983, Hizballah engineered the truck bombing that killed 241 U.S Marines and sailors in their Beirut headquarters. Six years later, Hizballah disposed of the hated American colonel, William Higgins. And Sayyid Bakhtiar firmly believed the group was behind the bombing of the French jet liner over Niger that same year, killing 171 passengers. On a daring raid into the Christian Quarter that same year, the team led by Bakhtiar had captured then executed fourteen Lebanese officers. His speed and ruthlessness on that raid earned Sayid Bakhtiar the nickname Zul-Junnah, "Winged Wolf," which he promptly took for his own.

As his reputation for leadership grew, this penchant for involving himself in combat actions brought him a tersely worded reprimand. A truly great leader, he was informed, does not expose himself to possible disablement or death.

"That would be cowardice!' he roared at the hapless messenger.

"Nevertheless," the cringing little man whined, "it is believed such a habit may lead to disaster."

"Habit?" Zul-Junnah roared. "*Habit?*" And the shaken messenger fled the room.

Habit, indeed. Whatever the risk, Zul-Junnah could not possibly sit in idleness while barely trustworthy minions jeopardized what he had been sent to accomplish here in the Mexican desert. He had to oversee every detail, a demanding yet necessary requirement for his kind of leadership.

He did not know who had conceived this brilliant plan. Someone, no doubt, with access to the incredibly specific American military publications. Someone disgusted with the current lack of initiative by the Abu Nidal Organization, or perhaps a defector from the now-moribund

Popular Front for the Liberation of Palestine. Both groups had been disappointments during the recently ended Gulf War.

But credit was unimportant. What mattered was that, through his contact with a man of indeterminate nationality in Lebanon, nearly thirty of the most impatient and aggressive defectors from those organizations were filtered into Mexico to unite here. The mission: produce a spectacular event that would stun the entire world with its audacity and destructive power.

The office trailer vibrated as someone mounted the steps outside. The plywood door was opened by Nasr Ilahi, the "Divine." Some name, Zul Junnah thought, for his ape-shaped foreman sent here from Teheran to oversee construction. Though Ilahi was a fellow Iranian, he did not have Zul-Junnah's full trust. But it was Zul-Junnah's policy to be distrustful of everyone until proof otherwise was demonstrated several times over.

He had not trusted the bespectacled contact man from the shadowy "Committee of Three" until the Committee's plan was revealed to him so many months ago. The nervous go-between with steel-rimmed glasses would not, or could not, identify the Committee. But it proved to have apparently unlimited resources, financial and otherwise, to support this project that set Zul-Junnah's heart racing.

"It is hot as the very gates of hell out there," Ilahi snorted in his northern-accented Farsi. He tossed his hardhat on the battered desk.

"You chose your words well," Zul-Junnah said. "When our work is completed, this will indeed be the gate of hell."

"Praise Allah that the brains behind this," he swept his brawny arm toward the activity beyond the trailer's windows. "This wondrous plan knows what they are doing."

Sayyid Zul-Junnah fixed his eyes on Ilahi's. Behind the foreman's thick features the man was impossible to read. Yet had not Ilahi been hand-picked by the Committee itself?

"I suggest you concentrate on the derricks," he said. "Should someone in authority we have not 'accommodated' appear here in search of an oil exploration site, we had better look and act like one."

"As we speak, the first derrick is about to rise," Ilahi the Divine said with irritating satisfaction. "Beyond the 'barracks' building. You cannot see it from here. It will be necessary for you to walk out on the site."

A carelessly thrown barb, Zul Junnah thought. Does not this construction minion realize who I am? But he stroked his ragged scar and hid his feelings behind a mask of equanimity.

"How much longer to complete the initial construction phase, Ilahi?"

The foreman fingered his thick mustache. "With all building materials now on site, we should finish that phase in no more than a week."

"A week?"

"One more week."

"We are dealing largely with local labor, Zul-Junnah, men inspired not by this glorious mission, but by paychecks. The second phase, after the locals have departed, should move faster. This initial construction is not so easy with so many unskilled workers."

"Do not expect me to sympathize, Nasr Ilahi."

Not after the week I've just gone through, Zul-Junnah thought. Two trips from Phoenix to Tucson. First to get the cursed crates moved to the fence; a complex operation in itself. Then back to Phoenix to arrange for the truck and crane. The wait for the driver from Chicago. The jouncing springless truck drive back to Tucson for the acquisition. Then the much longer ride to this Mexican desert shit hole. All of it exacting and exhausting. And here was Ilahi complaining.

Zul-Junnah glared straight into his wavering little pig eyes. "Yours is the easy part."

2.

A t 9:30 a.m. two days later, a borrowed Davis-Monthan AFB staff car nosed through the gate of the isolated junk-aircraft storage compound. Its passenger, a sixty-year-old, stoop-shouldered representative from the Elmo Gridley Foundation, sat in the front passenger seat exuding self-importance. The driver, a chubby young captain named Larssen, instinctively felt a degree of irreverence toward official civilian visitors.

"Were you ever in the military?" Larssen could not resist asking as he slid back into the car after unlocking and swinging open the compound's gate. The aircraft graveyard was deserted, personnel appearing only for occasional inspections and to meet specific requests such as today's.

The Foundation man, gazing through steel-rimmed glasses at the ranks of obsolete, dead-storage aircraft, said, "No."

He sure isn't one for conversation, the captain thought. Larssen had hoped for maybe a mellow World War II vet, a "Brownshoe Air Force" man who would help lighten this dull chore with a tale of Schweinfurt or Ploesti. No such luck. The Foundation man was buttoned-down business, here to select a... "What is it you're after, sir?"

"A B-25 Mitchell bomber. The Foundation hopes to find one in restorable flying condition."

"Why a B-25?"

"Because Mr. Gridley flew one in the Pacific." The man's tone hinted at disdain for this whole foray.

"Do you know anything about B-25s?"

"I don't have to know anything about B-25s, Captain. I just have to acquire one to satisfy a rich man's whim."

"If he flew in the Big War, he must be at least seventy or so now. He's not planning to fly a Mitchell himself?"

"No, no. He's planning to use it to raise money for the Elmo Gridley Military Aircraft Museum." The Foundation man took off his specs and polished them with his handkerchief. "My time here is limited, Captain. Could we...?"

"Sure thing." Larssen fed in a tad more gas, and the car bounced along the weed-strewn hardpan between the rows of deteriorating aircraft. Damned shame, all this. Talk about a throwaway society.

"Supposed to be one somewhere along the south fence...unless someone else got it since I checked the inventory runout after you called last month. World War II war birds are in demand these days."

He swung around the squatty nose of a battered C-130 Hercules. Those things were still in production. This one must have been one of the first off the assembly line in the 1950s.

A hundred feet further on, Larssen pointed. "Right along there... That's odd."

"What's odd, Captain?"

"Something's been removed from there, but we haven't received any record of that up at the base where the inventory is kept."

Larssen stopped the car and peered at the gap between two deteriorating helicopters. No tire imprints, but half a dozen eight-by-eight timbers lay evenly spaced in the scruffy ground along the fence. Timbers, Larssen knew, of the kind used to provide space beneath crates for front-end loaders' prongs.

"Captain, my time is quite limited."

Impatient son of a bitch. Larssen pressed the accelerator, and the car bounced on. In the southwest corner of the fencing, they did find a B-25. Its tires were flat and deteriorating but the airframe seemed not overly battered.

For the first time since the captain had picked him up at Davis-Monthan, the Foundation rep smiled. "Stop right here, Captain. I'll take a closer look."

When he stepped out, heat swirled into the air-conditioned car. Hell with this guy, Larssen decided. Let him look at it by himself. He stayed behind the wheel, engine running, A/C on MAX.

It was a go. Back at base HQ, Larssen signed the transfer documents. Then the thin, round-shouldered Easterner drove off in his Avis Dodge, back to Tucson International Airport.

Officially, that ended the captain's assignment, but he wasn't finished yet. He had his assistant, an efficient, ash-blonde, E-6 five-striper, call up the dead-storage crated inventory on her computer. He bent over her shoulder to squint at the readout. There were not a lot of crates in the graveyard down there. He asked her for a printout.

Good thing he hadn't yet turned in the borrowed car. Out in the broiling mid-day sun, he slid back behind the wheel now almost too hot to touch. "Dry heat," they bragged around here, as if that somehow made it less overpowering. So's an oven, he was fond of riposting, but look what it does to a turkey. He flipped the A/C back on MAX, drove out the main gate and headed south again.

An hour and forty-five minutes later, Larssen returned to base HQ, his suntans grubby with sweat and his face sunburned except for a wide, whitish V over his right eyebrow where the front of his "flight cap" had perched.

"All accounted for," he told his E-6, "except for these three particular crates." He showed her the storage location he had pencil-checked on the printout. "See what you can find out about these, Sergeant."

Within minutes, what she found out sent Larssen to the colonel in charge of the section. What he told the colonel prompted that senior officer to grab his phone and put through a priority call to a certain brigadier general at Fort Belvoir.

***

After he replaced the receiver, the general at Fort Belvoir, on the Virginia side of the Potomac south of Washington, gazed at the phone for a long moment. A former engineering officer, he was given to deliberate planning. Now nearing retirement age, he had become ever more evasive of potential pension threats.

Theft of the stored remains of Project Pluto? That call from the agitated colonel down there at Davis-Monthan was damned thought provoking. But was it the responsibility of the Air Force Intelligence Agency? Here at Belvoir, the AFIA supervised some 2,300 people worldwide — active duty, reserve and civilian—to collect and process information useful to Air Force brass. His people were trained as intelligence gatherers, and this Arizona thing did not quite fall into that category, did it? Developing the Global Awareness Program, preparing National Intelligence Estimates, and best-guessing Defense Intelligence Projections for Planning were solid AFIA responsibilities. But not the tracking of stolen AF artifacts, though the potential of this particular theft did send a chill along the general's aging spine.

He leaned back in his swivel and tented his fingers. Hadn't he gotten that call because the colonel at Davis-Montham had let one of his museum pieces wander away? That was a matter of a missing asset, the general decided. Whatever the importance of that asset, the fallout of its loss is "not in my department." The old bureaucratic lateral pass applied here. And the general knew in whose department this hot potato did belong. He reached for his phone again.

***

"You realize what that damned Pluto thing is, Ollie?" asked the one-star general at Fort Belvoir.

"I know what it *was*." Brigadier General Oliver Madden, a stumpy man built like an aging weight lifter, spun his chair to his office window's view across the junction of the Potomac and Anacostia Rivers, toward downtown Washington. "I think they called it the 'Weapon from Hell.' Cruise missile with a load of multiple A-bombs. Cute idea, but it was nuclear powered and would have laid a poisonous radioactive wake. It was bagged years ago. Too dangerous to fly over friendly territory."

"Why do you suppose anybody would want to steal such a thing?" asked the general at Belvoir. "How would they even know about it?"

"Declassified reports. The components were junked, I assume."

"Actually they were stored, according to the fax from Davis-Montham. Engine and all--well, without the nuclear fuel rods, of course. Now somebody has stolen it from storage. Why do you suppose anybody would want to steal such a thing, Ollie." The voice at Belvoir had become so pleasantly conversational. Madden suddenly realized he wants to lay this thing on me.

"I'll give you odds it's not going to be set on a concrete pylon in front of some American Legion hall," Madden offered. "But Pluto was deactivated years ago."

"But if it could possibly be reactivated..."

"The potential could be staggering. Even a news leak of the theft would generate national jitters." God save me, Madden thought, this situation *does* belong here at my Air Force Office of Special Investigations.

"Your department, Oliver." Fort Belvoir had recognized the import of his silence.

Madden smiled tightly. "Yeah, no doubt about it. My department." He heard a sigh of relief. "Fax me everything you might have on this, Henry. Then hope to God we're involved in no more than an elaborate prank." He hung up and ran stubby fingers through his close-cropped reddish hair. His AFOSI investigators, eighty-five percent of them military and the balance trained reservists or civilians, delved into crimes by and against the Air Force. Assault, drug trafficking, *theft*, rape, and murder. No question. This oddball case of relic thievery was an AFOSI responsibility.

General Madden shoved his solid bulk out of his chair, careful to put his weight first on his good right leg. The left one had been rebuilt by damned fine surgeons after it caught a walnut-sized piece of white-hot flak over Hanoi. But he still limped a bit as he walked to his office doorway. Having come up through the ranks, he was averse to summoning his nearby aide by interoffice phone like some potentate on high.

"Lieutenant," he said to the just-out-of-the-Academy kid at the desk outside the door, "I need Major Pappas."

Not quite eight minutes later, the major was located and summoned. Pete Pappas, Madden thought as the major strode in, always manages to look like a preoccupied college senior. Trim as a tennis pro; IQ way up there. He had posted the third highest grades of any graduate of the Special Investigations Academy, one slot behind a reserve captain named Steve Gammon.

"Shut the door, Pete. I want to keep this quiet." Madden nodded at the office's conference corner, and they huddled.

"We've been handed an odd one, Pete. You ever heard of the Pluto project?"

Pappas's heavy eyebrows arched. "Pluto? The Romans' Devil?"

"I'm talking about a weapon, Major."

"Can't say I have."

"I'll give you until fourteen-hundred this afternoon to familiarize yourself with Project Pluto, then get straight back here."

"It may take a while to get clearance."

"Project Pluto is no longer classified, Pete. You won't need clearance."

The Aegean Collegian, as Madden had heard his subordinates call the young major, gave Madden a snappy, "Yes, sir!" and rushed out.

Madden fidgeted with routine paperwork. He recalled the Pluto basics from an intelligence briefing maybe ten years ago. That exposition of chilling data was not the kind of thing you ever forgot.

Incredible that our side had come up with such a diabolical weapon. But weren't we the geniuses who had engineered the A-bomb? the ultimate in death-dealing until the H-bomb? That gem of mass slaughter was ours, too. At least we'd had the good sense to cancel Pluto. But if it were possible to resurrect the remains...

***

Precisely at 2:00 p.m., Pappas burst back in waving a sheaf of notes and near to bursting with newly acquired technical knowledge.

"Jesus, sir! What a fantastic—I mean, Pluto was one weird weapon."

"Details, Major. I remember the gist. I want the details."

Pete Pappas poured out his just-absorbed information as if he had been intimately associated with the project. When he finished, he paused. Then he said, "General, if I may ask, why do you want all this?"

"Because, Major, somebody has stolen the mothballed remains."

The Aegean Collegian's face paled under his normal tan. "Why?"

"You tell me. If the right—in this case, wrong—party has gotten hold of those preserved components, the potential is more than a little off-putting, wouldn't you say?"

"Only if whoever has it could reactivate the drive component. The fuel rods were disposed of when Pluto was stored. So were the booster rockets. The thing couldn't get off the ground without booster rockets."

"Umm." Trying to mask his left leg's weakness, Madden turned to stare through his window at the languid Potomac. "Whoever took that thing, Pete, the potential is there. Our problem is to get it back. Or destroy it. Can I assume you have given that some thought?"

"Yes, General, I have."

"And?"

"Without telling them why, we alert all our special agents to be aware of the theft. Three large crates, two of them some twenty-five feet long, can't just be carried in a minivan."

"Parallel agencies?"

"For the moment, General, I recommend it be considered strictly an Air Force assignment. Next, it might be helpful to find out if anyone who actually worked on that thing is still alive and rational. Get him here for an intense debriefing."

"Might be of use. Get on it."

"Finally, General, I strongly suggest we bring in one top AFOSI man as field investigator. Only he would be privileged to full disclosure."

"And your suggestion as to whom we should bring in as that field investigator?"

"We need somebody fast on his feet, with the initiative to act without worrying about career effect. Somebody who's not all that concerned with military procedure."

"Sounds to me you're talking about a loose cannon type, Major."

"I'm talking about a man who can do all that without churning a wake, sir." Pappas gave him a tight smile. "Something like a torpedo. Comes in nice and quiet, then gets the job done."

Madden sank into his desk chair. "Are you talking about who I think you're talking about?"

"Gammon, General. Reserve Captain Steve Gammon."

3.

Twenty minutes after landing at West Palm Beach International, I swung my rented Taurus off U.S. 1 into a broad Palm Beach driveway.

Hoping my rented car wouldn't drip on the drive's spotless ochre tiles, I rolled slowly past the four-car garage and pulled up to the low hedge across the end of the three-story mansion's parking area. Beyond the hedge stretched a hundred feet of beautifully tended Floritam lawn, one of the few grasses able to survive South Florida's scorching summers. The lawn ended at the top of a concrete seawall. Beyond the wall lay the beach, badly eroded by hurricane season tides.

I stepped out of the car—not easy at six-foot-two—took off my dark glasses and slipped them into the pocket of my flowered Aloha shirt. The mid-morning sun was blinding but comfortably warm on my bare arms after the car's ambitious A/C. I climbed the stone steps to the broad porch—the deck, in Sun State parlance.

I pressed the pearl doorbell button and wondered, should I be here at all? Our divorce was not quite a year old.

The broad door with its frosted-glass heron motif opened partway. A pleasant black face peered up at me. Then the door opened wide.

"Mister Steve! Oh my, it's good to see you again!"

"Hello, Della. How have you been?"

"Just fine. I've been just fine." She stepped aside to let me pass. Down the hall, I heard a woman call, "Who is it, Della?"

"It's Mister Steve!" Della shouted over her shoulder. "Come to visit Miss Lizabeth." She turned back to me. "Least I figure that's what brings you here this fine day."

"You figure correctly, Della. How is she?"

"She's doing o.k. She's..."

"Steve Gammon!" Mrs. Ellen Palmer burst out as she rushed into the hall. "How nice of you to come. Thank you, Della." She seized my hands, kissed me on the cheek, then stepped back. "Let me look at you."

My former mother-in-law was a strikingly tall, auburn-haired woman, resplendent this morning in cream colored slacks and a scarlet tank top. During my brief marriage to Lizabeth, I'd had a much smoother relationship with my mother-in-law than with my wife.

"How are you, Ellen?"

"Surely better than my daughter, at the moment. If only she'd had the sense to stay off that horse of hers. I've always said there's no horse more dangerous than an inconsistent jumper."

Together we walked toward the broad staircase at the end of the parquet-floored entrance hall. I felt empty handed. On the short drive from Palm Beach International, I'd deliberated over whether to seek out a florist shop but decided that would look too pat. Phony. Maybe this visit would seem that way, too. But for me, it wasn't. Call it compassion for a fallen woman, in the literal sense.

"Lizabeth is fine," Ellen said, unbidden. "Well, as fine as one can be with a fractured leg."

At the foot of the broad staircase, she paused. "I'll go up with you. I was about to check on her anyway. Then I'll leave you two alone."

At the top of the long climb—the ground floor had fourteen-foot ceilings—I followed Ellen down the wide corridor that led toward the magnificent view of the ocean from the second floor deck.

"Look who's here, darling."

On the front deck, Lizabeth Palmer Gammon reclined in a white wicker chaise facing the ocean. Below a pink sweater, a light blanket covered her to the waist. Her 25-carat gold hair framed the pale patrician face that had so beguiled me four years ago...almost to the day, I realized, with a quirky little lurch in my chest.

"Steve!" Lizabeth cried, a touch more dramatically, I thought, than the situation called for. But her emerald eyes danced.

"I've things to attend to," Ellen said abruptly. "I'm so glad you've come, Steve. It's very...nice of you." And she left us alone with our tensions.

"You should have married Mother," Lizabeth said, unsmiling. "You two get on so well."

Here it was already. The little conversational jab delivered with preppie tartness. I bent down, kissed her cheek. Soft and cool. "You seem to be in good shape..."

"...for the shape I'm in," she finished. We laughed at our old catch phrase.

"How are you really, Lizabeth?" Never "Beth," and positively never "Liz." She was always formally, sometimes formidably, "Lizabeth."

"Aside from this damned fractured tibia and the prospect of several weeks on crutches during the Palm Beach party season, I'm just peachy."

"Shoulda stayed off that horse."

"I was off that horse. That was the problem."

She hadn't lost her flair for quick humor. One of her redeeming qualities.

"But I was lucky," she added. "I didn't land on my head. My legs slapped the top rail of the jump. Broken legs mend a lot better than a broken neck."

"You did this in Virginia. How'd you get down here so fast?"

"Ambulance plane." The wicker chair creaked as she lay back and openly appraised me. Same slow smile hiding fast thinking.

"Oh, God, Steve. If I weren't such a wreck, I'd drag you into my bedroom right now." Her eyes clouded. "I've really missed you, big man! Missed that dashing busted beak of yours. And do I see a beguiling touch of gray at the temples?"

"That's from trying to build a constituency from scratch. After a two-decade hiatus, I'm finally getting some use out of my neglected urban planning degree."

"I'm so glad you're a success. I'll admit I never thought you'd make a go of it."

She sounded wistful, vulnerable. Then, as ever, she killed it. "I assume you flew over here in that damned little airplane."

"In the Super Cub, yes."

"Always hated that thing. It was the only competition I had."

"That and the Air Force assignments."

She nodded. "Those damned, always high-priority, spookily-secret Air Force assignments! Haven't you finally gotten enough sense to give them up?" Her scowl softened into the trace of a smile. "We could make it work again, Steve."

"It didn't work the first time."

"But I was good for you, wasn't I?"

Hell of a question. She'd been an insatiable bunny in bed, but just as demanding out of it. I'd had to be an iron man to keep my own life from being absorbed by her need to dominate — and by her family's prominence.

I walked to the deck's waist-high railing and peered along the beach. I could see the not-so-distant seawall that fronted the Kennedy estate with its rambling house. More space than grace. And no air conditioning, so rumor had it.

"Steve?" she prompted behind me, her voice small against the crump of surf.

"Yes, there were times when you were 'good for me,' " I hedged.

"But not enough of them."

I turned back to her. "When we were good together, we were very good, Lizabeth."

"But when we were bad, we were horrid?"

We both laughed, but it was true.

"I loved you, Steve. I think I still do. But we always seemed to be on divergent courses."

More like collision courses, I didn't say. In our silence, I heard a phone ring.

Her compelling eyes were fixed on mine. "Do you think we could ever..."

The deck's French doors swung open. "I'm so sorry," Ellen Palmer said. "Phone call for you, Steve. A General Madden."

Lizabeth laughed coldly. "Well, that just proves a point, doesn't it?"

"Sorry," I felt saved in a way. She had been zeroing in on a personal level where I never felt comfortable. "I'll have to take it."

When the commanding general of the Air Force Office of Special Investigation called, it was never trivial.

The phone was at the end of the second-floor hallway, an old rotary dial type. The tradition-bound Palmers were never quick to change anything.

"Steve Gammon, General."

"Your associate in Fort Myers gave me this number." Madden's raspy voice sounded unusually tense. "Thank God I've caught up with you."

"That bad, General?"

"Potentially, yes. Under wraps and we want to keep it that way. I want you to drop whatever you're doing. We desperately need you up here ASAP."

"All due respect, General, but you've got a hundred investigators just as good. Some of them already on active duty."

"You're the one I need. Eighteen years active duty, two with AFOSI, now on reserve status. All that in general. In particular, because of the missing C-130 case last year. You stuck with your conviction we had a corrupt major on our hands. Something I didn't want to believe until you proved me wrong."

"I was lucky."

"Luck had nothing to do with it. And there was your work on your brother's murder."

"That wasn't AFOSI work, though, General."

"I kept tabs on it anyway. Everybody in the Maui PD thought he'd died in an accident until you went out there and proved otherwise."

Madden paused. Then he said, in what I recognized as his sales-pitch tone, "I want you because you are possibly our most persistent and self-motivated agent, reserve or otherwise. And the one I most depend on to keep his mouth tightly shut."

And one, I thought, with a critical business meeting scheduled tomorrow. "General."

"You remember Pete Pappas?" Madden said. "I'll tell you exactly what he said to me not an hour ago. 'We could call in any number of bulldogs,' Pete told me, 'but we need a bloodhound on this one.' You're that bloodhound."

"Sounds serious."

"It can be. Or, frankly, it may not be. We need you to find out."

"Can you give me two days, General? Tomorrow, I've got..."

"I can't give you even one," Madden broke in. "This isn't a misplaced airplane or a security leak thing. It has truly frightening potential. Whatever you're working on, turn it over to that capable associate of yours. Then get yourself over to Southwest International early tomorrow morning. You're already booked on Delta. Takes off at seven thirty a.m. Change in Atlanta. You'll be met by one of my staffers at Washington National."

The general paused for breath, then, "Steve, this is Priority Scarlet."

Jesus, that was one short of Attack in Progress!

"As of now, you are on active duty with the temporary rank of lieutenant colonel. You roger that?"

Well, that was a couple steps up. "Yes, I roger that, General. I'll be there tomorrow, sir." I smiled. Madden was a sharp military man, but sometimes he sounded like a frustrated actor playing a relished role.

With reluctance that surprised me, I walked back to the deck. "Lizabeth, I'm sorry."

"You have to go. The damned Air Force was always part of the problem, wasn't it?"

"You're right, but I wasn't willing to give up serving my..." that sounded pompous; "...to give up my AFOSI work for the sake of a few charity balls."

"That's not fair. I needed a life, too."

"Hell, Lizabeth, it was a situation we just couldn't work out. You be good, now." I bent to kiss her gently on the forehead. "Get back on your feet and stay away from horses."

"Sure. Like you'd stay away from that damned plane of yours, even if it dumped you in the Everglades."

"I've got to go."

"Of course you have," she said icily. "I do appreciate your coming *all* the way across Florida to see me."

I pondered that through my goodbye to Ellen and Della then to my car. Fort Myers to Palm Beach was only 115 air miles. Lizabeth had a technique of sinking a barb so deftly you didn't feel it until it festered awhile. I drove out of the Palmer driveway and out of Lizabeth's life.

At West Palm Beach International, I turned in the Taurus. An acne-scarred youth on an airport tug gave me a lift to the general aviation flight line.

"You the guy with that old Cub out there? You must really like flying to do it in an old crock like that."

I gave him a quick smile but said nothing. My Piper tail-dragger was no "old crock." It did look like the now ancient Piper J-3, the once-ubiquitous yellow Cub with the black lightning bolt along its fabric-covered fuselage. As a private joke, I'd ordered my Piper PA-18 Super Cub painted like the old J-3. It looked like its ancestor, but it had almost two-and-a-half times the horsepower, plus flaps. Its take-off run was a mere 140 feet, less than the wingspan of a Boeing 747 jet liner.

Like the old J-3 Cub, the PA-18 had two tandem seats. Unlike the hand cranked J-3, mine had a starter and was radio-equipped. I buckled into the front seat and pressed the starter button. In a burst of raw power, the big Lycoming caught. I adjusted the headset and was given taxi then take-off clearance.

The thing climbed like a rocket. I wondered if the line boy was watching, slack-jawed. I cleared out of West Palm airspace and set the compass on due west. The 115 mph cruising speed and light tailwind would get me to Florida's gulf side in less than an hour.

Some contrast to my Cold War missions, first in the vulnerable U-2R, then in the SR-71 Blackbird. At max speed above 78,000 feet, the Blackbird would have crossed the Florida peninsula in just over three minutes. Unlike the slower, lower altitude U-2s, the huge SR-71 recon jet could outrun any Soviet SAM, but all my thirty-seven missions in U-2s had been high tension.

Leisurely soaring a couple thousand feet over South Florida's sparsely settled interior was the reverse. Yet, despite the risk of those trans-USSR flights, I had experienced disaster only once. Departing Azerbaijan SSR westward at 65,000 feet, my U-2R's turbojet abruptly failed. Essentially a powered glider, the plane sailed dead-stick over the Turkish border. But I knew I couldn't make it to the USAF base almost 400 miles further west at Incirlik.

Three thousand feet over the mountain town of Mus, I bailed out. The only lasting effect of that nighttime plunge into eastern Turkey woods was a broken nose. Its bridge permanently showed a boxer's break that apparently gave me a rakish look oddly appealing to women. But to date, I'd had an unenviable record in that department.

Six hundred feet over the casual sprawl of Fort Myers, I throttled back for the base leg then the final approach glide. Over the closely-spaced homes of the Tanglewood subdivision, I levered down the flaps. The Super Cub's descent steepened. The multiple lanes of the Tamiami Trail flashed below the donut tires. I flared out and set her down precisely three-point on the wide macadam of Page Field.

Levering the flaps up, I swung onto a taxi strip and pulled into my slot on the tie-down line near the general aviation terminal.

I checked in at the operations office then guided my pearl gray Buick out of the airport's entrance drive into Route 41, the Tamiami Trail. The summer traffic was comfortably sparse. At Cypress Lake Drive, I turned westward toward McGregor Boulevard. Four miles south on McGregor, I pulled into Seagrape Plaza, a small U-shaped strip mall.

My office was discreetly tucked away in a corner of the unspectacular plaza. I parked, opened the frosted glass door marked simply *Gammon Associates*, and walked into my barnlike office dominated by two big drafting tables. Both were covered with development plat maps. His and hers tables; neither of us had a desk.

As I stepped in, Erica Bannerman straightened up from her drafting table. Dark haired, slender, in her early thirties, nearly as tall as I was, she wore a look of imperturbable confidence. Her tan skirt reached a precise three inches below her knees, and her skirt-lengths never varied with fashion's whims. Her white blouse was always unadorned except for a tiny pin with a scarlet head, discreetly tucked into her left lapel; the red-headed pin of Mensa, the society of major IQs.

Erica had all the attributes of the classic bachelor career woman except for the fact she was married to the proprietor of a Fort Myers body-building salon. Despite their seemingly incompatible lifestyles, she occasionally appeared at work flushed and smiling. Beauty and the Beast seemed to hit it off just fine.

"General Madden got through to you?" Her voice was low and silky.

"Oh, he did that, all right."

"You took to the air this morning." Her aquamarine eyes held a mischievous glint. "Better to joy ride than to jog?"

"I did both, partner. Jogged Punta Rassa's byways at dawn. Cleared the ground-borne cobwebs thereafter with a quick flight to Palm Beach."

Erica's eyes held mine. "How is she, Steve?"

"Mending."

"Mending," she repeated, but I wasn't going to be drawn into saying anything more than that. It was over. Lizabeth was the past; some of it sweet, too much of it bitter. "I gather the general has a dire need," she prompted into my silence.

"And his dire need is what I don't need, with tomorrow's deadline on our Coppersmith Green feasibility study."

I sat down at my work table and leafed through our recommended changes for that projected Sarasota strip mall development. Talk about lousy timing.

I sat back from my sheaf of notes. "Looks like you inherit tomorrow's meeting with Coppersmith, Erica. You ready to tell him he should increase his parking area by ten percent?"

"Of course." I knew she relished filling in when I was called away.

"You're aware old Frederick Coppersmith has a low regard for working women?"

"But a high regard for Princeton, I've noticed during his visits here."

"And you are a daughter of Old Nassau."

"Tiger Inn. Class of '88."

"You are chillingly sharp. Ms. Bannerman." I tossed my stapled notes across my table to hers. "As of now, the Coppersmith Green evaluation is all yours."

"*All* mine? But you've done so much of the preliminary work."

"I don't know what General Madden has in mind, Erica. It sounded like more than a day's work. Besides, it's time you head up a project. You've been doing most of the detail work on Coppersmith. You deserve to take it over."

Her eyes glittered. "God, yes! But I want to be open to consult with you if I..."

"That's nicely politically correct of you, partner, but you're capable of handling the whole thing by yourself. Still, if you need... Hell, I'll probably be back in a couple days if you need me."

"Oh, sure."

When I left to pack, she wore a confident grin.

...Priority Scarlet?

4.

A t daybreak the morning after General Madden's call, I showered, dressed, and chugged down a mug of instant coffee. Then I drove my Buick out of my South Fort Myers town house driveway, wound down to Summerlin Road and headed north for Regional Southwest Airport.

As Madden told me, my ticket to D.C. and a boarding pass were handed over at the Delta counter. In a concourse restaurant, I had time for a second coffee, plus grits, toast, and a perusal of the *Washington Post*. Saddam Hussein had enough of an army left to drive Iraq's northern Kurds toward the borders of Iran and Turkey...The USSR was in a state of unrest...Gorbachev was said to be seriously ill. But I found nothing that even hinted at a situation that would warrant an AFOSI Priority Scarlet.

I boarded Delta's twin-jet DC-9 feeling totally uninformed. I hate to feel uninformed.

***

As the 737 I'd boarded in Atlanta's plane-change banked out of the holding pattern and into its approach to Washington National, I watched the rows of markers on Arlington National Cemetery's slope drift below, dim in the hazy summer drizzle. We banked to follow the Potomac's swing. Helluva place for a busy airport. Smack in the center of D.C.'s metro sprawl.

I heard the landing gear rumble down and lock into place. Then we touched down hard, as if the captain was thankful to have picked his way in here and was making sure he stayed safely glued to the runway.

At the end of the off-loading ramp stood a smartly-uniformed female E-4, her mahogany hair neatly trimmed just above her blouse collar. The nameplate over her right breast read LOPEZ. She had obviously been briefed with the aid of my photograph, and she stepped right up to me.

"Colonel Gammon?" She looked a touch uncertain, and I didn't blame her. Dressed in khaki slacks and one of my vivid Aloha shirts, I looked like a displaced vacationer in this bastion of navy-blue power suits.

I gave her a smile and a nod.

"We'll pick up your luggage, Colonel, then be on our way."

I held up my carry-on bag. "This is it, Sergeant. We're already on our way."

I elected to sit up front in the staff car. "Crystal clear and oven warm in Florida," I offered as we swung through the airport's exit onto traffic-clogged Route 1.

"Yes, sir."

"And a misty drizzle here."

"Yes, sir." She glued her coal-chip eyes ahead, expertly anticipating slow-downs and stops.

"City gets more congested every year."

"Yes, sir," said Sgt. Lopez.

I gave up. The Plymouth rolled across the Rochambeau Memorial Bridge spanning the Potomac, skirted the Jefferson Memorial, then plunged in the traffic swirl of the freeway along Washington's bottom side. A few minutes later, Sgt. Lopez whipped us off the expressway into South Capitol Street, across the Frederick Douglas Bridge, then past the Naval Station, and finally into Bolling AFB.

No stranger to Washington, I wondered why she had taken the long way. But I was more intrigued by whatever had prompted Brigadier General Oliver Madden to summon me here on this muggy July Tuesday. As an acting lieutenant colonel, no less. Two steps above my reserve grade.

Sgt Lopez flashed her gate pass. The air police two-striper bent down to peer past her. "Your ID, sir?"

I handed over my Reserve ID card. The E-3 checked his clipboard. "Right, sir." He returned the card and stepped back to let us roll onto the base.

Sgt. Lopez pulled up in front of base headquarters, leaped out, dashed around the rear of the car and whipped my door open while I was reaching in the back for my travel bag.

"Well done, Sergeant. Thanks for the scenic ride."

"You're wondering why I passed up the south route and took the long way."

Sgt. Lopez was a mind reader.

"The Wilson Bridge is being repaired, sir. Traffic in that direction is a mess." For the first time, she showed a trace of a smile.

***

In his office doorway. General Madden seized my hand in both of his, but his expression was on a par with Curtis LeMay's during a bad day.

"My God!" he said in a rare burst of mild profanity. "Where did you get that shirt?" Then he smiled…briefly. "It's good to see you, Steve. I appreciate your taking this on with such short notice."

As if I had a choice, I thought. But it was decent of Madden to imply this was voluntary. Just about now, Erica would be in Sarasota recommending to a prickly Frederick Coppersmith that his proposed Green include less concrete and more grass.

"How have you been, Steve? Still puttering around Fort Myers in that little puddle jumper of yours?"

"I've been fine, General, and I had the Super Cub in the air just yesterday."

"Come on in," Madden urged, standing aside to let me pass. "You've met Major Pappas."

"Pete, how are you?"

Standing at the conference table, The Aegean Collegian's heavy brows lifted in a quick smile. "Aside from the business at hand, Steve, I'm fine. Glad you're here."

The other man in Madden's office was unfamiliar, a civilian in a rumpled tan suit, medium height and rail-thin, with wavy white hair surprisingly full for a man I judged to be in his seventies.

"Dr. Cornelius Joiner," Madden said. "Dr. Joiner has just flown in from San Diego as a special consultant on this situation."

Joiner switched to his left hand a large manila envelope he held, and extended his right. His grip was unexpectedly powerful.

Madden nodded toward the office conference table. "Gentlemen, let's get on with this. We aren't at all sure what we are up against, but time could well be of the essence."

We settled in. "Coffee?" Madden offered. I nodded, and Madden poured from the carafe in the circular table's center. It wasn't often that a reservist colonel, nee captain, had his coffee served by an active-duty general.

"Steve, I'll come straight to the point." Madden's pale blue eyes showed strain. "Sometime after a routine inventory six weeks ago, an item mothballed at an aircraft boneyard near Tucson was stolen. The theft wasn't discovered until yesterday. We don't know why the thing was taken, or by whom. What we do know is this: the stolen item is a potentially goddamned frightening piece of weaponry."

Madden paused to take a long drag at his coffee. For the general, that was strong language.

"Dr. Joiner," the general said, "thirty years ago you worked on that project. Bring the colonel up to speed."

The elderly civilian rubbed his palms together like a man about to relish a meal. "Have you ever heard of Project Pluto, Colonel Gammon?"

"Afraid not," I said. "Secret?"

"It was at the time, back in the late nineteen fifties and early sixties. A nuclear-powered, supersonic, low-altitude cruise missile."

"*Nuclear* powered?"

"Why not? Back then, the atom was going to be our salvation in a world predicted soon to run out of fossil fuels. It may yet be our salvation, Colonel. Nuclear power is plentiful. Properly designed and maintained, it's relatively clean. Back then, the *Nautilus*, our first nuclear-powered submarine, was already under construction. So why not nuclear-powered aircraft, even spacecraft?"

Joiner tapped his large envelope with a forefinger. "Why not a nuclear-powered cruise missile? Thus Project Pluto, powered by a nuclear-powered ramjet. You're familiar with the Nazis' V-1 flying bomb? It had a small, dorsal-mounted ramjet engine that consisted of not much more than a set of air-intake flappers up front, a combustion chamber, and an exhaust tube. Air rushed in through the flappers, a fuel-air mixture was ignited in the combustion chamber, the flappers closed, and the reaction to the escaping exhaust gasses drove the V-1 forward."

"So for Pluto, the idea was to heat the incoming air with a small nuclear reactor."

Joiner beamed at me. "Very good, Colonel." His smile faded. "I was convinced the project held tremendous promise. Using a terrain avoidance system, Pluto would travel a few hundred feet above the ground at a calculated Mach three. Its payload of small, delay-fused hydrogen bombs would be released on transmitted signals. We determined that a single Pluto cruise missile could incinerate half a dozen cities in one launch."

"What was your connection with Pluto, Mr. Joiner?" I asked him.

"I was a young nuclear scientist then, Colonel, already convinced atomic power was the answer to a world facing an ultimate energy crisis. I was a member of the Pluto development team."

Joiner leaned back in his chair and folded his arms. "What an awesome project that was. First in the design labs outside Oakland on the West Coast, then at the reactor test site in Nevada."

"At aptly-named Jackass Flats," Pete Pappas put in.

Joiner shot him a sour look.

General Madden cleared his throat. "No editorials, Major. Under Cold War pressure, it obviously seemed a valid project."

"Did it work?" I asked.

"Yes, the engine did work. Beautifully. It was off the drawing board, and so was the air frame. But they never got in the air. By then, tests showed the Atlas, Titan and Polaris missiles could reach their targets in minutes, striking from space—far more efficiently than the terrain-hugging Pluto. So the government shut down our project."

Remarkable, I thought. Thirty years of smoldering resentment still colors his chalky cheeks.

From his thick envelope, Joiner pulled out a collection of 8-by-10 photos. He held up a shot that looked like a bundle of ceramic rods. "This is the nuclear reactor, not quite six feet long and little more than a yard across. This next one is a schematic of Pluto's terrain avoidance unit in the nose cone. The electronic control system is just behind it, next to the bomb compartment, then the engine section aft."

He shuffled through the rest of the photos. "And here's an artist's impression of the weapon taking off. Stubby wings, vertical fin, ventral air-scoop, and the two solid-fuel booster rockets not yet jettisoned."

I studied the photo spread. "This thing could deliver a bellyful of hydrogen bombs at supersonic speed. In certain circumstances, that would seem to make it a viable system. Am I missing something here?"

"A major problem, Colonel. The nuclear engine would commence output well clear of the launching crew. But after that, the reactor would have laid a swath of gamma and neutron radiation several miles wide wherever it flew. With this weapon traveling at three times the speed of sound, it would be past you before you heard it. But in its wake, you would be hit with a shock wave and a blast of horrendous noise that could burst your eardrums. And if you were in or near the flight path, you'd also be radiation-dosed. To what extent, we were not certain."

He nodded at his photo pile. "Quite a weapon," he said with a little smile I found chilling. He was still in love with this God-awful thing he'd helped create.

"After the project was cancelled," he added, "the airframe and engine were crated and stored with the idea they would eventually be reassembled for static display at the Smithsonian's Air and Space Museum in Washington or the historic aircraft park at Chanute Field."

"And out of that act of historical preservation," I couldn't resist putting in, "comes our current problem. Can the components actually be made operable, Mr. Joiner?"

He frowned. "Everything was crated but the fuel rods and booster rockets. The rods would require sophisticated manufacture by a qualified ceramics company. There were hundreds of those rods, little octagonal 'cigars,' each with a hollow core. Made of uranium and beryllium oxides. We were ordered to junk the fuel rods before the missile's engine was stored. They would not be easy to replace."

"But not impossible?" I pressed.

"Not for a determined group with sufficient financial and logistical resources."

Even in this air-conditioned office, I felt hot under my out-of-place tropical clothes. "So somebody could activate and actually *launch* this horror?"

"And who," Pete Pappas put in, "is 'somebody'? College pranksters? Highly unlikely that a bunch of beer-steeped frat brothers would go to the trouble and expense of acquiring the equipment to hoist those big crates over an eight-foot-fence. Then there's the matter of its location in the depot."

"Such as?" Madden prompted.

"Our records show it was moved from an interior site to its position along the south fence. That made it accessible from the outside."

"Presumably by truck-mounted crane."

"My guess, too, Steve. The fence is still intact. Now consider a possible ultimate recipient of those Pluto parts: a foreign power or powers. In between, some fanatical terrorist organization. Take your pick. The problem is to locate the damned thing and recover it... Or take it out."

I gave Pete a little smile. "Am I expected to be a one-man brigade?"

"Not quite, Steve." General Madden leaned toward me. "We've notified all AFOSI agents to report sightings or shipments of specific-sized crates. We need you assigned full-time in the field to gather every scintilla of information available to locate the thing. Then we'll determine where to go from that point. For all we know at present, it may indeed be stacked in the shadow of an Arizona mesa with the high-spirited sons of U of A laughing up their sweatshirts at us."

"Or," Pete Pappas said, "on a North Korean freighter, heading west out of San Francisco."

Madden nodded. "We've thought of that, too. All our seaports have been alerted. Those crates are pretty big to hide. So is what's in them."

"How about satellite recon?" I wondered.

"Good point," Pappas said. "But unfortunately, none of our current close-detail surveillance orbits was set up to spy on ourselves. At the moment, we want to keep this in the family, so to speak."

"Why, Pete? Surely not the damage to professional pride over having lost a potentially dangerous classified relic."

"Pluto hasn't been classified for some years," Madden told me. "There have been a few articles about it in technical magazines, which may be where the thieves got the idea. But it's classified now, gentlemen, especially including the fact that it's missing. Imagine the brouhaha were the media to start speculating on the potential. 'Weapon from Hell in Hands of Unknown Thieves.' Makes a great headline, Steve."

"I'll do what I can, General."

"We're damned sorry there's so little to go on."

"Tucson will be a start."

***

The Beech T-1A Jayhawk cruised west-southwest at 530 mph. A student pilot occupied the left seat, with his instructor pilot in the right seat, and me, newly brevetted Lt. Col. Steve Gammon, dead-heading behind them. The impressive performance of the T-1A's twin turbofan engines would put me into Davis-Monthan just a few minutes over four hours after take-off from Bolling.

My presence on the flight was courtesy of the Air Training Command instructor's willingness to make an intermediate stop at Tucson on his scheduled return to Williams AFB near Mesa.

Thanks to Madden's call to Supply, I was in uniform now, my new silver leaves mint shiny. The uniform had been the general's suggestion. "You'll be interrogating service personnel. They should respond more positively to a uniform."

Late in the afternoon, the Jayhawk began the long descent, its blunt nose aimed at the city of Tucson materializing in the lengthening shadows of the surrounding mountains.

By nightfall, I'd grabbed a quick supper at the Officers Club and was checked into a militarily functional single room at VOQ, Visiting Officers Quarters. It offered a small refrigerator stocked with snack foods, and a cabinet of miniature liquors and mixers, all on the "use what you want, pay when you check out" arrangement.

And there was a phone. I glanced at my watch. Five-forty here, eight forty back in Florida. By now, Erica would be in her South Fort Myers condo. Got her on the second ring.

"How'd it go in Sarasota?"

"He took me to lunch," she said, as if that were an unusual happening. Which it was.

"No kidding? I don't think Old Frederick ever takes anybody to lunch. Does that mean he's going along with our recommendations?"

"He said it would cost him two units, but he'll do that to meet the requirements for another five acres of open space."

"Great going, partner! You've made more progress with crotchety Fred than I ever have. Stay on the case, okay? Looks like I'll be otherwise occupied for a while."

"A while?"

I knew that was all she would ask. She was well aware that specific questions on my AFOSI work were taboo—sometimes for her own protection as much as for general security purposes.

"No telling how long, Erica. Can you start the prelim study of the Bordenfield Estates project, along with finishing up Coppersmith?"

"My pleasure."

I knew it was. She delighted in working on her own. "Tell you what," I said, "now that Coppersmith is nearly finished, you can head up Borderfield along with it. I'll be your back-up."

"Are you serious? That's a whole new project. Steve, you're a...you're a very... Well, let's just say I really appreciate that."

"You be good, Ms. Project Director."

"You, too."

I hung up. Lucky to have her. Lucky in business; unlucky in love.

I put together a light scotch and soda, loosened my tie and settled into a chair at the small writing table. Maybe tomorrow's already arranged briefing with Davis-Monthan Air Police Major Mollison would give me more of a handle on this urgent but still uncomfortably vague assignment.

Cornelius Joiner had left me with the impression that in capable hands, the hellish thing could actually be launched—if fuel rods and boosters were acquired. Hundreds of fuel rods...Hell, fabrication of that many custom-made ceramic fuel rods could take months. And it could be hard, if not impossible, to keep secret. Might General Madden be a bit on the pessimistic side?

...Unless, I realized with a sudden chill rippling across my shoulders, unless fabrication of the rods and acquisition of the boosters had been underway before Pluto was stolen.

5.

Four months before the theft of the Pluto crates, Abdul Arif, a muscular, heavily-mustached captain of Iraq's elite Republican Guard, peered down the line of twelve missile transporter/ launchers. The blue exhaust of their idling engines mingled with the tan twilight haze. The rumbling engines sounded, Arif thought, chillingly like that of a distant "carpet" bombing by the American B-52s. Such an attack had pulverized this Basrah-based unit before last month's cease fire.

Now, his transporter with its complement of three missiles still aboard, was at the tail end of a convoy ordered back to Baghdad. The vehicles ahead began to move, but Arif's refused to start. The driver ground the engine over and over, sweat glistening on his pockmarked cheeks.

Captain Arif climbed up on the step. He stuck his face in the driver's open window. *"Fee eyh?"* he asked. What's the matter?

The driver, a date farmer before he joined the Guard, shrugged. "Fuel pump? Bad gasoline? Who knows? ...Sir," he added hastily.

"Get out," Arif ordered. "The whole line has stopped to wait for us. Run ahead and tell the major this vehicle is dead. The convoy will have to move without it. I will stay, repair it myself, then follow. You find a ride on another vehicle."

In view of the increasing hit-and-run Shiite guerilla attacks in the area, the driver looked only too happy to obey. He stepped down from the high cab, saluted, and scurried forward along the line of idling vehicles.

The acrid stink of burning crude mingled with the smell of exhaust. A southwest wind began to veil the darkening sky with the smoke of Saddam's lunatic parting gift, the oil fires in nearby Kuwait.

Five minutes passed. Then the convoy started to pull away. The tracked transporters spaced themselves fifty meters apart. Eleven of the operational vehicles under the major's command would clank up the highway along the Tigris from Basrah to Al-Kut. There, Arif knew, Saddam hoped to conceal the transporters and their missiles from the UN inspection teams even now being formed.

The irony of all this, Captain Arif realized as he watched the dust of the highway swallow the last vehicle in the convoy, was that through the hell of recent combat, not one of their missiles had been fired. Not one. If they had been Scuds, Arif's battery might have seen some action. But they were surface-to-air missiles, Soviet-made SA-6s, three to a vehicle, the same missiles that had been so successful against Israeli fighter-bombers during 1973's October War.

When his air force fled to Iran, his army surrendered, and when turning on a tracking radar attracted the missiles of Coalition fighters, Saddam ordered the SA-6 batteries to conserve their rockets. Conserve? For what Arif could only guess. But it seemed no omen of continuing the cease fire.

In the increasing darkness, he ran his eyes over what he had here. A Soviet-made launch vehicle with three SA-6 solid-propellant rockets, each seven meters long, a third of a meter in diameter. Each was capable of tracking and destroying an enemy aircraft as high as 20,000 meters.

But that was not to be. Arif's euphoria as an officer in the world's fourth most-powerful army was blasted into reality with its prompt defeat by what had been derided as the paper tiger of the West. And by the pathetic performance of the "Knight of the Arab Nation," Saddam, himself. The chunky American general, who looked like somebody's jolly uncle, out-thought, out-maneuvered, and out-fought him then added the insult of pronouncing Saddam "no soldier."

Even many of the so-called elite Republican Guard forgot their blood commitment to the Great Father-Leader of all Arabs, threw away their rifles, ran in the face of the hellish bombings. This, Arif had witnessed. And it was the reason for what he did now.

The broad engine hood of the transporter squealed as he unlatched its catches and raised the heavy cover. He reattached the cable from the coil to the distributor cap and banged the hood back down. He swung up into the cab and pressed the starter. The big engine groaned, snorted, then roared into life.

Arif rammed the gearshift into low and eased out the clutch. The transporter lurched forward, up the deserted roadway. By now, he judged, he trailed the convoy by at least five kilometers. He welcomed the breeze fluttering through the open windows. Soon he would be out of these wretched flatlands.

As the road began its swing around the great lake north of Basrah, Arif shifted through successive gearings up to fast cruise. The transporter, its metal tracks clanking, lumbered toward the highway intersection in the town of Al Amarah, the place where he would have to make the irrevocable final decision about his future.

***

Ten days before, a little man, his face hidden in the shadow of his head cloth, had silently appeared at the captain's table in a Basrah café. Arif prepared himself to stave off yet another pathetic personal-item sales offer or begging plea from another desperate local. But the little man surprised him.

"No, Captain, I have nothing to sell. I wish to buy."

"I have nothing to sell."

"Of course you do. But first, I will buy us coffee. We will talk over coffee." He himself brought the two cups from the counter, and there was no way Arif could not permit him to sit at the rickety table. The café was barely back in operation after its owner cleared away the stone shards after a British bomb hit on the power relay station across the street.

Was the little man forty or sixty? In the absence of electricity, Arif could not make out the stranger's face in the candle-lit folds of his red-checked *gotra*. As the man talked, one thing did become clear. This self-invited table companion was no Saddam sympathizer.

"He is a madman whose name will spell the end of Iraq." The little man leaned close. "The air force has wisely spared itself from a lost cause by flying into Iran. The army stopped its own massacre only by honorable surrender. Yet your unit's major recognizes none of this. He continues subservient to this madman who has led all of us to defeat."

"You speak treason!" But Arif kept his voice low.

The man reached into the folds of his robe and produced a roll of bills that he flashed, then again concealed.

"Iranian rials," he said in a near-whisper. "An initial stipend simply for you to consider my offer."

"Offer?"

"Let us save words, my friend. I wish to buy one of your transporter/launcher trucks with its three-rocket cargo."

Arif grinned. This man was demented. "Only one?" he asked with an indulgent grin.

"Only one."

"You plan to shoot down a bird or two, is that it?"

The man chuckled. "The rockets' use will not be traceable. You will have no risk from that."

"Only the risk of having my hands or my head chopped off for stealing government property."

"Only if you are stupid enough to remain in the Guard afterward."

"Lose my hands for stealing, then be killed for desertion."

"Stealing from a government that has stolen an entire country, and departure from a military force that now barely exists. Be practical, Captain. Saddam will eventually get you killed, but I offer you the riches of a lifetime. Think it over, then return here in two days' time." The small man stood and took Arif's hand, deftly slipped him the rolled bills, then strode out of the café.

Arif continued to believe the man was demented until he unfurled the tight roll beneath the table top. He held in his hand Iranian rials exceeding an entire year's pay in Saddam's Republican Guard. If the little man could give away this kind of money just to have him think over the proposition, what might Arif expect as full payment?

Idiocy! This was idiocy even to contemplate the theft of an SA-6 unit. And yet... what truly was his future in the now-disgraced Republican Guard? Already there were rumors the Guard would be sent north to quell a growing revolt among the Kurds. He had known many Kurds in his preliminary life as a clerk of licenses in Tuz Khurmatu. They were not a bad sort of people. Yet Saddam had already used lethal gas to kill everyone in Halabjah, a Kurdish town east of Tuz Khurmatu. What further atrocities might his troops be forced to inflict upon their own countrymen?

...How would one go about the theft of a loaded transporter/launcher? Arif could not resist being intrigued by such a bold proposal. And when two days had passed, he knew how to do it.

As promised, the little man reappeared in the café. He bought two coffees then joined Arif at their secluded table.

"Have you given my project thought?" His voice was a near whisper in the folds of his voluminous headcloth.

"It can be done."

"I am certain it can."

"I did not say I will do it."

"My friend, you have not yet heard the entire proposal." He raised his cup and sipped. "On delivery, you will receive three times what I have already given you."

More than *four years'* pay! "When..." Arif struggled to control his voice. "When and exactly where?"

"When it can be done without causing a problem fatal to you. Where? To an address I will give you. An address in Iran."

"Iran! How will I get across the border?"

"The way will be paved. You are 'Captain Tereekh, on special assignment.' Remember those words."

"Captain 'History'?"

"A nice touch, do you not agree?"

Arif glanced around the dimly-lit café then leaned close. "We are scheduled to leave the Basrah area in eight days."

"That will be suitable." The man placed some dinars on the table, beneath them, a folded scrap of paper. Then he rose and walked out of the café.

***

As the major's executive officer, Captain Arif had no difficulty in arranging to ride in the convoy's last transporter. Nor had it posed any problem to encourage the driver to inspect the engine, then to divert his attention long enough to pull loose the distributor lead...

Then send the driver off into the departing convoy.

Now, as darkness closed around him, Arif waited fifteen minutes. Then he gunned the roaring transporter northward along the Tigris River to begin the trek through 100 kilometers of desolate marshland to the bridge at Al-Amarah.

Stars speckled the moonless sky. A night for love, not traitorous thievery, Arif thought, as he thundered through the tiny settlement of Al-Uzayr on the west bank of the Tigris. To his right, he caught glimpses of its sluggish glitter beyond the town's low buildings. Then the highway curved back through the desolate marsh.

An hour later, he still followed the route of the convoy, some twenty minutes ahead of him. But when he rumbled over the bridge across the Tigris at Al-Amarah and stopped at the intersection just beyond the bridge, the moment of irrevocable decision had come. To the left, the road led to Al-Kut, his unit's final destination. To the right, some 70 kilometers east lay the Iranian border with the crossing point written in the instructions left on the café table with the small man's dinars.

Captain Arif drummed clammy fingers on the steering wheel. A thief and a traitor if he turned east. But a thief even if he turned west and rejoined his unit. If he failed to follow through after taking their first payment, surely the little man's organization would track him down and have no hesitation one dark night in slitting his throat.

Arif drew a deep breath, eased out the clutch and turned the steering wheel hard right.

***

The border crossing had a small guard shack on each side of the road, with a barrier between: a thick pole painted with alternating strips of red, white and green. In the glare of Arif's approaching headlights, the Iranian guard — a teen-aged boy wearing his field cap almost down to his ears — stepped to the barrier and held up his hand. Arif braked his ponderous track-laying truck to a jittering stop.

The boy trotted around the front of the transporter, his assault rifle at the ready, and craned his head up at Arif. Across the road, the Iraqi guard appeared barely interested in all this. No question; he had been reached. But Arif was not at all sure about this over-armed Iranian kid.

"Papers?" the guard demanded.

"I am Captain Tareekh, on special assignment," Arif recited. In the tense, exhaust-fumed night, the words sounded inane. And if the little man in the café had been too confident — or if the attempt to bribe this armed boy had failed — or if he was not the guard they had gotten to... Arif slid his right hand toward the holster on his hip.

"What was that you said?" In the wan light from the guard shack's low-watt flood, the boy border guard looked dangerously over-eager. Arif unsnapped the holster's flap. But, he realized, if this child decides to whip up the muzzle of his rifle and fire, my pistol will never make it out of its holster.

"I am Captain Tareekh," Arif restated icily, "on special assignment."

The boy grinned. "Pass, Captain 'Tareekh.'" Yes, he was in on this. The cocky little bastard had been playing with him. The barrier pole swung up. Arif tramped the accelerator. Let the clutch out too fast. The transporter crossed the border in an elephantine jump. Arif nursed the vehicle up to speed and rolled into Iran.

Five kilometers later, he tuned south into a narrow roadway that snaked through night-blackened fields then through the darkened village of Huzgan. In the new morning's first hour, he passed Ahwaz. More than a hundred kilometers still to go.

Just before dawn, he spotted a distant glow in the mist rising from the Shatt al-Arab, the waterway to the Persian Gulf. The lights of Abadan. Just short of the bridge onto Abadan's island, he turned into a narrow road paralleling the waterway.

This far, the route here had been through sleeping hamlets on deserted country roads, but now he felt as obvious as a rhinoceros in a chicken yard. Yet the few vehicles he passed took no heed of him; or, if they transported officials at this dismal hour, none felt the urge to challenge his monstrous military vehicle.

Along this unlighted roadway, scattered industrial buildings appeared. Two kilometers farther, he found the numbered building described in the small man's note, a cinderblock warehouse. He slowed the transporter, clanked into the gravel drive and pulled up in front of the building near several parked automobiles. He switched off the engine. Silence closed in like a damp blanket, broken only by the ticks of the cooling engine.

He waited. Sweat began to bead his forehead. Could this be the wrong place? Might I have somehow misread the...

A small door opened. Its yellow rectangle silhouetted a man who stepped out, a slender man in western shirt and slacks, but wearing a head cloth that obscured his face. He reached in his hip pocket, and Arif tensed. He could be shot right here, his corpse robbed of the partial payment he carried beneath his shirt, his body dumped in the river not fifty meters distant.

But the man withdrew an envelope and thrust it up at Arif. "The balance. I will take you into Abadan, then you are on your own. It would be well to get rid of that Iraqi uniform quickly."

Arif had thought of that and brought civilian clothes with him. His contact waited while he changed in the roomy cab. Then they both stepped into one of the automobiles, a German Audi that had seen better days, and rattled off toward Abadan.

***

As the Audi dwindled in the distance, a much larger entrance opened in the building's front, its overhead door hauled smoothly upward by an electric motor. A man in greasy coveralls climbed into the transporter's cab, studied the unfamiliar controls for a few moments, then started the engine. Gnashing the gears, he maneuvered the huge vehicle into the building, braked it near a truck loaded with big, corrugated drainage pipes, and switched off the engine. The building's big access door sank into place, and silence again surrounded the darkened warehouse.

Inside, a crew of six mechanics set to work. Using a block-and-tackle suspended from an overhead traveling crane, they unloaded two of the three slender SA-6 rockets, leaving the central one in place. They removed the 80-kilo warheads from the two missiles now on the concrete floor. Then the crew extracted the guidance modules and dismantled the fins.

What remained were two one-foot-diameter tapered cylinders some twenty feet long, each packed with solid fuel propellant. With the help of the overhead crane, the work crew laboriously inserted the two stripped SA-6s into two of the drainage pipes aboard the adjacent commercial truck.

Two hours after Captain Arif, with the equivalent of four years' pay concealed inside his shirt, was let out in central Abadan to shift for himself, the drainage pipe truck rolled out of the warehouse. Through the early morning haze, it drummed into Abadan, headed for the international dock area.

The two stripped SA-6 rockets, now no more than booster casings and propellants, would traverse the length of the Persian Gulf. Concealed deep in a shipment of Russian-made corrugated drainage pipes, they would skirt the Arabian Peninsula, journey up the Red Sea, then through the Suez Canal into the Mediterranean, cross the Atlantic, and finally dock in Tampico, Mexico.

There some of the pipes, especially including the two code-marked sections containing the SA-6 propellant bodies, would be off-loaded onto a waiting truck. Then they would be driven to their final destination in the Sonoran desert. At every critical stage of the long journey, agents of The Committee of Three would generously grease the palms of those who were to expedite the crucial shipment.

6.

In a secluded suite on the third floor of Cairo's palace hotel several months before Captain Arif deserted with his SA-6 transporter, three men shared thick, sweet *ziyada* coffee. Below the double windows of the luxurious living room, midmorning traffic clogged Tahrir Square. The stutter of stressed engines and the grind of clashing gears mingled with the shrill cries of sidewalk hawkers. A screen of tan dust hung in the exhaust-ridden air.

But the central room of the hotel suite, with its windows closed to the clamor and dust below, was cool and quiet. The three men who sat stiffly around the small conference table near the window cared not about the view. What they did care about was the business at hand. A brass tray with a silver pot of coffee, three cups and a plate of nut-filled *kunafa* pastries lay on the table, but not a briefcase, voice recorder, note pad, nor even a single sheet of paper.

Records of their meetings were kept only in the minds of "Cheetah," the tall, nattily mustached man from Iraq; "Stallion," the stumpy, pockmarked man from Libya; and "Lynx," the man from Iran, whose eyes blazed fiercely above his prominent, death's-head cheekbones. For secrecy and convenience, each had selected his code name. At their first meeting a year ago, when the froglike Libyan had announced that his would be Stallion, the eyes of the Iraqi and the Irani had met in bemusement.

After the mandatory pleasantries of greeting, a silence settled over the Committee of Three. Lynx, the Iranian with the blazing eyes, was acutely aware that Iraqi Cheetah and Libyan Stallion trusted each other as one Arab trusted another, but they did not necessarily trust Lynx in that way. He was a Persian. But, he assured himself, all of us are here in common purpose. He lifted the coffee pot.

"Coffee, gentlemen?" He poured for all three, thus establishing himself as host and chairman of this meeting.

Aristocratic Cheetah sipped his coffee through thin, purplish lips. "Excellent, Lynx. Excellent." He selected a pastry and remained perched on the edge of his chair.

The Iranian turned his intense gaze to the squat, pockmarked man, who also indicated approval of the coffee's quality. Lynx permitted himself an inward sigh of relief. It was he who had suggested Cairo as this meeting's place, and he who selected the hotel.

"Let us hope this pleasant weather is an omen." Cheetah smiled thinly and stroked his mustache with thumb and forefinger.

He spoke in English. Though he and dumpy Stallion were Arabs with Arabic as their tongue, the Persian Lynx spoke Farsi with Arabic as a barely adequate second language. Thus they agreed to conduct these delicate matters in the infidel language in which all three, through business necessity, had become proficient.

"The weather was not so agreeable at ten thousand meters over the Gulf of Sidra," Stallion grumped from the depths of his cushioned chair.

"But a safe flight, nonetheless," Lynx said, with a forced smile that masked his irritation. The toy-like beeping of a Japanese or European auto drifted up from the street, then was drowned in the arrogant bray of an American-made car.

Lynx darted a hard-eyed glance at the others and thought, all three of us might be more comfortable dressed in desert *thob* and *gotra*. But there are no telephones in the desert, and immediately after this meeting, carefully worded telephone communication would be essential. So here we sit in drab iron-gray business suits, looking like an OPEC executive committee dressed western for CNN cameras.

But, Lynx reflected, our common interest is not oil pricing. We are here to guarantee maximum confusion to the Great Satan. Contrary to our expectations, America came through the Persian Gulf crisis united and a major power in the Middle East. Now, all three of us agree, we need to strike a blow that will make world-class fools of the Great Satan's leadership.

Lynx set his cup on the tray, sat back and tented his fingers. "Gentlemen, I can now report," he said with a confident smile, "that the plan to obtain two SA-6 rockets is underway, though it will take some time to find the essential cooperative defector."

Stallion offered a satisfied nod, but Cheetah had a question.

"And as to acquiring the Pluto missile itself...?"

"On schedule. Now we must deal with the critical matter of propulsion."

"I thought the SA-6 conversions..."

"They are to get the missile off the ground, Stallion. I am speaking about in-flight propulsion by the missile itself. Through study of the remarkably available declassified data in the project, we know the engine was stripped of its nuclear fuel rods, but the compact reactor remains. Only the rods were disposed of. So our challenge is replacement fuel rods." Lynx turned to Cheetah. "We count on you for that."

The Iraqi stroked his mustache. "Now that the cease-fire is permanent, that requirement should be easier to meet. But there could be further complications. The Kurds to the north, the Shiites to the south"

"Without the rods," Lynx broke in, "everything we have planned will be of no consequence." He could see that the tall Iraqi was nettled by his interruption, but Cheetah managed to keep his voice level.

"I am aware of that, Lynx, but surely you are aware that Baghdad is not now so eager to condone such...adventuring."

"Which is precisely why we are here," the Libyan broke in. "Can you guarantee that the rods will be supplied, Lynx?"

"It will not be easy. The question is: can it be done? The answer lies here with the three of us. We all are at great risk in acting counter to the official views of our governments. None of this has been nor will be easy."

Lynx reached for his coffee, sipped, put the cup back on the tray. "Listen to me. We have made excellent progress to this point. Funding has been slipped undetected from government monies. The booster rockets will soon be in our hands. Our possession of the weapon itself is all but assured. And each of us continues to be known outside this room only as a successful business man in each of our countries."

He paused to regard Cheetah and Stallion in turn. "We are in common bond here, my friends, joined in protest against the softening of our governments' resolves toward the Great Satan of the West. We are the last hope to turn the course back to purity."

Again he paused, this time for dramatic effect.

"So I ask you again, Cheetah, can you assure delivery of the fuel rods?"

"The answer is, again, it will not be easy."

"That is not the reassuring answer we require. Remember we all three have sworn to success or death. If you cannot guarantee delivery..." Lynx shrugged and was pleased to note sudden tenseness beneath Cheetah's smooth tan. Were the power rods not forthcoming from Iraq, the whole project would collapse.

"Are you sure there is enough material available? The specifications state that thousands of rods are needed."

"Yes, yes," Cheetah insisted. "Thousands, fabricated of uranium and beryllium oxide. Hexagonal for tight stacking, longitudinally drilled to permit air passage. Each no larger than a thick pencil." He sat back with a self-satisfied smile.

"So many rods," said the squat man from Tripoli. "In view of the Israeli attack on your reactor at Tuwaitha, then the devastating effects of the Eight-Year War, how have you been able to secure such amounts of uranium and beryllium oxide?"

"That cowardly attack took place a decade ago, my friend. The turmoil of the recent war actually helped us. We relieved the government of such materials during Tuwaitha's reconstruction. The balance was spirited out of the hard-hit nuclear facility at al-Qaim and from the research center at Mosul University."

Cheetah's smug smile told Lynx the Iraqi was holding back something more to impress them with at the proper moment.

"Gentlemen," Cheetah continued dramatically, "the project for fabrication of the fuel rods will soon be underway at a minimally damaged facility near Zakho in northern Iraq."

Lynx and Stallion nodded approvingly. Then Stallion's unpleasant rasp demanded, "Who, if I may ask, is to oversee the fabrication of the fuel rods?"

The Iraqi gave him an almost mocking smile. "Dr. Muzaffer Ghavam."

"*The* Muzaffer Ghavam?" Stallion was visibly impressed. "*He* has agreed to this?"

"Not as yet. But, I assure you both, he will."

"Surely not for money," Stallion said. "His knowledge has already made him a rich man."

"Not money," Cheetah agreed. "A far more compelling motivation has been arranged."

"I must ask you," Lynx said to Cheetah, "when the rods are ready for transport, will you be able to arrange for safe passage?"

"It is assured. But I will need advance notice."

"How much advance notice?" Lynx asked.

The Iraqi frowned, apparently irritated by Lynx's persistence. "Not less than thirty-six hours."

"You personally guarantee that passage?" Lynx pressed.

"As confidently as I can guarantee the fuel rod fabrication," Cheetah said with a tight smile.

In the silence that followed, Lynx refilled his coffee cup. Then he asked, "And when will that be?"

"Within months. But it will take more money." Cheetah turned expectantly to the chunky man from Libya.

Stallion nodded. "Money is not a major problem. During the Gulf crisis, the price of Libyan oil rose along with the world price. Colonel al-Qaddafi has become increasingly reluctant to underwrite international... ventures. But he has also become increasingly careless about his government's finances. I have a man in the proper place, so it will not be difficult to apply the siphon as needed."

"This man of yours," Lynx pressed, "surely he is not aware of the destination of such funds?"

The Libyan smiled. "He has been led to believe he and I are engaged in a 'reallocation' for his and my benefit. When there is no longer a need for such funding, he will meet with an unfortunate accident."

"Once we could have counted on our respective governments to back such an enterprise as this, Cheetah reminded them. "Now we must take all the risks personally."

"An American missile to be launched against Americans," Stallion murmured. "What is the expression?" Then his teeth flashed in a grin. "Poetic justice!"

"Are there other matters we should consider?" Lynx asked.

"Yes," said Stallion in his irritating rasp. "I have serious concern about our man 'in the field.'"

"Zul-Junnah?" Lynx was taken aback by this reservation toward the man he himself had so highly recommended. "Zul-Junnah's very existence is devoted to bringing the Great Satan to its knees. What is—"

"Does a wise general expose himself to gunfire?" Stallion interrupted. "Your Zul-Junnah is commanding a complex mission, yet he is personally involving himself in activities best left to subordinates, activities that risk his exposure. That would jeopardize the entire mission."

Lynx dismissed the Libyan's caveat with a wave of his hand. "He is a devoted activist. He is wedded to our cause."

"But I still—" Stallion began, and Lynx knew this was the moment to adjourn.

"We will meet again two weeks from today," he said, closing further discussion.

"Again here?" asked Cheetah.

"Unless there is reason otherwise. If so, you will be notified." Lynx stood.

"Death to the Great Satan!" Stallion rasped.

"In time," Lynx said calmly, "but this is a beginning."

7.

"**M**ajor Mollison, take a seat." I nodded at the armless chair on the other side of the government issue metal desk in the stark room the base exec officer had made available.

A career man with four years to retirement, the major was built like a middleweight boxer with his gray-blond hair cropped close. His salute had been snappy, almost challenging. I read that as an indication the CO of the air police detachment would cooperate but not necessarily open up.

Burke Mollison sat stiffly, knees close together, hands cupped over them.

"You are charged with base security, Major?"

"Correct, Colonel Gammon."

"That includes, I assume, the remote aircraft storage yard south of here?"

Mollison gave me a cold look. "That includes 'reasonable precautions,' since the yard stores only obsolete aircraft with museum potential."

"What constitutes 'reasonable precaution,' Major?"

Mollison's hard blue eyes were unwavering. "Basically, the eight-foot-high chainlink fence surrounding the area. And a two-man patrol in an ATV once a day, primarily to assure the fencing is secure. It's unlikely anyone would want to steal an inoperative obsolete aircraft, Colonel."

"Someone did steal one, Major."

Mollison's face reddened. "My people have operated to the letter of security regulations, sir, and I personally—"

I held up a restraining hand. "Mollison, I'm not interested in blame assessment. My responsibility is to find, then help recover or destroy the damned Pluto missile components. If there is anything you can tell me that might help us do it, I'd like to hear it. Your men searched the area?"

"My people cordoned off the immediate area where the theft took place. Then I personally searched inside the fence only. I found several footprints, apparently made by a large man and a smaller man."

"You assume these were made by the thieves, not by whoever moved the crates to the fence location?"

"Yes, I do," Mollison said with obvious satisfaction, "because it rained out there at dusk the night the containers were taken. The prints were made after the rain. So it's a fairly safe assumption they were made after the yard closed for the night and, presumably, after the crates were already in place adjacent to the fence."

"You took castings?"

"Under the thin crust formed by the light rain, the sand was too dry and loose for castings, Colonel. That's a problem out here."

"You searched inside the fence. What about outside?"

"I thought it was best to leave that until a formal investigation was convened. The stretch of road I assume they came in on is several miles long. We've blocked it off and posted guards. No one has been permitted in there since."

I realized Mollison wasn't intimidated by a stiff military approach; he relished it.

"Major, I'm just passing through. You're an old hand here. Any ideas you might have will be appreciated."

Mollison's eyes were steady on mine. Then they flicked to the pilot's wings on my blouse. Silver wings on an Air Force base are a respected badge of accomplishment. Mollison's brittle gaze softened.

"It's my opinion the theft was no prank, Colonel. The crates had recently been moved from the interior of the yard to that location adjacent to the fence. Moved, I assume, by the part-time civilian work crew using the forklift. But the yard's records show no orders to move the crates."

I consulted a folder on the desk. "Captain Larssen is responsible for storage yard inventory and personnel?"

"Yes, sir."

"That will be all for the moment, Major. I'll give you a call when I'm ready to check the storage yard."

Mollison stood, saluted crisply and strode from the room.

Captain Larssen was due in eight minutes, time for a cup of coffee. As if by telepathy, Sgt. Almond, my temporarily-assigned, red-haired E-4, stuck his head in the open door. "Coffee, Colonel?"

"You read my mind, Sarge. Black, please." I perused the file again. Ernest Larssen was charged with storage yard supervision, including inventory control, preservation procedures and disposals. He was in his third year as a supply officer. His service record said straight arrow. But if Mollison was correct, there was a weak link somewhere in the storage yard operation.

Like Mollison, Larssen arrived on the minute. There, though, similarity ended. The air police CO had been hard holster leather. Overweight Captain Larssen was more like soft suede. His chunky-fingered salute lacked snap. He sank onto the armless chair like a man settling in for lunch, surely not a career officer. On the other hand, this was the man who had discovered and reported the theft.

"Tell me about it."

Which Larssen did, with an obvious love for detail.

"So," I said when he finished, "it looks like we have two possibilities here. Either someone broke in to move the crates, or one or more of your part-time crew moved them. But Mollison reported no sign of a machinery access break-in. So that puts the situation squarely in your lap."

Larssen nodded. "Yes, it does. And that's damned disturbing. I did not authorize any such relocation. That was done without any contact from my people here at the base."

"Which puts it on the part-time yard personnel. I want to interview each of those four civilian employees ASAP."

"I anticipated that, Colonel. All four are here now, with Sergeant Almond."

This was one hell of a cooperative officer.

"I do appreciate that, Captain. You're dismissed. Tell Almond I'll have them in, one at a time. Starting with the one in charge."

The first storage yard worker was a green card holder named Carlos Estevez, a tall, stringy Mexican.

"You may sit," I told him.

He perched stiffly with his fingers clenching the front of the chair seat.

"I see you have been employed part-time at the storage yard for more than a year."

"Si. I am boss of workers."

"The wages are adequate?"

"One can always use more, Jefe, but what I am paid here for part-time work is many more times what I would get for same work in my country."

"What are your duties in the storage yard, Mr. Estevez?"

He shrugged. "To see everything is okay. To check on stored aeros. To work with Capitán Larssen when an aero comes in or sometimes goes out." He smiled wanly. "To boss my three workers."

"What is the equipment in the yard?"

"Forklift and tug."

"Who is the last to leave the yard at end of the days you work?"

Estevez's thin eyebrows rose high on his forehead. "I am. I lock yard at five." He paused, frowned, then said softly, "But not that day."

"Which day?"

"Thursday before night of stealing. We work only on Thursdays."

"You didn't work that day?"

"I leave early. Mi esposa...my wife." The man looked anguished.

"What about your wife, Carlos?" I asked in a softer tone.

"In afternoon, police call me. A purse-taker...purse-snatcher? In shopping mall. Some boy take it. He hurt her arm. Police take her to estación and they call me. So I go."

"About what time was this?"

"Maybe four. An hour before we quit anyway. My three workers, they close up yard that day."

Coincidence, or...? "In which shopping mall did this purse snatching happen, Carlos?"

"El Carnaval Mall," he said with no hesitation.

"When you left the yard early that day, where exactly were the three crates that were stolen that night?"

Estevez gave me a bemused look. "I was not so worried about the crates then, Jefe. But I think row medio... in middle of yard."

"Where they were supposed to be?"

"Si."

"Not by the fence?"

He shook his head slowly. "I do not think so."

"You would have noticed if they had been moved?"

"Si. I would know something is changed."

I pushed back my chair and stood. "That will be all for now, Carlos. Gracias."

The foreman smiled, bowed slightly and strode out. I followed him to the door, and waited until he left the room.

"Sergeant Almond," I called, "in here, please."

Almond stepped in.

"Close the door." No need for the other three yardmen out there to hear this. When the door clicked shut, I told him, "Get on the horn to whatever Tucson precinct has jurisdiction over El Carnival shopping mall if there is such a mall. Estevez claims his wife ran into a purse-snatcher there. I want anything you can get, including who did it—if they caught him—and what happened to him. Need that ASAP."

"Yes, sir."

"Now you can send in the next storage-yard man."

Joseph Longeye was six feet of rangy muscle, his blue-black hair cut shoulder-length. A tightly wrapped package of young, hard-eyed American Indian.

"What tribe?" I asked.

Longeye's composure cracked a little. "Zuni." Then he said, "Do you care?"

"Come on, Longeye. This doesn't have to be an adversarial confrontation."

"What do you call it, then?"

"Depends on you. Sit down, Joseph. Tell me about your duties in the storage yard."

The Indian sat stiffly and folded his arms. "I do what the Mexican tells me to do."

"Which is?"

"Scut work. Weeding, clean-up, help bring in the old heaps. Help dismantle and load the ones that go out to museums."

"You run the forklift?"

His dark gaze hardened further. "We all run the forklift."

"You recall anything unusual the day before the crates were stolen?"

"Unusual?" The man's bronze face went blank.

"Don't play games with me, Joseph. Different that day from other days."

'I'm just a dumb red man, Colonel."

I glanced at the file on Joseph Longeye. Tucson high school grad, two years of junior college, major in English. "I'd say you're quite an educated red man, Joseph."

"Then why am I humping dead airplanes around a graveyard?"

"That's a question you have to answer for yourself, but it says here your record out there is nothing to be ashamed of. Let's get back to what I asked you."

His tightly folded arms relaxed a little. "Nothing unusual in the yard that day."

"Exactly the same as every Thursday you work?"

"Exactly."

"What about Estevez?"

"What about him, Colonel?"

"He locked up at five as usual?"

Longeye said nothing.

"Are you trying to protect this man?"

"Protect a Mexican green carder who supervises three U.S. citizens? Why would I protect him?"

"Come on, Joseph. Level with me. Either you're covering for your boss, or you're trying to do him in."

"You already know, don't you?"

"Know what, Joseph?"

The young Indian surprised me with a grin. "White man speaks with forked tongue, as they say. Okay, so I'm trying to keep the Mex out of trouble. I've worked for worse."

"So tell me what went on out there."

Longeye dropped his hands to his lap and shrugged. "He left early."

"How early?"

"An hour early. Around four. Said his wife needed him, and he left."

"Who locked up that day?"

Longeye stared at the wall behind my head. "I left right at five. The other two were still there."

"You each have your own car?"

"Yeah. Parked outside the yard gate."

"When you left, where were the three crates that were stolen?"

"I didn't notice, Colonel. I had a date with a chick in town. When I left, I wasn't thinking about crates."

"Think about them now. That's why we're going through all this."

"Yeah, I know. What in hell was in them?"

That was a surprise. "You don't know what was in them?"

"I don't care about any of that stuff out there. It's just a job. But whatever was in those boxes must really be something else to cause all this."

"Good guess, Joseph. You think of anything else unusual about that day, I'd appreciate your getting back to me, okay?"

He nodded. "That's it?"

"For now."

After Joseph Longeye strode out of my little interrogation room, Sgt. Almond appeared in the doorway. "I've got that info for you, Colonel."

"Bring it in, Sergeant. And close the door behind you."

Almond squinted at his page of notes. "At fifteen-twenty hours, Corporal Tasco, Southwestern District, Tucson Police, responded to a call from El Carnaval Mall's security office to apprehend a Howard Bedlow, Caucasian, age sixteen, on an assault and robbery charge."

"In a little plainer English, Sergeant."

"Yes, sir. The kid grabbed Mrs. Estevez's handbag and roughed her up."

"Assaulted her?"

"After he had the purse, he slammed her against the stucco wall of the corridor to the ladies room. She got some pretty nasty abrasions on her left arm before a mall security officer heard her screaming and got there in time to apprehend Bedlow. The Tucson cop—"

"Corporal Tasco."

"Yes, sir. He took her and the Bedlow kid to the local precinct, where Mrs. Estevez called her husband. She was pretty well shaken up. So was he, when he got that call. He left the storage yard immediately to go pick her up and take her home."

"What happened to young Bedlow?"

"They held him overnight for a juvenile hearing the next day. It was his first offense, so he was released in his mother's custody, pending final disposition."

"You got his address?"

"Right here, sir." Almond tore off the bottom third of his note sheet and handed it to me. "Not a nice part of town, sir."

"Can you get us a car?"

"But I've got all the info here."

"You have what the police reported. Official bare bones."

Bare bones might be all there was, but I was struck by the coincidence. The storage yard's foreman leaves an hour before closing time on the day the Pluto missile components are illicitly moved to the fence.

"See about a car, Sergeant."

"What about the other two yard workers, Colonel?"

"Tell them they can go have lunch. But they're not to leave the base. I'll interview them after we get back."

8.

Almond was right about this part of Tucson. The Bedlow boy and his mother lived on a narrow, crumbling side street in the city's outskirts. The gray frame house begged for paint.

My knock got me only silence from inside the house. Then the curtain obscuring the adjacent window moved.

"Mrs. Bedlow?" I called. "I'm Colonel Gammon from the air base. I'd like to talk with you for just a moment."

Her words came thinly through the flimsy door. "You ain't the police?"

"No, ma'am. I'm Air Force."

The door opened a few inches. The reek of cigarettes gusted through the crack. She was short and slack-faced. Probably in her forties, she looked hard-used.

"Your boy, Mrs. Bedlow. I'd like to talk to him."

"Why? Ain't he been through enough?"

"He did take that woman's purse. I'd like to know why."

She stared up at me, on the verge of tears. "I'd like to know why, too. He don't do things like this. I don't know what got into him."

"Is he here, Mrs. Bedlow?"

She nodded.

"Could I talk with him, out here alone?"

She nodded again, miserably, and shut the door in my face. I waited. The door opened, and a skinny kid slid out, blinking in the sun.

"You're Howard?"

Looking more like a frightened, lank-haired fourteen-year-old than a wised-up sixteener, he bobbed his head.

"I know you've got troubles, Howard, and I'm not here to make them any worse. I've got troubles of my own, and I'm hoping you can help me out."

"You kidding?" For all his grade-B Huckleberry Finn looks, Howard Bedlow had the whiny voice of a young squirt.

"No, I'm not kidding. What's got me confused is that until the other day, you had a clean record. Then you screwed it up. Grabbing the purse was bad enough, but ramming Mrs. Estevez into the wall...I don't understand why you had to rough her up?"

Howard's hands began to twitch. He stuffed them into the pockets of his rumpled jeans.

"I've got a funny feeling about this, Howard. I think there's more to it than you've been telling."

The boy's head jerked up. "Look, Captain...what are you, anyway?"

"Colonel. Lieutenant Colonel Steve Gammon."

"Bigger than a captain."

"A couple of cuts, Howard. What do you want to tell me?"

"Does it go back to the cops?"

"Maybe you'll want to take it to the cops yourself. I don't see how you can make things much worse for you than they are right now."

He stared at me. I kept my eyes on his.

Then he swung his arm toward the house. "Look at this place!" he burst out.

"Could stand some paint."

"Could stand a hell of a lot more than paint. So this guy says he'll give me fifty bucks to grab the Mex woman's purse."

"What guy, Howard? Where'd you meet him?"

"In the parking lot at the mall. I hang out there, carry grocery bags for tips. So he says he'll give me *fifty bucks* to grab her purse. Said he dropped his car keys and she walked away with them."

"You believed that?"

"Not really, but I believed the twenty he showed me. Said it was mine after he got the purse."

"You said he offered you fifty."

"Yeah." Howard looked at the ground again. "Another thirty if I, you know, sorta pushed her around. Teach her a lesson for stealing his keys."

"You get the money?"

"Hell, no! When I got back to where he said to meet him, he wasn't nowhere around. I stood there like a dork, and that's when the mall cop grabbed me."

I resisted my impulse to give this kid the chewing-out of his life, but that wasn't my mission here.

"Where's your dad?"

He stared at the ground. "I don't even know *who* he is."

"Pretty tough to face, Howard, but purse-snatching can't make it any better. What did this sleaze look like?"

"Big, real big. With a big nose and a mustache and a scar. Right here." Howard ran his finger from the right side of his mouth up his cheek. "And he had some kind of accent."

"Southern, Yankee, what?"

"Not American."

"Mexican?"

"Huh uh, I know Mex."

"He sound like anyone you've seen on TV?"

"Not American, that's all."

"Okay. What color skin? Light, dark? A black man?"

"Not black. But dark, and he had real curly hair."

"Wearing…?"

"Dark pants, white shirt."

"A hat?"

"Who wears a hat?" Howard muttered.

"Shoes?"

"I wasn't looking at shoes. I was looking at two twenties and a ten."

"Anything else you can tell me, Howard?"

"Isn't that enough to show you how dumb I was?"

"Yes, it is. Look, Howard, it's up to you whether you want to tell the cops all this. Might help you, might not. It does help me, and I appreciate it."

I thrust out my hand and Howard took it with a hesitant, clammy grasp. One scared kid.

"At least, tell your mother everything. She should know what you thought you were doing for her."

I walked back to the car. Sgt. Almond leaped out to open the door for me.

"What was that all about, Colonel?"

"Nothing good, Sergeant. Let's get back to the base and have at those last two yard guys."

***

Samuel Trask reminded me of an aging wire-haired terrier. Under his flapping surplus army fatigues, he seemed to be all stringy muscle. His hair stuck up in a bushy gray halo around his thinning crown. He looked fifty, but his employment record said he was forty-one.

"I see you're from New York, Mr. Trask."

"Hey, Chief, call me Sammy. Yeah, the Bronx."

"What brought you out here?"

"Wanted to see something besides traffic and people. Some joke, right? Twenty years of knocking around the U S of A, and here I am sweating my balls off on three part-time jobs to make enough for a flop, food to live on, and gas to keep my junker going."

"Tell me about the Thursday before the crates were taken, Sammy."

Trask cleared his throat. "What about it?"

"Was there anything different about it?"

"You mean the Mex leaving early?"

"You tell me."

"Not much to it, Chief. He gets an emergency call 'bout an hour before we-close up, and he's gone."

"Who locked up? Look at me, Sammy."

"The rest of us."

"Who left first?"

"You mean after the Mex?"

I nodded.

Again Trask's eyes avoided mine. He picked at the frayed cuff of his shirtsleeve. "The Indian, I think."

That would corroborate Longeye's story—unless these two had worked it out between them.

"Who was the last to leave the yard that afternoon, Sammy?"

"Me and Petrillo."

"You left together?"

"Right." Sammy Trask cleared his throat again. "You got a problem with something?"

A lot of throat clearing, I thought. Eyes that won't meet mine. This man is lying.

"I have one hell of a problem, Sammy. I'm hoping you can help me with it."

"Like I said, I snapped the pad on the gate, then me and Petrillo got in our cars and left."

"You remember where the three crates were at that point?"

"Right where they was supposed to be. At the end of the center row. That's where we store boxed units. Airplanes mostly around the fence, boxes in the middle."

"All right, Sammy. Thanks for your help. That'll be all for now.'

I followed Trask to the door and motioned to Sgt Almond to come in as Sammy walked out.

"Two things, Sergeant. When you bring in the next man, give him a friendly tip that it looks like the colonel has given the other three a clean bill. And put in a call out front to detain Mr. Sammy Trask."

As I expected, hulking Frank Petrillo arrived in an obviously nervous state. Moisture beaded his wide forehead. His restless fingers kneaded his sweat-stained baseball cap.

"Sit down, Mr. Petrillo. You know why you're here?"

"It's about them three crates that was ripped off."

"What do you know about that incident, Petrillo?"

He fingered one of the curly sideburns framing his chubby face. "I don't know nothing about it. When I left that day, everything was okay. Next day, Captain Larssen brings some museum guy to the yard and finds the crates gone."

"How did you leave the yard that day?"

"We left it secure, like every Thursday."

"I don't mean that, Petrillo. Who left first?"

"Oh. Estevez left first. He left early. Personal problem, he said. We heard later that somebody beat up his wife."

"Who left next?"

"I think it was the Indian out first. At five. That's when we close. Then me and Sammy left together."

"Who locked up?"

"We done it together, like I said."

"You handled the padlock yourself?"

Petrillo scowled in concentration. "No. Sammy did."

"You each had a car there?"

He nodded. "In the parking area outside the gate."

"Who drove away first?"

"Like I said, we drove away together." Petrillo frowned. "No, wait a minute. Sammy decided to empty his car's ash tray, so I pulled around him and left."

Bingo!

"Thanks, Petrillo. You can go."

"Sergeant!" I called when Petrillo's footsteps faded. "Get Trask back in here. Now!"

Four minutes later, Sammy Trask again sat uneasily in the chair in front of my desk. For this interview I stood, walked from behind the desk, and towered over the skinny yard worker.

"Colonel, I already told you"

"Mr. Sammy Trask, you are in deep shit."

He looked stunned. Cleared his damned throat.

"You faked snapping the padlock shut, fiddled with your car's ashtray until everybody else was gone. Then you went back in there and fired up one of the forklifts."

"That's crazy!"

"No, that's moonlighting. How much did you get paid for that little piece of relocation work?"

Now Sammy had a hard time getting his throat clear.

"Participating in the theft of government property. Taking a bribe to do it. How much was it, Trask? A thousand? Two? What did the big man with the scar pay you?" I was gambling on that.

Trask's face went two shades paler.

"You know about...him?"

I watched Sammy crumple.

"Christ, Colonel. They was only three crates of some damned obsolete I-don't-know-what. He told me all I had to do was move them next to the south fence on the Thursday after next. Then give each crate a little orange squirt from a spray can he gave me."

"You set up a burglary of government property, Trask. At the least, you're going to be charged with complicity in theft. You come up with all the details, it might help you."

"Ain't you supposed to be reading me my rights, or something?"

"I'm not the police, Sammy. This is a military matter."

I put my foot up on the edge of Trask's chair and leaned over him. "Where did this guy contact you?"

Sammy let out a long, ragged sigh. "He came up to me in the parking lot near where I have a crummy room. Had an accent I never heard before."

I strode off a few feet, then turned back. "And?"

"And we got talking. And he said how I could make some easy money just by moving three crates up to the fence."

"That didn't bother you?"

"I figured some antique airplane freak was out to get himself a free artifak."

"Come on , Sammy."

"Hell, I don't know what I thought."

"You thought about money."

Trask nodded. "Yeah, ten Cs. In advance."

"Showed real trust."

"Told me he'd cut my nuts off if I blew it. If you call that trust, then he showed trust."

"You're a real sweetheart, Sammy. But you may have just done yourself some good." I picked up the desk phone. "Sergeant, take this man into custody. Then see if you can find me a sandwich somewhere."

In this murky situation, I'd made a small break. I picked up my phone and called Mollison.

***

In the dead-still afternoon, the storage yard's oily sand exhaled the stale breath of desert heat.

"The crates originally were there, Colonel." Major Mollison pointed at the end of a central row of variously-sized crates, most of them weather-aged, some of them newer.

"And the three we are concerned with were moved —"

"Courtesy of Samuel Trask."

"Yes, him. Using one of the forklifts. Put them where you can see I've taped off the area."

We walked to the empty space between two sad-looking antique helicopters. "You told me you searched here, inside the fence."

Mollison pulled off his flight cap and mopped his forehead with a handkerchief. "Yes, sir. Found nothing except those loose footprints. There…" He pointed. "And over there. You can see why castings couldn't be made in this loose stuff."

"And outside the fence?"

"I took a look, saw nothing. But I was rushed, and with all the grass and weeds out there, I thought I'd better tape it off for a more detailed search."

Outside, the yellow tape had been strung in a square U from the fence on either side of the theft site to a pair of stakes some thirty feet out in the weeds.

"You told me a daily patrol drives along that perimeter road out there."

"Since Captain Larssen discovered the theft, I've had the patrol swing outside the taped area."

I surveyed the fence. Eight feet high, with wire twists sticking straight up along the top.

"We'll go back to the vehicle," Mollison suggested. "I'll drive us out the gate and back here to the taped area."

"Hell with that, Major. I'll climb over."

I trotted to my left, past the point where the tape was tied to the chain link, ducked under the nose of the hulking 'copter, and pulled myself up the rippled wire fencing. My uniform shoes gave me just enough purchase. When I dropped down outside, I was sweating.

"Shit," I heard Mollison mutter. Then he clambered up and over the fence to join me outside.

Six feet apart, we ducked under the tape, then slowly walked inside the marked perimeter, eyes to the ground, noting every disturbed stone and crushed leaf. One laborious, time-eating sweat job. No wonder Mollison had hoped to lay it on somebody else. But I'd managed to stick him with a share of it anyway.

The deep, wide-spread tracks in the sand roadway near the fence had obviously been made by one hell of a big truck. No surprise. Mollison already surmised that much.

"Grease stains here." The major squatted and fingered an oily blotch between the tire tracks and the fence. "No, it's hydraulic fluid. My guess, the truck had a crane with a minor hydraulic leak." He stood. "Whoever did this was damned well-organized."

"Mollison, over here."

He stepped close and leaned over my shoulder.

"Saw a glint in this clump of grass. Ballpoint pen."

"Yeah," he said. "Cheap dark green plastic, but with a nice, shiny clip. Tells me it hasn't been here long."

"Fingerprints?"

"If we're lucky." Mollison pulled out a key ring, slipped a key through the pen's clip, extracted the pen from the grass clump, then held it up for closer inspection.

"What's that yellow lettering?"

"Kind of faded. BLACK... something, Then LONG," Mollison read. "And there's a third word. Looks like HAUL."

"Let me have a look at that, Major."

Mollison handed over his keys with the clip-supported pen.

In the scorching sunlight, I squinted. "That's BLACKHAWK. And you're right. The nearly scratched-off third word is HAUL. BLACKHAWK LONG HAUL."

"Could have been dropped by our missile thieves," Mollison said. "Or a hiker. Could have passed through a couple hands and mean nothing at all." He pulled an evidence envelope from a pocket and slid in the pen. "We'll check it for prints, but I'll lay odds this and a charge card will take you on any wild goose chase you want to buy."

"On the other hand, it's the only potential lead we have." My mind raced.

Blackhawk. A sports name. Hockey. The Chicago Blackhawks.

Thirty minutes later, back in the welcome air conditioning of base HQ, I called to the E-4 outside the door of my temporary office, "Sergeant Almond, see if you can find me a 1991 Chicago phone book."

9.

Two days after the Cairo meeting of the Committee of Three, and five months before the theft of the Pluto missile components, Maha Baiji stepped from her doorway onto the narrow sidewalk. In her *abaya*, she looked no different from the gaggle of women on this gritty street in the small Iraqi town some eight kilometers south of Baghdad; no different except for her bright green shopping bag. She took no notice of the dusty tan Fiat that prowled along the street fifty meters ahead of her. Morning heat already pressed down on the street. She hoped to reach the market square and complete her food purchases before the sun rose much higher.

Her bright green bag made her easy to follow. From observing her for a week, the three men in the Fiat knew she would cross at the intersection just ahead. When they stopped just short of the cross street, the halted Fiat caused no particular interest. Then the right front and rear doors burst open. Two men leaped out, seized Maha and thrust her into the Fiat's rear seat so rapidly her scream froze in her throat. One of the men pushed in behind her. The other slid back into the front passenger seat. The doors slammed shut. The driver floored the accelerator, careened the Fiat into the side street, and it vanished.

Not one of the stunned women on the sidewalk would recall anything helpful to the late-arriving local police. Two men in dark trousers and white shirts had seized a woman from the sidewalk. They had been tall, short, average—according to which witness was speaking. No one had thought to take the Fiat's plate number. No one, in fact, even reported the car was a Fiat.

Nor was the handful of police officers particularly interested in pressing the matter. The descriptions of the incident had sounded too much like an activity of the KGB-trained Amn, the Iraqi Department of State security. Even the local police found it not healthy to become involved in potential Amn affairs, especially with Saddam still in control of ever-shakier central Iraq.

The authorities did not learn who the young woman was until late in the evening when her husband reported her missing. He worked as a plasterer. She was a dutiful housewife. The motive behind her abduction was not clear until the following day, and then only to her brother in Baghdad.

***

Muzaffer Ghavam, a burly, yet placid forty-year-old bachelor with a doctorate in nuclear physics from MIT, took no notice of the man striding past his table in the busy coffee house. Not until he realized the man had left something in passing—a small piece of paper, folded once. Ghavam spun around to see only the coffee house door swinging shut. With a puzzled scowl, he unfolded the paper.

> Do what we demand, your sister Maha will be released. Refuse, and she will be defiled then never seen again. Inform the authorities of this note, or disobey instructions to follow, she is dead.

Ghavam stared at the alarming unsigned note. Could it be a cruel joke? He shoved back his chair and rushed to the café's telephone.

"Muhammet, this is your brother-in-law. May I speak to Maha?" He held his breath.

Muhammet's voice was a near-sob. "She has been taken, Muzaffer. I meant to call you, but in the—"

"Taken?"

"By men in a car. When she walked to market. That's all the police have told me. What should I do, Muzaffer? What *can* I do?"

"You can do what the police ask. And you can pray, Muhammet. We both can pray. If I learn anything, I will of course call you," he lied. Lying was inescapable. He hung up with his fingers jittering in fear for Maha, and in disgust at himself for his enforced withholding of the truth.

The instructions came that evening, by telephone to his obscure lodgings on the east bank of the Tigris. He hoped the ringing might be his awaited notice of reassignment in the government's nuclear program, or the police with helpful news. But he feared otherwise.

And he was right. The male voice was chillingly toneless. "Maha is in our hands. You will supervise the manufacture and delivery of certain ceramic items, specifications to be forthcoming by messenger. This will be done at the Al-Mansur ceramics plant near Zakho."

Zakho? An isolated Kurdish town in the northern mountains of Iraqi Kurdestan, a place of rumored turmoil. Ghavam had heard hazy reports of nuclear research there just as the fighting broke out in Kuwait.

"The director of the factory," the flat voice on the phone told Ghavam, "has been told you will be fulfilling a Jordanian government contract. The raw materials are already delivered, beryllium and uranium oxides. Specifications will arrive by messenger."

"May Allah curse you!" Ghavam burst out. But his words were spat into a dead phone.

The next morning, he found the specifications slipped beneath his loose-fitting front door — eight pages of them. The project called for sixty-thousand beryllium-uranium oxide hexagonal rods, cigar-sized and center-drilled down their length. Included in the papers were a Zakho street address — his lodgings-to-be — and a letter from an official of the Iraqi Freedom movement in Saudi Arabian exile, granting his safe passage into Iraqi Kurdestan. A forgery, Ghavam suspected, but a convincing one.

Also enclosed in the flat packet: something that looked like a dried brown berry. It took Ghavam a full minute to realize what it was. A chill broke between his shoulder blades. His cold fingers dropped the amputated nipple.

He found an operating fuel station and filled the tank of his battered gray Mercedes. By dusk, he had driven well north on the roadway along the Tigris; through Tikrit, Saddam's hometown, to Mosul. Here, he crossed the river.

At the far end of the bridge, he was stopped by a half-dozen bearded and turbaned Kurdish men armed with automatic weapons. How many more could be in the nearby bushes? Ghavam's hand trembled as he offered the purported letter of passage to the tallest among them. The man wore a flowing red mustache. His piercing eyes, black as midnight, scanned the paper. The glaring eyes were not the most disturbing part of this encounter. What really focused Ghavam's attention was the cold muzzle of the man's assault rifle pressed against Ghavam's throat.

The towering Kurd looked up from the letter. "You are to work in the ceramics factory?" His Arabic was accented, ever so slightly, but accented nonetheless. The gun muzzle pressed hard against Ghavam's jugular.

"What the letter says is correct," he managed.

"Piss on Saddam!" the Kurd burst out.

"By a hundred camels with bad kidneys!" cried Muzaffer Ghavam without hesitation.

Shouts of laughter rose from the men grouped around the road-weary Mercedes. The dark-eyed leader jerked his rifle skyward. The roadway cleared, and Ghavam rolled off the bridge onto the road to Zakho. For a hundred more kilometers, the narrow pavement wound through foothills. Then the road steepened into the mountains along the Iraq-Turkey border.

As Ghavam drove into isolated Zakho, night black as the pit of hell had fallen. He found the address easily enough, an ancient, mold-smelling, two-story inn.

"*Andee hagz,*" he told the wheezing old guy at the counter. "I have a reservation. Ghavam."

The old man gave him the key to a room on the second floor, with a view of the street, for what that might be worth. Ghavam felt trapped, and by people without conscience. His sister's mutilation, if indeed the grisly token sent him was hers, was dreadful. But equally distressing was the very act of mutilation involved. Flagrant defiance of the laws protecting women. What kind of people were these?

***

In the next morning's wan light, Ghavam drove northward on the dusty road toward the town. Three kilometers out, he found the ceramics factory, an undistinguished, two-story cement-block building of considerable size. Ceramic manufacturing here, so many kilometers into virtual isolation? Or was this place devoted to work more closely associated with his own assignment?

He left the Mercedes in the moderately-occupied parking area and walked into the stark plaster-walled lobby. Behind a metal reception desk, a skinny man in a long-sleeved white shirt glanced up from a rumpled newspaper. Then he hopped to his feet.

"*Ductoor* Ghavam! We have been expecting you." Ghavam towered over the scuttling little man, who turned out to be director of operations. The warm reception gave Ghavam a touch of confidence, but he quickly realized that could be entirely false. He was not a casually-visiting fellow scientist here; he was a hostage of some ruthless gang, of which he knew nothing.

But they apparently knew much about him; probably knew he had been raised by his sister after their parents were killed in a Kurdish uprising; evidently knew how close they had become; obviously knew he was one of Iraq's foremost nuclear experts, and that his name would gain him instant status in any scientific organization in the nation.

And so it did at Al-Mansur Ceramics. He was given an office, even a secretary who seemed required to do little more than fend off any caller not directly related to Project *Seegaar*, as it was informally termed. He was ordered to supervise the seegaars' production, quality control and manufacturing pace.

Ghavam soon realized pert little Noor was increasingly bored by her inactivity. And as her small part in the project wore on, he began to hope her boredom and his isolation might lead to mutual...adventuring.

He was trapped by the stark vision of Maha lying in some filthy cellar, her breast painfully suppurating, her mind choked with terror at the next horror they might inflict on her. He would do what they asked here, get it over with, then trust in Allah to make them let her go.

In three weeks, he fell into a trap within this trap: Noor. Raven-haired, petite perfection, she was no more than nineteen, fresh as a desert flower. Ghavam had been strong enough to resist Saddam's drive toward nuclear statehood. That fortitude had cost him the top spot at the nuclear research facility at Tuwaitha, rebuilt after its 1981 bombing by the Israelis, and had sent him into on-call isolation in Baghdad. But now, concerning Noor's obvious willingness to cooperate beyond office hours, he was elatedly weak.

In the months required to produce the thousands of precisely-shaped ceramic seegaars, his compliant secretary continued to grace his office — and his bed in the shabby little apartment provided him in nearby Zakho. Her easy compliance, he suspected, could have two purposes; to provide him with some necessary relief from the rushed pace of his close supervision work. And to report to his keepers any sign of non-compliance.

Noor...Light. Could be, Noor...Bittersweet.

***

This night, Muzaffer Ghavam lay beside her on his damp sheet and stared at the crack-veined plaster ceiling. Sixty-thousand seegaars were complete, packed in three specially designed crates, ready for shipment. At last, his part in this unfathomable project was over.

Naked, Noor rose leisurely from the bed, turned to offer a smile, then reached into her clothing she had neatly folded on a chair.

"Muzaffer, my love, this came for you this afternoon."

He took the envelope in some confusion. "You wait until now to give it to me?"

Her smile tightened into a hardness he had not seen before. And her voice was different. As if she had aged in his arms.

"As instructed," she said.

He opened it with fingers that had just developed an annoying tremor. Thanks largely to her, these bastards knew everything he did.

The envelope contained an unsigned typed note:

```
7 am tomorrow. You will ride the truck to Mosul.
The cargo will be transferred by the truck
crew. You will board the flight and accompany
the shipment to its final destination. When
the project is completed, your sister will be
released. Your Mercedes will be returned. If
you fail to comply, your career will abruptly
end. Your sister will become a memory.
```

Through his suddenly dry throat, he finally managed, "Wh...Who gave you this?"

"It was on my desk, Muzaffer."

"I thought you said you were instructed to give it to me at this time."

"There was a note for me as well."

"Which said what?"

"To give you the envelope tonight. At least I waited until we —"

"Oh, thanks for small favors, Noor. No doubt a log has been kept of our 'love' affair. Tapes of our conversations." He glanced around the tiny room. "Hidden cameras here, perhaps?"

"I was only..." She buried her face in her hands and wept.

Ghavam glared at her. Whoever these bastards were, they believed in the surety of overkill.

***

With the crates of seegaars and Muzaffer Ghavam aboard, the aircraft taxied toward the Mosul Airport runway close to noon. A twin-engine Beech Super King Air. He had glimpsed its nameplate when he was motioned aboard by the beak-nosed pilot. That nose, Ghavam thought, gave the man a bird-of-prey look. A real contrast to his dumpy co-pilot. Both wore travel-worn, leather flight jackets over tan shirts.

Ghavam found himself the only passenger in two rows of six seats each. He sank into one of the seats halfway down the left row and marveled uneasily at all this aerial luxury. The money invested in whatever this was leading to seemed limitless. When the Beech, its twin turboprops whining, took off a few minutes later, he remained the only passenger.

The first leg traversed the length of Iraq all the way to the Persian Gulf, with a nighttime landing in Oman for refueling. The next day, they flew for hours offshore, land continuously visible a few miles to the right. Then, at eight or ten thousand feet, Ghavam guessed, they rushed on with land on both sides of what he decided had to be the Gulf of Aden. He felt totally helpless, caught up in what had to be a complex project leading to something horrendous.

When the gulf fell behind, and the Beech roared over solid land, he assumed they cruised over Ethiopia. Right. They landed at Addis Ababa. The Beech was refueled. The co-pilot delivered Ghavam a sandwich supper. Next morning, off again. With the sun behind them, he knew they headed west. Across Africa? Ghavam was already exhausted.

Tension. Apprehension. Trapped in flying prison. Hours slumped in one of the sea of empty seats. Day-into-night-into-day. The inevitable refueling stop after some six or so hours of monotonous droning in a sky relentlessly blue. Heavy money had to be greasing their multi-nation flight path and its daily take-off and landing clearances.

During the long aerial hours, the pilot and co-pilot alternately napped in their seats. When either of them made his way aft to the lavatory, he looked haggard.

In the empty cabin, Ghavam felt treated as a piece of barely animated baggage. I'd welcome another face. Any face. Even Noor... that'd be two faces, damned deceptive little imp.

Then, an overnight at a small airport with water visible on the west horizon Guinea...Ivory coast? Take-off early next morning to head west over open water. Horizon-to horizon. Had to be the Atlantic, apparently at its narrowest point for this lavish but limited-range airplane.

He dozed… Stared into empty blue above, rolling green below… Slept… Landing. Where? When the tri-cycle wheels chirped down, he deduced — from…Portuguese — he was in Brazil.

Not the plane's destination, though. More days over land, then skirting land, now on his left. South America's northern flank. He was navigating by sun, and knew they flew northwestward.

Two more dreary overnight stops, with the co-pilot delivering the inevitable plastic foam cup of coffee and slices of bread each morning; more coffee with the monotonous two sandwiches for a lonely supper.

When the empty ocean gave way to islands, he deduced they were over the Caribbean. Yet another refueling stop, this one in…that sign says *Maiquetia Airport, Caracus.* Could easily escape here, Ghavam thought. Could have at every stop. Pilot and co-pilot off to the terminal. I could just walk away

And kill my sister.

At every stop, he had stayed aboard. And he stayed aboard here. The co-pilot returned with the evening's two sandwiches — these were too spicy, but he forced himself to eat.

Late the next day, the Beech greased down, then taxied to a stop in the area reserved for non-scheduled, privately owned aircraft. The pilot cut his switches then called over his shoulder as if he had a planeful. "Last stop. Hermosillo."

Where the hell is that? Ghavam wondered. The co-pilot stepped back to open the cabin exit door. Ghavam spotted a flag on the distant terminal. Vertical green, white and red stripes, with some complex design in the middle. Mexico, he decided.

A windowless van pulled up. Three musclemen transferred the crates, then motioned him into the back with the big boxes. He felt stiff, grubby, and in dire need of a shower and shave. Then the van, with the vital uranium/beryllium crates and Iraq's leading nuclear scientist aboard, rumbled northwestward.

10.

"Can I get you anything, Mr. Gammon?"

I looked up from my window seat, and something thudded in my chest. My God, the flight attendant was almost a clone of Lizabeth. Same swirl of champagne hair. Same sleek figure. Almost the same silvery voice.

On its northeasterly heading, the 727 rode so smoothly that only the urgency of what I was hoping to do kept me from being lulled to sleep. Another break late yesterday gave me a sense of progress, but now I felt that could be a false impression. Mollison had conducted his own interrogation of Larssen's people and had struck pay dirt. The captain's assistant E-6 five-striper admitted that several months ago she had mailed a listing of the storage yard's inventory to a representative of the so-called Miami Museum of the Air. "Keep it quiet," the museum's rep told her. "Another museum may be after the same items we are."

Mollison thought he had made real progress—until that lead dead-ended at the Miami post office box number the caller had given the E-6. The renter had briefly taken it in the name of the non-existent museum, and that box number was now rented to a mail order house.

The faded imprint on the Blackhawk ballpoint pen remained the only lead. I'd debated a phone call to Blackhawk Long Haul vs. my appearance up there. Too easy for a potential source to lie on the phone or simply hang up. So here I sat, Chicago-bound.

Before I left Tucson, I reported all this to General Madden at Bolling, along with the descriptions young Bedlow and Sammy Trask had given me of the man with the cheek scar. Now only Blackhawk Long Haul, listed in my borrowed Chicago phone book, offered a lead.

***

Under a gray, drizzling overcast, O'Hare was its usual enclave of supercharged bustle in Chicago's western suburbs. In gray slacks and navy sports coat, I checked my bag in a terminal locker and stepped into the murky Illinois afternoon.

The taxi ride south was a lengthy trip through traffic to an industrial street near South Chicago's lakefront. Blackhawk Long Haul's warehouse terminal occupied the whole block. The hulking corrugated steel building was flanked by a chainlinked yard crowded with blue semis and trailers.

The cab bumped over a railroad siding then pulled close to the west end of the building.

"Wait here," I told the driver.

"Your dime, buddy. Meter keeps running."

Behind a dented steel entrance door, the small reception area was neater than I'd expected; paneled in birch plywood with a brown linoleum floor. The heron-like woman on the other side of a glassed partition appeared to be dressed in a collection of multi-colored scarves. She had reddish bangs down to her sandy eyebrows and squinted at me as I walked in. The thick security glass had a three-inch speaking hole placed low.

She hunched down. "Yeah?"

I bent down to the hole in the glass. "I'd like to speak with the manager, please."

"Mr. McReedy?"

"If he's the manager."

"He's the owner. And the manager, too."

"Is he here?"

"Yeah."

Absurdly, we faced each other in our crouches. "Well?" I prompted.

"Who wants to see him?"

"Steve Gammon. On a critical matter."

She grinned, showing oversized teeth. "You kidding?" She hit a button on her counter, and I heard her amplified voice reverberate beyond the lobby's rear door. Three minutes later, McReedy banged through that door, and I realized why he put up with this obstinate woman-behind-glass. In baggy khakis, McReedy had the same angular height, the same sandy eyebrows and washed-out red hair, though his was receding. He looked to be in his fifties. A father-daughter act.

"Yeah?"

I stuck out my hand. "Steve Gammon, Mr. McReedy. I'm here on government business."

McReedy's grip went limp. "IRS?" His voice had gone limp, too.

"No, no. Not IRS." I took the beat-up pen from my shirt pocket. "You recognize this?"

McReedy took the pen hesitantly, peered at me, then at the fragmented lettering.

"Where'd you get it?"

"Did it come from here?"

"Well, yeah. Gave them out for a while. Turned out the lousy printing wore off, like you see here. So we didn't reorder."

"How many did you give out?"

McReedy scowled. "What's this all about, Gammon?"

"There was a theft of government property, Mr. McReedy. We found this pen of yours at the scene."

"And you're hoping I have a list of people who got these? Fat chance. We gave out a gross of the damned things. This one coulda passed through a coupla hands by now. No way I can tie this lousy pen to anybody, if that's why you're here."

I pondered a moment. "Let's go at this another way. Have any of your drivers been dispatched to the Southwest recently? Specifically, to Arizona. Hauling a flatbed?"

McReedy's washed-out eyebrows rose. "No and no. Not to Arizona, and we don't have any flatbeds."

Dead end. A gross of pens given out, and McReedy was right. Any of them could have been passed on to others.

"How does your set-up work, Mr. McReedy? You rent rigs to independents, or do you have your own drivers?"

"This ain't U-Drive It. I got near thirty drivers on the road at any given time."

Final try. "Any of them missing?"

"What do you mean, missing?"

"Unaccounted for, Mr. McReedy. Not on the road, not on vacation, not sick at home. Unaccounted for."

"I got an idea. Delilah!" he shouted through the blow hole in the glass. "You got any driver, uh, unaccounted for?"

"Minute, Dad." She turned to a computer in a corner of her cubicle. The screen flashed green then began to scroll. A moment later, she bent back to the hole in the glass.

"Four out sick, five on vacation, rest on the road."

"Print 'em out, Hon."

After a few minutes of muffled dot matrix zipping, Delilah ripped the sheet from the cubicle's printer, rolled it into a tight tube and passed it through the talk hole.

McReedy handed over the print-out "That do you?"

"Admirably. My thanks."

"You wanna check my warehouse?"

"I don't think that's necessary."

"I run an honest business."

"I'm sure you do."

"Always cooperate with the government. You sure you're not IRS?"

"Positive."

"Who, then?"

"Air Force."

"You gotta be kidding."

"Not at all. You have a phone I can use?"

"Sure thing. Use the one in my office. I gotta do a coupla things out in the yard anyway."

McReedy's office, a partitioned-off corner of the warehouse, stank of cigarette smoke. I sank into his squeaky swivel, shoved a jar of reeking butts to the desk's far corner, and pulled the finger-grimed phone closer.

I tried the homes of the five vacationers, got four no-answers and one house sitter. The no-answers were inconclusive, but all four were listed as married, and it seemed unlikely a driver bent on big-time thievery would take his wife along.

Next, I asked to speak directly with the drivers on the sick list. Got the first three. This looks hopeless, I thought, as I dialed the number listed on the printout for Ahmed Fadlallah.

"He is not here," said the accented female voice.

"I'm calling from Blackhawk Long Haul, ma'am. He's listed out sick."

I got a long pause. Then she asked, almost in a whisper, "Mr. McReedy?'

"No, but I'm working with Mr. McReedy."

Another silence. I could hear her ragged breathing. Then she cleared her throat. "Ahmed told me... He said to say he is sick."

"Do you know where he is, ma'am?"

"He said... He said he would be gone maybe three days, but now it is more than three."

"You haven't heard from him?"

"*La*... No."

I checked the address. Cicero. Hadn't I seen a Cicero sign on the way here?

"Mrs. Fadlallah, this is Colonel Steve Gammon. I'm with the Air Force. I'd like to come to your home to talk to you, if I may. Right now."

"Air Force?" Her voice had climbed an octave. "What's wrong?"

"I want to discuss it with you in person, Mrs. Fadlallah. I'll be there shortly."

***

"I hope you've got the cash, pal," the cabbie muttered as he shoved us westward through late afternoon traffic. "I don't take credit cards."

The brick house was from another time on a side street from another era. The front door was three steps up between cement pillars. I pressed the doorbell button, heard its buzz clearly through the varnished door with its eye-level glass diamond. The door opened a cautious three inches.

"Mrs. Fadlallah? Steve Gammon. I called you earlier."

She was no taller than chest-high to me, with her black hair combed straight down, a stark frame for the walnut planes of her narrow face. Her light blue house dress contrasted with her dark eyes.

"Ahmed is in trouble?"

"I don't know, Mrs. Fadlallah. Is he?"

She stared past me for several seconds, then she opened the door. "You can come in."

Décor by Sears, impeccably cleaned and dusted. I sensed she was a painfully dutiful wife in Middle-Eastern custom.

"Sit, please, Mr...."

"Gammon."

"Coffee? I made coffee."

That could ease the tension. "Fine, thank you."

She brought into the small living room a hammered brass tray bearing a heavy brew already laced with sugar.

"You are from where, Mrs. Fadlallah?"

"Iran. From Shiraz. My husband, too."

"And you have been in this country since…?"

"We come in 1980, just before the war starts."

"The Eight-Year War."

She nodded.

I set my cup and saucer on an end table. "Mrs. Fadlallah, the trucking company has listed your husband absent because of illness."

In her chair opposite me, she stared at the braided rug. "He tells me to tell them that."

"Why? Where has he gone?"

"I do not know. He says he will be gone three days. But he does not come back."

"You have no idea where he is?"

She shook her head, again failing to meet my eyes.

"Does he take such trips often?"

"No, never before." But she didn't appear to be curious about his going off on an unexplained journey; only disturbed that he had overstayed his expected three-day absence.

"What clothes did he take?"

"Only two *blooze*…shirts, extra pants, sweater. And his gloves."

Not much of a wardrobe for a three-day stay. Working man's garb. That could rule out a passionate sojourn with a woman other than the one sitting here nervously overstirring her coffee.

"Was there anything he said that could suggest where he might be going?"

She gazed intently at the window behind me. A decade ago, she would have been a beautiful woman. Now her face showed signs of middle-age creasing.

"When I pack for him, I ask Ahmed if he will be warm enough with only a sweater."

" 'Where I go,' he says, 'it will be warm. Do not worry.' "

The temperature warm, or what he was getting into? Or both? Arizona was warm this time of year.

"You said he packed gloves."

"For driving. He always wear gloves to drive trucks."

Another slender tie-in.

"I am a good American," she blurted.

"I haven't questioned that, Mrs. Fadlallah. Not at all."

She fell silent. Then, as if she had come to a significant decision, she leaned toward me. "I tell you all I know."

"How did he leave here?"

"Leave?"

"In a taxi? His own car? Did someone pick him up?"

"Ah. I take him to airport."

I fought my impulse to roar at her, but maybe the problem was one of miss-meshing cultures.

"*You* took him to the *airport?*"

"In our Honda."

"When?"

"Thursday, last week."

"What time of day?"

"An hour before midday."

"What airline?"

"Like a... a... Like this." She drew a figure in the air.

Interlocking U's. "United?"

"*Aywa!* United!"

"Where was he going?"

"He did not say."

"Might you have a photograph of your husband I can borrow?"

She stood and handed me a small framed photo from a corner table, a color snapshot of the two of them standing on a lake shore. Lake Michigan, I assumed. Ahmed Fadlallah looked a few years older than his wife, a surprisingly frail man, clean-shaven, probably in his late forties.

I slipped the photo out of its ceramic frame. "I'll return the picture, Mrs. Fadlallah. Is there anything else you remember about your husband's leaving? Anything at all?"

She shook her head.

"You've been a real help," I told her as we walked to the door, "and I thank you."

"Why Air Force?" Now her face showed real concern. "Why does the Air Force ask about Ahmed?"

"It may be nothing," I said at the door. A sympathetic lie.

***

"We have a whole lot of flights that depart around noon, sir." The trim United agent at O'Hare had a rigid helmet of hair dyed lusterless black.

"I'd appreciate a list." I showed her my AFOSI ID card, and she began to tap her keyboard.

I studied the printout she handed me. A lot of midday departures to warm weather destinations, including one with a stop in Phoenix.

I marked it on the runout and handed it back to her. "If it can be done, I'd appreciate a list of the passengers on this one." Then I found a public phone, and dialed my temporary office down in Tucson.

"Sergeant Almond, what I need in a hurry is the name of any truck rental outfit in Phoenix or Tucson that leased a flatbed with a crane just before the incident at the storage depot—and hasn't gotten it back yet, or isn't sure where it is."

I thought it unlikely the perpetrators of such a large-scale thievery would take the risk of returning the rented rig. More likely, they would simply abandon it.

Back at the United counter, the agent handed me another computer print-out. Here it was: *Fadlallah, Ahmed.* Didn't even disguise his name. He was booked for Phoenix.

"Two outfits, Colonel," Sgt Almond reported when I called him again. "Both in Phoenix. One of them says they're not sure where their flatbed is at the moment, but they can vouch for the renter. The other outfit has no idea where their flatbed and crane may be. It was rented six days ago, and the owner is concerned because the rental contract called for only three."

"I'll check that personally, Sergeant. Name?"

"Navhop Truck Leasing. Owner's name is Peach, Leonard Peach." Almond read off the Phoenix address.

"I'll stop over in Phoenix tonight, and talk with them tomorrow. Good work." The next available flight would get me to Phoenix around 9:00 p.m. Down there I'd rent a car, find a motel, then have a go at Navhop in the morning. Some name to pin shaky hopes on. If hope was the word. I was acting on hunch-and-luck, the investigator's last ditch fall-backs.

***

After Hadeeya Fadlallah watched Mr. Gammon's taxi pull away, she shifted her eyes to the little house across the street. In less than a minute, she knew.

Behind her, the phone shrilled. So predictable.

"*Aloh,*" she said. Arabic, because these conversations with the man across the street were always in Arabic.

"Who was your visitor?"

"A salesman."

"No salesman arrives in a taxi. Do you want to see your husband alive again?"

To her silence, he said, "You and he agreed to become part of the Silent Jihad. You will do as we direct. You will tell me the name of your visitor."

What choice did she have? Surely the Americans would not forgive Ahmed and her coming here with aggressive intent. And she was certain that defiance of the omnipresent man in the house over there would have serious consequences.

She felt sick. "A man from the Air Force." Her mouth was dry as desert sand.

"His name?"

"Gammon." Almost a whisper.

"His rank? Where did he come from? What did he want?"

"He did not tell me."

"I am fast running out of patience, Hadeeya."

"He told me none of those things!" She felt her fear melt into hot anger.

"What did he look like?"

"You have no need to ask," she snapped with American-like defiance that surprised her as she said it. "You have pictures. I see you making pictures of everyone who comes here."

She slammed down the receiver and slumped in a chair, trembling.

11.

I found Navhop Truck Leasing housed in a big corrugated metal garage on a hard-scrabble side street in an industrial fringe of Phoenix. Some contrast to the glitz of the resort area, I thought, as I parked my borrowed Ford in a space marked VISITOR near the office entrance. The sun's aggressive heat bounced off the parking area's macadam and made even the latch of the building's steel door hot to my touch.

The office looked like a throwback to the 1950s. No paneled reception lobby here; only a cluttered drywall cubicle dominated by a scarred wooden desk, a brace of over-stuffed steel filing cabinets, and a rattly window A/C unit. Despite its crusted casing, the struggling A/C made the office winter-chilly.

Pawing through one of the filing cabinets crouched a man who groaned to his feet as I walked in. Of middling height, he wore a startling orange leisure suit.

"Mr. Peach?"

"That'd be me, friend. What can I do for you?"

A white fringe ringed his bald crown. He flashed a crinkly smile.

"I'm Colonel Gammon, Mr. Peach." I wore civvies this morning. "Air Force."

In a sidling dance, Peach moved around the desk and offered me a pudgy hand. "You been expected, Colonel. A sergeant from the base down Tucson way called me yesterday. I told him, yes, two fellas rented a hoist-equipped flatbed on the date he mentioned. He sounded like that wasn't the end of it, and here you are."

"What specifically did they rent, Mr. Peach?"

"My Fruehauf flatbed mounted with a hydraulic crane. A three-day rental, they told me. And now it's overdue."

"Can you describe the men who rented it?"

"One big, one not so big. Foreigners, by the way they talked."

I dug Fadlallah's photo out of my shirt pocket. "Is this one of them?"

Peach peered at the photo. Then he frowned. "Look, Colonel. I'm just a simple country boy. What am I getting into here?"

"No trouble for you at all, if you're being up front with me, Mr. Peach. Is this one of the men who rented your rig?"

His pale gray eyes flicked back down to the photo. "Yep. Yep, it is. He's the short one."

"And the other? What did he look like?"

"Big, like I told you. With a mustache."

"And a long scar from the corner of his mouth?"

"You got them pegged, Colonel. What'd they do with my rig?"

"I wish I could tell you, Mr. Peach. We want them as much as you do. I'd like to take a look at the paperwork on the rental."

"Got a signed contract with the guy's name and driver license number."

He rummaged through the mess on his desk and plucked out a yellow form. Here it was: confirmation in writing: *A. Fadlallah.* A for adios? Whoever was masterminding this didn't appear to worry about Fadlallah's paper trail. Which, I realized, pointed to his being expendable.

"Do you require payment in advance, Mr. Peach? Or at least a credit card?"

"They offered a cash deposit. Twenty-five hundred. A cashier's check drawn on a Chicago bank. I cashed it after the third day. They bring back my flatbed, I'll credit the deposit to what they owe me."

I handed back the contract form. He squinted at it. "A-rab fellas, right?"

"Possibly."

"Try to work with minorities," Peach snorted, "and what does it get you? Named this place Navhop to honor the Navajos and the Hopis. Now they're both mad at me."

"At least you're trying, Mr. Peach. Look, if you get your rig back..."

"*If!*" Peach's rosy face went pale.

"...or if you hear anything at all concerning that rental, I'll really appreciate your calling this number immediately." I gave him Major Mollison's office number. Peach dredged a much-chewed yellow pencil from his desk debris and scrawled the number on the bottom of the contract form.

When I opened the door to leave, the inward gust of Phoenix noontime heat seared my throat. Behind me, Peach called, "Let's have any new info go both ways, Colonel. You hear?"

***

At a scrambler phone in the base commander's office that afternoon, I waited for General Madden to come on the line. A buzz, two clicks, then the general said, in an oddly subdued voice, "What have you got, Steve?"

"The missile crates were taken out of here on a crane-mounted flatbed leased from a Phoenix truck rental company, driven by one Ahmed Fadlallah, a south Chicagoan immigrant of Iraqi descent, now — according to Immigration — a naturalized American citizen. He departed O'Hare at noon, July five. Rented the rig in Phoenix late that afternoon. He was accompanied at the rental by another man, presumably a Mid-Easterner with a noticeable facial scar. The flatbed was rented for three days, but now it's overdue."

"Fairly impressive, Steve, for a couple days' work."

"You're being generous. I'm able to tell you only where the truck has been, but not where it's gone, General. What we really need to know is where it is now."

"At least we can depth-check this Ahmed fellow. What was that name again?"

"Fadlallah. Ahmed Fadlallah." I spelled it and added the Chicago street address.

"We'll handle that at this end. Anything specific about the other man?"

"I'm ninety-eight percent sure he's the same guy who was in Tucson a few days before the theft of the Pluto. Bribed one of the storage yard workers to move the crates to an easy access point, and arranged to get the yard boss out of the way."

"Any lead on who he might be?"

"Only a description, General, with three helpful ID characteristics. Big guy, with a mustache, which, of course, he could shave off. And a prominent facial scar."

As I gave Madden a more detailed report on my activities from my first day on this assignment, I felt increasingly frustrated. Not a single lead concerning the whereabouts of the Navhop truck and its potentially lethal cargo.

And, of course, the general sensed my frustration. After a long pause, he said, "You've done an excellent piece of work Steve. So far. Now we are certain the theft was no college prank, but an event with far more serious implications. So stay with it at your end."

"This may be a dead end, General."

"I refuse to accept that. I want a report the instant you have something more. In the meantime, I'm requesting a high priority overhead imagery search, initially within a five hundred mile radius.

"Satellite recon."

"One of our recent launchings out of Vandenburg put up a wide-scan recon satellite with an adjustable orbit. We'll give it a try.'

I took a quick swallow of the potent coffee one of the C.O.'s aides had left me. "They could be whistle clean, but we should have background checks run on Blackhawk Long Haul in Chicago, and Navhop Truck Leasing in Phoenix. How about a rundown on ceramics fabricators?"

"To uncover any that might be turning out little hollow rods of uranium and beryllium. Not a bad idea, Steve, but it could take a while. Stay at Davis-Monthan tonight. Check with me this time tomorrow."

That, I felt, was one of the worst orders I could be given: do nothing. Almost anything was preferable to just sitting here.

***

Dr. Cornelius Joiner was glad he'd made it back from that remarkable meeting at Bolling in time for the quarterly dinner of the Society of Retired Aerospace Engineers. That get-together at San Diego's Holiday Inn at the Embarcadero had been most pleasant, Joiner thought, as he and wife Eleanor walked out the hotel's entrance and began their customary stroll along Harbor Drive. A decent cut of roast beef and the program on the liquid-fueled rocket experiments of Johannes Winkler in pre-World War II Germany had made the evening most worthwhile.

The best part was that Eleanor seemed perfectly happy to accompany her husband on these quarterly events. She had no interest in the programs, but she did like to get out of their small Hillcrest house and "go out on the town." And she enjoyed their traditional walk along Harbor Drive after the meetings ended.

On the brightly-lighted sidewalk, Joiner glanced at his watch. A little after 10:00 p.m. They told Marty they would be back home before 11:00. Joiner had felt guilty leaving Marty alone in the house, but as Eleanor told him on the short drive here down rapidly descending 4th Avenue, "A surprise house guest is at the host's mercy." Marty Bekker, one of Joiner's former co-workers at Lawrence Lab, had dropped out of the blue today. Joiner encouraged him to go with them to the SRAE meeting, but Marty had demurred. "Rather not see all those deteriorating poops again, Corney. I'll be fine here, keeping your TV warm."

At Lawrence Radiation Lab, someone had tagged Marty as a graduate of the Oscar Levant School of Social Graces, and here he was, thirty years later, with no discernable mellowing.

Joiner fought the urge to lay the whole Pluto thing on the table for whatever Marty might have to offer. But General Madden had sworn him to secrecy. So this was like the tight-mouthed old days, when Joiner had been thrilled to be in on a high-security project, but frustrated that he couldn't gab a damned word about it, even to Eleanor.

She strode quietly beside him now, much shorter than he, her arm linked with his, her hair silvery in the streetlights' glow. In her early seventies, she still managed a hint of the pixie attractiveness that had captivated him nearly fifty — good God, *fifty* — years ago.

Beyond the B Street Pier and Broadway Pier, the tiered lights of Coronado and the North Island Naval Air Station spattered golden glints across the mile-wide arm of San Diego Bay. The cool, moist night air carried the salt and creosote tangs of the waterfront. Joiner loved these post-meeting strolls, but tonight his thoughts had strayed far eastward. That command visit to Bolling was frightening in its potential. Yet the theft of the Pluto components made Joiner's heart thump invigoratingly faster for an added reason. His quiet retirement life had a new edge. He was more observant, more aware, more...

Oh, hell, he told himself as they headed back toward the hotel, you're just an old fart playing at new importance. Trying to relive what will never be again. Seeing what isn't there at all... Like the blue delivery truck I spotted when Eleanor and I pulled out of our driveway tonight. Thought I saw it again, behind us on 4th. Same van? Of course not. The city was full of blue vans. And I didn't see it when we pulled into the Holiday's parking lot.

"Corney, dear?"

"Eh?" She had brought him back to the harborfront.

"We're here."

"Oh, sorry."

They left the sidewalk to amble toward the parking area. Harbor Drive's traffic noise faded into the silence back here. Now he felt the air was oddly warm. Warm and still. For no discernable reason, Joiner felt a prickle across the nape of his neck.

Ridiculous.

Their little tan Subaru hunched in the row along the north side of the lot, between a larger car and a delivery van. In the diminished lighting, he couldn't make out its color. Blue? He was becoming paranoid.

Eleanor's grip tightened on his arm. Did she, too, sense odd tension? Their footsteps gritted on the blacktop. He winced at the sound.

As he fitted the key into the door lock on her side, he heard the scrape of a shoe. Someone else was out here, someone he hadn't seen as they traversed the lot.

Then he heard rapid footfalls. In sudden fright, he jerked up. A black form swung around the van's hood. Another whirled from its rear doors. Two men suddenly sandwiched him and Eleanor in the narrow space between their Subaru and the van.

For God's sake! A mugging!

12.

"**M**y wallet is in my right-hand breast pocket." Cornelius Joiner was surprised at the steadiness of his voice, but his body was instantly in a cold sweat. This simply could not be happening.

"Oh, my!" Eleanor gasped. She thrust out her purse.

"Take what you want," Joiner fought back the threat of a voice quaver. "Then please leave."

"You will come with us," the man nearest him ordered, a big bastard with a scar from his bushy mustache up to his right ear. English was not his native language. Joiner could not place the accent. Not Spanish, not ghetto patois. He peered up at the man's dark facial planes and glittering hard eyes. He felt a sharp prod in his side and glanced down.

"Gun," the big man said. "You come with us."

"*Corney!*" Now Eleanor's voice was shrill with accelerating panic.

"Leave her alone!"

"She come or she dies," the other assailant ordered. A squat man with a voice like a toad's croak, also in that unidentifiable accent.

"We'll do nothing of the kind!" Anger boiled in Joiner's chest. Who did these sons of bitches think they were?

"You both come or you both die." The scarred man amended in a tone of deadly assurance. "She dies first."

A bluff? Would these two thugs actually shoot them? Here, in a parking lot in the middle of San Diego? As Joiner began to weigh the probability, Toad-Voice seized Eleanor's arm, twisted it behind her. Slapped his other hand across her mouth to shut off her scream of pain before it began.

"All right! *All right!*" Joiner cried. He looked around wildly. Where in hell was anybody at all? This was way out of hand.

"In the van," ordered the man with the pistol.

They herded Joiner and Eleanor to the rear of the van. Blue van, Joiner noted. What an ass he'd been. Obviously—now—these two thugs had kept watch on their house, followed the Subaru, waited in the parking lot until they could pull up next to it. Then sat here until he and Eleanor walked right into their arms.

"I don't know what the hell you're after," he said as Toad-Voice flung open the van's pair of rear doors, "but you don't need her. Leave her here."

God, wasn't she too old for rape? Or was it true that rape was an act of violence, not sex? His hands began to shake.

The pistol prodded his side. "Inside," the thug ordered.

Joiner felt a surge of hot anger. He forced it down, climbed in, then turned to see Toad-Voice grab Eleanor and boost her aboard.

In the parking lot's dim light, Joiner made out a dark lump and a cardboard box against the front end of the otherwise empty cargo space.

"Behave, old man," Toad-Voice grated, "and you will not be tied. Do not behave, and we will tie you and cripple your woman."

The doors slammed shut. Seconds later, the engine kicked in. On his knees, Joiner scuttled back to the doors. If they could drop out while the van rolled slowly through the lot... Maybe when it paused for a break in the Harbor Drive traffic.

"*Damn!*"

"What?" Eleanor's voice sounded parched.

"No door handles in here."

But there was a small window between the cargo area and the front seats. In the dash lights' glow up there, he could make out Toad-Voice's hump of a shoulder and see the flashes of street lights as they swung to the right.

In the near pitch darkness, Joiner and Eleanor huddled against the van's cold steel side. He slipped his arm around her shoulders. The poor woman had to be petrified. But his analytical mind refused to give way to panic. What was the purpose of this crude kidnapping? In a van with no inside handles on the rear doors, a little spy window up front. And now he noticed a lingering smell of unwashed bodies. His scientific mind stopped its slide toward panic.

"Coyote van."

"Coyotes?" Eleanor sounded dazed but fighting it. "In here?"

"It's a term for the guys who transport illegal aliens up to U.S. border areas 'easy to cross.'"

But that surely wasn't the point now. And robbery hadn't been the motive. What in hell was going on here?

Then a frigid wave broke over his shoulders. He knew. And he knew why they, of all people, were sprawled on this damned steel floor.

In a sharp swing of the van, something soft slid against his leg. That dark clump he'd spotted when they were forced aboard. He reached down. "It's a blanket," he told Eleanor. He began to pull it over them. "Two blankets, in fact."

"Thoughtful bastards."

At her defiant sarcasm, he felt a surge of warmth. "Their way of keeping us reasonably healthy, kiddo." He hadn't called her kiddo in twenty years.

So what was in that box he'd spotted? He crawled across the knee-crunching steel floor. His exploring hands found two bottles of—he unscrewed a top. "Water," he told Eleanor. "And..." He reached back in the box. "Feels like a loaf of bread. Yeah, it's bread."

"Bread and water. For prisoners. But why?"

"Good question." He scuttled back to her, draped one of the blankets over her trembling shoulders. "To keep us in reasonably good shape. I'm beginning to get this. They need me."

"Need you? Why?"

Security be damned now, Joiner decided. "We're in this together. If I'm correct, these people, or whoever they're working for, stole an old cruise missile. One I worked on decades ago. And now I suspect they need me to get it operational."

"After forty *years,* Corney? An old *cruise missile?"*

"Not the kind you read about now. We designed it to deliver a succession of H-bombs that could flatten up to a dozen cities in one flight."

"My God! You were part of that?"

"I'm afraid so. In the Cold War, we were all science. Very little humanity. Until we tested the thing's nuclear engine."

"What happened? It didn't work?"

"It worked fine. But then we realized it would lay a swath of radiation across the friendly countries it would have to overfly to reach Russia. So humanity won out. We dismantled it and packed it away in crates."

"And now these guys have stolen the crates and science could eclipse humanity after all?"

"Very astute, kiddo."

"Who has them?

"Who knows? Some hate-America group."

"And they want to use that thing in a crazy attack?"

"That could very well be the case."

"Oh, Corney! And they want me along so you—but you *can't!* I don't care what they do to me. You just can't!"

He gave her what he hoped was a reassuring hug. "Without the fuel components, it's just so much dead metal. When we stored the thing, those components were disposed of. So it won't matter what they force me to do. The nuclear engine won't run without fuel. I can putter and dither, and somehow we'll get out of this."

His head was working, but his heart hit bottom. All he could do now was comfort Eleanor as best he could and "hang in there," to use one of friend Marty's favorite catch phrases. Marty… Surely house guest Marty would report their failure to return home after the SRAE meeting. Their car would be found in the Holiday Inn parking lot. But then…?

In the next two miserable hours, they learned just one thing: lying on the blankets folded several times lengthwise offered relief from the unyielding floor. They chanced a few swallows from one of the water bottles. Dozed...

…Then awoke to the slowing of the van's jostle. Then its squealy stop.

Joiner peered through the tiny window forward. "Looks like a border crossing point. Not a big one like Nogales. I'd guess remote and sleepy Lukeville."

Jabber up front. A Spanish-and-tortured-English palaver with a compliant-sounding border guard. Bribery at work? Then the van rushed on, too quickly for a kick-and-scream effort. And, Joiner suspected from the brevity of the stop, that would be futile anyway, with bribed border guards.

Another miserable hour. Another jittering stop. He peered through the little window. In the early morning gloom out there, a lonely neon Pemex sign glowed.

"Gas station," he told Eleanor. They heard the rattle of the gas cap, clank of the inserted nozzle, the rush of incoming fuel.

"Corney?" Eleanor whispered. "Kick and scream?"

"I'm afraid the station attendant wouldn't have a chance against two armed kidnappers, kiddo."

They rolled off again, along a winding road increasingly hilly.

Another stop, this time with cactus-studded desert visible through the spy window. The rear doors squealed open. Toad-Voice stuck his head in.

"*Twalitt,*" he announced.

"What?" The inflow of fresh morning air was welcome despite its heat, but what did this guy want now?

"Bathroom!" came a muffled shout from the front seat.

"Oh." Joiner turned to Eleanor. "About time."

He helped her out into hilly wasteland. Not a building, nor another vehicle in sight. She looked at leering Toad-Voice, then at Joiner. "Corney...?"

"Behind those bushes over there. They know we're not going to run off into this wilderness."

Yet, after these few moments free of their mobile prison, he felt returning meekly to the damned Coyote van demeaned them somehow. Then off they rolled. Southward, Joiner determined, when the mid-morning sun gleamed on the driver's side of the little window.

Joiner unwrapped the loaf of surprisingly fresh white bread. He handed Eleanor two slices. She shook her head.

"You're not punishing them by punishing yourself. Be a sensible bread-and-water prisoner."

An hour after that, they felt the van swerve off the pavement onto a bouncy side road. Finally, long miles of bone-rattling slowed to a winding crawl. Then a stop. And silence. Until the rear doors were thrown open.

"*Barra!*" Toad-Voice shouted. "Out!"

They clambered from the dank cargo area to stand between the van and a crude wooden shack. In the deepening dusk beyond the van, Joiner made out several towering oil rigs. An oil exploration site? What sense did that make? He scanned the darkening valley, then focused on a big building in the valley's center. Two stories of wood siding.

He heard a muted growl of generators, and a scatter of lights flicked on.

Mustache-Scar's hand grabbed his shoulder, shoved him toward the shack. The big thug unbolted the door and pulled it open.

"You live here."

As he and Eleanor stumbled in, Joiner thought the "you live" of that gruff comment was reassuring.

But the "here" was chilling.

13.

J ust after midnight in the Holiday Inn at the Embarcadero, where
General Madden had instructed me to await contact in my room, I
opened the door to a discreet knock. There, just after midnight, stood
Major Pete Pappas, Madden's Aegean Collegian aide. Pete's tight smile
failed to disguise the grimness in his eyes.

"Come in, Pete. Come in." With the Air Force Office of Special
Investigations sending the sharp, young major across the U.S. for a
personal conference, the situation had reached a stage beyond tense. "You
had any dinner?"

"On the plane. Just signed in. Got a room a floor down and came
straight here."

"How about some coffee – with a dash of brandy? I think the situation
calls for it."

"With urgency, Colonel." Pappas kicked the door shut and set down
what looked like a fat file case.

I poured from a room service carafe and a mini brandy, then we sat at
the little table near the window.

"I want you to understand, Steve, Madden sent me to fill you in on the
overall picture. Then I'm to stay here to follow the Joiner disappearance.
That frees you to follow up on satellite intel."

"In the meantime, we can apply our frustrated intellects to the Joiners.
I left Tucson as soon as their disappearance hit this morning's news. Got

here only a couple hours ago. Reported that to Madden, and he said sit tight until you got here. What've you been able to get at your end?"

The young AFOSI major took a long pull of coffee, set down the heavy china cup, and squinted through the window at the nighttime view of San Diego Bay. Then he turned back to me. "Before I blew out of Bolling, the San Diego police reported to Madden that the desk clerk here saw Joiner and his wife leave the front exit around nine last night. Just before midnight, a house guest of the Joiners called here. The Joiners were long overdue home, and he was getting antsy. The Holiday contacted the police, who found the Joiners' Subaru still in the parking lot out back. That's where the trail ends. If they don't show up after forty-eight hours, the police will issue a BOLO."

"I have a far from reassuring idea what's happening, Pete. I'm sure you do, too. Joiner worked on the Pluto back in the 1950s. Ergo…"

"Ergo whoever took those crated parts needs an expert to reassemble the thing. Who else but the top scientist who helped build it?"

As Pete picked up his coffee cup, I noticed its little jitter. "Any report on the satellite sweeps," I asked him.

"Since yesterday, there've been sweeps from central Texas through all of New Mexico and Arizona and Southern California. Even into northern Mexico. A team of analysts is still going over big scale printouts, but small scale showed nada we might be interested in. So I don't hold out much for the more detailed study. That's a lot of area to cover to find a flatbed-crane truck. And by now, your scar-faced guy and his buddy could have the truck and crates under cover."

"Our needle-in-a-hayfield approach may not be the way to go about this." I poured myself another cup of the strong coffee.

"Yeah. The best bet was the APB we had the police issue just after the theft was discovered. Unfortunately, there was a delay in that, but we've screened more than twenty local and state police intercepts of crane-equipped flatbeds, loaded and empty, from Texas north to the Dakotas, and west to Washington State and California. *Nada*. Nothing that fits the INCRIT."

I gazed out at the moving lights of boats in San Diego Bay. Red, green. Purposeful. At least out there, they knew where they were going.

I turned back to Pete. "I think by now they've already unloaded and hidden or disposed of the flatbed. What else you got?"

"This next HUMINT gave us a cold jolt in the spine. Pure coincidence, maybe, but worrisome. One of the CIA's airport people—"

"Airport people?"

"Yeah, they have a rotation of observers assigned to key foreign airports to spot anything worth spotting. In the jittery wake of the Iraqi cease-fire, Mosul Airport, way up in Kurdish land, is of particular interest. Among others. Three weeks ago, one of these CIA observers noticed a bunch of big boxes being crammed aboard a privately-owned Beech Super King Air. That's an upscale twelve-passenger job. But it took off with only one passenger aboard—a 'person of interest' named Musaffer Ghavam."

"I don't recognize the name, Pete. Does this Ghavam guy belong to any known terrorist outfit."

"CIA ran him through the Langley computers, and he's not in any group. But he just might be more dangerous than your standard bomb planter. Turns out he's an Iraqi nuclear physicist."

I let that sink in, and it sank in hard. "Where was that plane headed?"

"It took off south. Next spotted a couple days later at Lungi Airport in Sierra Leone. So it had crossed Africa. From Sierra Leone, it headed west over the Atlantic, and the CIA lost track of it"

"Hell!"

"Lost track of it—until it landed some days later in Hermosillo."

"Northwestern Mexico."

"Yep. The cargo was transferred to a van, which drove off with Ghavam in the passenger seat. And at that point, the CIA's spotter blew it. Couldn't get his old Chevy started. He ran for a rental, but by the time he got one, the van was long gone."

"Headed where?"

"Out of the airport, Steve. The CIA guy—actually an unofficial helpful-citizen adjunct—has no clue where the van was headed."

"So we have an Iraqi nuclear scientist last seen in northwestern Mexico. And now Joiner, also a nuclear scientist, has disappeared. Abducted, we can reasonably assume."

"And whoever did it also took Joiner's wife because she was a witness to the abduction."

"Come on, Pete. You can do better than that. If removing a witness was all they had in mind, they would have left her dead in the parking lot behind this hotel." I gave him a hard look. "Let's hope that won't turn out to have been a more merciful alternative for her."

Pete nodded glumly. "I see where you're going with the wife aspect. I agree. They'll keep her alive to get all they can out of Joiner. As far as we know, he's a loyal American. So they need her for leverage. Christ, Steve, she's a woman in her seventies."

"What do they care about that? I'd guess they're the same kind of people who gun down passengers in airport waiting rooms and blow up department stores in some sacred cause. What's one senior citizen to them? Two, after Joiner has done the work for them."

"If you're right, and if he does it."

"You got anyone you really love, Pete?"

"Sure. My wife. My two kids."

"So some ruthless son-of-a-bitch makes off with one of them and says, 'You turn over the AFOSI file on such-and-such, or we take a pair of pliers—'"

"I get the picture. I don't know what I'd do."

"You'd know what you couldn't do, Pete. And that's exactly what can be facing Joiner."

"And here we sit talking while the Joiners face God-knows-what." He paused. Then he said, "All right. Let's go with the Mexico angle. We don't know where the van went from Hermosillo, but how 'bout we concentrate satellite recon on northwest Mexico. That could narrow things down to something useful."

Pete stood, picked up the boxy case he'd brought with him, brought it to the table and extracted a telephone handset.

"You always travel with a scrambler?"

"Whenever a group of crazies steals a nuclear-powered cruise missile, Steve, and I have to call a general at his home."

Four minutes later, Madden came on the line. After giving him a three-minute update, Pete handed me the phone.

"So it looks like Mexico," Madden said without preamble.

"Northwestern Mexico, General. I'd be willing to put a fair amount of money on that."

"Such specific locationing could help, but at the same time, it adds a problem to our problem."

I thought Madden sounded unusually testy—a general with more than enough worries for one evening.

"We can't just send in the U.S. Army to sweep the area clean, Steve. And with the current tension over the Mexican fair trade proposal, plus the usual political picture down there, all we can do is concentrate our satellite sweeps there."

The line fell silent. Then Madden said, "How sure are you about this northwestern Mexico info? Scale one to ten."

"I'd give it an eight, General. And I want to go down there."

"It's a big area. You stay where you are until our first south-of-the-border detailed imagery comes in."

A conditional go-ahead, but the general was right. Racing down to Mexico without a real lead would be as much an emotional act as a rational one. In fact, a lone gringo prowling around down there would be no cover at all. But, I thought, a typical American tourist couple would excite no curiosity whatever.

"General, if satellite recon comes up with anything at all, I want to go in — as a tourist. Man with wife."

"Not a bad cover."

"Who's available?" I asked.

"Polly McLean comes to mind."

"She's easy to work with, General, but she's more of a researcher than a hard field type."

"A hard field type..." I heard paper rustle. Then, despite Madden's attempt to hide it, I detected hesitation in his tone as he said, "Laura Gorcy."

Gorcy-the-Divorcee. Personality like a disgruntled porcupine. Married twice, blew it twice. Then back to her maiden name. Crack shot with a handgun — and with her mouth.

"How's your Spanish, Steve?"

"Rudimentary."

"Hers is a lot better than that."

What I was trying not to say was that Laura Gorcy was bull-headed, over-confident, domineering and generally distrustful of male supervision. Probably a conditioned reflex brought to full bloom, first by marriage to a hopeless alcoholic, then to a wife batterer, who himself ended up in a St.Louis hospital after Laura took him on with an ice-cream dipper. An interesting defensive weapon, it left him with a half-moon scar linking his eyebrows. This was the woman I was to take into Mexico as my "wife."

"Steve?" General Madden pushed for corroboration.

"She's a natural, General." God save us all.

"Good. Stand by. You're going on hold for a moment."

When Madden came back on the line, I heard more paper rustling. "Got a run-out here on satellite avails. First large scale sweeps will begin at daylight tomorrow. At that point, I'll ask Langley to give us a probability estimate, based on what we've assumed tonight. Stay in San Diego with Pete until I contact you tomorrow."

"I've had worse company, General." Laura Gorcy came to mind. I heard Madden click off, and I returned the scrambler handset to its case.

"How long do you think this thing can stay out of the media?" Pete wondered.

"Requesting the satellite scans has surely alerted more than a couple of agencies by now. The FBI and CIA shouldn't be security problems. And AFOSI certainly isn't. The Joiners' disappearance could stay a local story, if the media doesn't get into speculation."

"Hope so. The bastards engineering this mess could be the major security problem. When it suits their purpose, they'll no doubt make a point of paniking the public, hold the whole damn nation hostage for whatever they have in mind."

"I'm not so sure." I poured us both refills of our spiked coffee. This was turning into a late-late-nighter. "Know what I'd do in their place? I'd keep the project under wraps until the missile is operational. Once it flies, the whole Western Hemisphere will turn upside down looking for them. If big-scale extortion is what they're cooking up, they'll get the launch set and make their public pitch with a minimum deadline."

"Maybe they've dumped the thing somewhere, and they'll try a colossal bluff."

I nodded. "Possible. But I suspect we're complicating what can be simple. Launch the Pluto with its radioactive wake as insane revenge for Desert Storm. No warning. And people die in a swath a mile wide across the U.S."

Pete stared at me. "You think whoever took that thing can actually make it operational?"

"You know better than I do what condition it was in. What do you think?"

"Joiner thought the airframe, engine and the guidance system should be in fairly good shape. All components were sealed in airtight containers. The only missing elements are the fuel rods, sixty thousand of them. And booster rockets to launch the thing."

"You've answered your own question, Pete. Given fuel rods and boosters, it sounds to me as if the thing could fly. The CIA informant saw large containers being unloaded from the Beech King Air at Hermosillo. I'd say it's possible—even probable—they were the fuel rods. And Ghavam came with them."

"I hate to agree with you on that. But, yeah, it looks like they've gotten their fuel rods along with two nuclear scientists: Joiner and Ghavam. Jesus!"

"What have you found out about this Ghavam guy, Pete?"

"Born in 1950 in Baghdad, graduated from Baghdad University with a major in science, minor in English. Exchange student in the 1970s. Masters and doctorate in nuclear physics at MIT and, I think, Caltech. Last heard of, he was employed in Saddam's embryo nuclear development program."

"Willingly?"

Pete shrugged. "We don't know. Does it matter? As you so eloquently pointed out the last time we worked together, there's always a way to control behavior if the controller has no conscience."

14.

With the more concentrated satellite sweeps not practical until daylight, Pete returned to his room. I requested a 5:30 a.m. wake-up call and went to bed.

A couple minutes after I hit the pillow, the phone rang. I thought the operator made a mistake. Until I checked my watch. Five-thirty on the nose. Four hours' sleep wasn't enough. I wobbled to my feet, shaved, dressed and rode an otherwise empty elevator down to the restaurant to wait for Pete, who was already there.

"What kept you, Steve?"

Damned kid. Already had bacon and eggs in front of him. I ordered an omelet, and we ate with not much to say. Hundreds of miles overhead, invisible satellites relayed data to intel downlinks for conversion into visual scans for interpretive analysts.

Back in my room, with Pete and his scrambler at the ready, I tried to concentrate on the newspaper I'd picked up in the lobby. But the words kept merging into unintelligible jumbles.

"Goddammit, Pete!" I burst out at one point in what was becoming a miserably long morning. "The Joiners can be going through hell. That guy Ghavam could already be putting that engine together. And we sit here on our hands, waiting for the lousy phone to ring."

At 8:55, nearly noon back East, it rang. General Madden himself. Pete plugged in the scrambler unit, spoke briefly, then passed me the handset.

"Hectic morning at this end, Steve," Madden's metallic voice sounded less than elated. "Here's how it shapes up. As of this moment, no confirmable sighting of anything that looks like the truck and/or its cargo. That's from large-scale scans of Mexico north of a line from Laredo, Texas, to Obregón on Mexico's Gulf of California coast. Of course, our non-sightings aren't confirmation the Pluto isn't there. That's a lot of territory, and the truck and missile crates could be fairly easy to conceal.

"But a launch site isn't, General."

"That's a Roger. And assuming that's what those people have in mind, we've checked for isolated construction sites. In northwestern Mexico, our overhead imaging specialists have picked up what look like three oil-drilling operations. With State Department help, we ran a quick, discreet check with the Mexican equivalent of our Department of Commerce. And we got a surprise—at least, it was a surprise to me. The set-ups are Saudi. Did you know the Saudis have been drilling for Mexican oil?"

"Had no idea, sir. Oil-rich Saudis drilling for oil over here?"

"They've been at it for several years."

"Which of the three sites is the newest one, General?"

"Very cogent question. Two of the drilling set-ups have been in operation since 1989. The third, in the Sonora Desert, went under construction just a month ago."

"I'm willing to bet that with enough 'fee' money and some clever paperwork forgery, a third 'Saudi' operation could be..."

"Precisely, Steve. So the thinking here is to keep a close eye on that one. Continue the overhead imaging."

Here it came, as I suspected it would: bureaucratic foot-dragging. Now that other agencies had been brought in on this, Madden had no doubt been "talked to." Problems with the Mexican government. Potential intrusion of foreign territory. I could almost hear the caveats.

"Sorry, General, but I think we both know sitting and watching is the most dangerous course we could follow."

"No argument there. Officially I'm watching and waiting. Unofficially, I've contacted Captain Gorcy. She's a go. I want you to take a commercial flight back to Tucson today. Return to Davis-Monthan. She's scheduled to be there at 0900 tomorrow. She will give you an update briefing."

Here comes Gorcy, I thought. She'll have the latest detailed info, which she will inevitably believe gives her the upper hand to start with. Great.

But all I said was, "Roger, sir. I'm on my way."

"Good luck, Colonel," Madden offered. "Possibly for the sake of a whole lot of people."

Pete stored the scrambler headset and disconnected the unit from the room's phone jack.

"A recent oil op in the northwestern Sonora Desert, Pete. "That's where combined intelligence points to."

"Nice isolated location for a high-altitude bomb drop. They'd never know what hit them."

"Neither would the Joiners. And they're only part of the problem."

Ten minutes later, Pete Pappas and his scrambler departed, headed for an up-date briefing on the Joiners' disappearance. Eager to get out of here, myself — and, hopefully, into action — I was snapping my travel bag shut when I heard a subdued tapping at the door.

I squinted through the security lens. Not the maid, but a youngish-looking blond man with a precisely parted haircut and the unworldly face of a recent college grad.

The face was replaced by an ID card with an eagle's head surmounting a white shield emblazoned with a red and blue compass rose. In an arc above the eagle was the wording CENTRAL INTELLIGENCE AGENCY.

What in hell was the CIA doing here? I opened the door.

The guy glanced at a small photo in his hand then studied my face. "Lieutenant Colonel Gammon."

And he walked right in. Now I noted this agent, dressed in the mandatory Washington navy-blue suit, was not as young as he had appeared through the security peeper. As he eyed my sport shirt and khakis, his near-colorless lips took on a cynical little droop. Crow's-feet pinched the corners of his pale gray eyes. Closer to forty then thirty, I judged.

"And who might you be?" I asked, ID card notwithstanding. I was tired of talk. I needed to walk out of here and into action.

My self-assured arrival offered his leather folder, with its ID card replay. "Agent Ernest Bellingham. Tell you something, Colonel. For an AFOSI agent, you've been absurdly easy to find. You've left a credit card trail a mile wide."

"Are you coordinating with AFOSI?"

"To a degree."

"In that case, you should be aware I didn't come to San Diego undercover. Instead of your computer chase through AMEX records, why didn't you just ask AFOSI where I was?"

"Beside the point."

"What is the point, Bellingham?"

"The point is you should not have run off on this thing unilaterally without establishing an adequate pre-procedural sub-base. As we have done."

"A 'pre-procedural sub-base'?" In a computer blink, the Pluto crisis — Priority Scarlet was AFOSI's code for crisis — had just acquired what I suspected could be a bureaucratic wheel-spin.

Bellingham threw me a cold smile. "I'm here to convey to you the official notification that this matter is now an approved CIA mission. We are currently in the construct phase of establishing a multi-faceted cope mode."

"You've got to be kidding."

"To the contrary. I am deadly serious. We are committing major assets to Project Grapple."

"You *are* kidding."

"That's all I'm authorized to tell you about our investigation. I am authorized to insist that, in order to avoid compromising our maximum effectiveness, you withdraw from this uncoordinated, one-man effort of yours."

"In short, CIA wants to take over. You'll have to go up a couple notches and tell that to General Madden."

Bellingham scowled. "I sense less than 100 percent cooperation."

"You have a talent for acute perception."

"I also have orders directly from Washington."

"So have I."

"But not from Langley, Colonel."

"From the Air Force, Bellingham."

"What we don't need," Bellingham looked as if he was to savor this one, "is a loose Gammon on our gun deck."

I suspected he'd worked on that all the way from D.C. "You're a civilian agency with an information-gathering mission. This is a military problem."

"It's a concern of national scope, Gammon."

"So AFOSI realizes, and you're holding me up. I've got a plane to catch."

"Back to Fort Myers."

"You have no jurisdiction over AFOSI, Bellingham."

"In Mexico, that's debatable."

He knew about the Mexico aspect? In irritation, I paced to the window. Then I swung around. "You plod down there with your ponderous 'pre-procedural sub-base' approach, and that lethal bird could fly before you get your Project Grapple into rented filing cabinets."

"We don't work that way, Colonel. Your negative reaction has been anticipated. Fully anticipated. Unfortunately, I don't have the authority to order you off the project. Can I ask your cooperation by staying out of our way?"

"With pleasure." A meaningless concession. Gorcy and I would be working entirely and quietly on our own. "May I ask the same of you?" A comment not so meaningless, in view of this whole damned conversation.

Bellingham gave me the smile of a man who considered his competition hopelessly inept. "If needs be," he said vaguely. Uninvited, he plunked down in one of the chairs by the window. And gave me a shrug of resignation. "An exchange of pertinent information could be mutually useful."

I stayed on my feet behind the other chair. "I assume you have the specifications of the missing item?" Might this be the real reason he'd tracked me down?

"Got that directly from the Lawrence Livermore Labs, Colonel."

More alert than I'd expected. Might his bureaucratic attitude be a pose?

"Have your people considered the time-frame?"

"In our estimate, we have a window of at least several weeks. If, indeed, the vehicle is viable at all."

I swung around the chair and sat down. Maybe this guy wasn't quite operating at the bureaucratic slug-speed he'd led me to believe. How much did he really know?

"Consider Joiner and Ghavam," Bellingham said. "Joiner is a loyal American, How much can they expect out of him?"

"You're aware they also have his wife?"

"Certainly, Colonel. Stop testing me. Nevertheless, it's my opinion a loyal American scientist surely would find the means to delay, perhaps even to forestall the launch of such a complex vehicle. Or even program it to crash after launch."

"I met Joiner at an AFOSI meeting on this thing, Bellingham. He's still in love with that damned bird."

"I'm sure he loves his country more."

"We can't count on that to exceed his concern for his wife."

Bellingham smiled. "Aren't you going to ask me about Ghavam?"

"I know the CIA lost track of him when he landed in Hermosillo."

"Concerns about Joiner and Ghavam may well be beside the point, Colonel. Even assuming the seemingly impossible challenge of acquiring sixty thousand fuel rods is somehow met, there is another consideration that probably dooms the whole complex project. If there really is such a project."

"Jesus, Bellingham, quit trying to sidetrack me with windy wishful thinking."

He leaned toward me. "Boosters, Colonel. Where would they get booster rockets big enough to shove that thing up to sufficient speed for the ramjet to take over?"

Bellingham was officious and overconfident, but he sounded well within the loop on this thing. He sat back and gave me a little deprecating smile. "We've already notified all potential military sources to establish maximum security of any rocket propulsion ordnance of the magnitude that would be required."

"Logical," I conceded, though I didn't think importing boosters would be insurmountable to an organization that had apparently built a whole damned base right under our negligent noses.

"Be aware, Gammon, our apprehension of the perpetrators of this attempted terror act will be a significant coup for an Administration increasingly criticized for not disposing of Saddam Hussein. *Don't screw it up!*"

"I gather your time-frame is urgent but not critical."

Bellingham nodded. "You could put it that way. Now what HUMINT might you have stumbled on to add to what we already have?"

"Sorry. You seem to be way ahead of me in the 'human source intelligence gathering' department. Sounds as if you've got it all."

Bellingham stood. "See you in Hermosillo, then," he said airily.

Great. Had Project Grapple's info sources churned out even that?

15.

Cornelius Joiner could not recall a more miserable night in his entire life. Snatches of sleep interrupted by sudden sweats... Flashes of hopeless entrapment... Eleanor's ragged sighs... Then at daybreak, the struggle to pull his scrambled senses into focus.

He stared up at two-by-four framing, sheathed with some sort of black composition board. This made no sense. They were in a shack? A damned hot shack. He'd slept in his shirtsleeves. Sweat had wilted the collar.

He heard a creak. He swung around. Eleanor sprawled on a cot on the other side of the plank floor. And this craziness snapped into focus. Two bastards and their blue van in San Diego last night. The long, hard ride into an isolated valley. Then he and Eleanor had been shoved in here.

Stiff muscles protesting, he swung his feet to the splintery floor. The light that penetrated this windowless hovel speared through nail holes and cracks in the loose fitting sheets of dry-wall sheathing. Joiner pressed his eye to one of the larger gaps.

Three drilling rigs spaced along the narrow valley. Looked like an oil exploration site, with more shacks like this one scattered about. A long, low one that could be a mess hall.

And in the middle of all this, what in hell was that huge, windowless, slab-sided structure?

He squinted back into the shack's gloom. On the floor near the far wall, he saw an oil lantern and a book of matches. He fired up the lantern and stared at an empty paint bucket and a roll of toilet paper in a corner. Ye Gods!

In disgust, he used the bucket, zipped up and stood in the middle of the shack, unshaven, stomach growling, teeth gritting in hot anger.

The other cot groaned. Eleanor sat up, hair askew, eyes wide. "Corney? What...what are they doing to us?"

He sank beside her. "Nothing to you, kiddo. As long as I behave. They want me to work on the missile. Out there in that giant barn, I'd be willing to bet. As long as I'm a good boy, they won't do anything to us."

Until the work is finished, he thought, but he wouldn't tell her that.

The door banged open. Joiner squinted into its almost unbearably bright rectangle. The looming silhouette in the glare said in halting English, "I am Nasr Ilahi. I am foreman. You come."

They rose together.

Ilahi pointed at Joiner, "You. Not woman." He stepped into the shack, a hulking man in dusty jeans and a sweat-stained work shirt. Now Joiner saw he carried a cardboard box. He set it on the floor beside Eleanor. "You eat here." She looked down at two thick slices of bread, a tin bowl of soup, and black coffee in a metal mug.

"You," Ilahi said to Joiner. "You come with me."

Joiner looked helplessly at his wife, caught her staring at the plastic bucket in the corner.

"I'll be fine, Corney," she managed, but her voice sounded ragged.

He caught her by the arms, held her frightened eyes with his. Then he kissed her. "Yes." He tried to project a confidence that had long since drained away. "Yes, of course you will." He walked out ahead of the heavy-set Arab and heard a bolt slam home behind him.

The motionless morning air smelled of hot sand and carried the muffled sound of hammering. Now he had a better look at this God-forsaken place—a quarter-mile-wide valley between high rocky ridges. With a cut in the near ridge for the road they had jounced in on. And on each shoulder of that deep notch, he saw a man with a rifle.

Now Joiner realized this was an oil exploration site only in appearance. Just a few loitering workers manned each inactive derrick. The sole visible action was straggly foot traffic in and out of the long shack at the bottom of the nearest ridge. A thread of smoke from its jutting stovepipe told Joiner that was indeed the mess building.

What riveted his interest was the big structure in the middle of all this, that huge, windowless barn of a building out there.

Then, like a fuzzy projector slide heated by the light, everything snapped into sharp focus. All this was cover for what went on in that big central building.

Along the foot of the ridge, Ilahi urged him toward what appeared to be a construction trailer. "In here."

Joiner climbed three plank steps, turned the sun-heated knob and stepped in. He hoped for a welcome rush of air-conditioning. But the trailer's interior was as hot as the air outside.

At a worktable, he recognized Mustache-Scar, the taller of the two bastards who had kidnapped him and Eleanor last night. Eyes hard as black glass, the man said in passable English, "Your woman will not be touched when you do as we say. You understand?"

Joiner nodded.

"She stays in hut. You work there." He pointed through the trailer's front window at the big central structure.

"With me boss," Ilahi put in with, what Joiner felt was a degree of self-satisfaction. Did he detect a trace of competition between these two?

"And," the scarred Arab continued as if Ilahi hadn't spoken, "You will also sleep out there."

"*No!*" Joiner snapped. "*That* is out of the question."

The scarred man stood impassively through Joiner's outburst. Then he said, "Can it be you do not understand your situation?"

"I understand it precisely, but I am not going to be isolated from my wife. That, damn it, is the..."

Mustache-Scar held up a silencing hand. "Small matter."

"Maybe to you," Joiner bristled.

"*Tayyib*. All right. But I warn you. If work does not go fast, woman will be taken. By many. You do what we say."

Joiner tried not to show his spark of elation, then the icy ripple down his spine. He had won a concession, but the situation remained grim.

The scarred man stepped close. "*You do what we say,*" he repeated. He turned to Ilahi and said something in a tongue Joiner did not recognize.

"Out," Ilahi rumbled. "You eat."

Like a prisoner in a work camp, Joiner walked back into the shimmering heat. *Like* a prisoner? Hell, he *was* a prisoner in a work camp. He struggled to subdue his mounting anger.

In the rude structure he had correctly identified as a "mess hall," he was given a bowl of murky brown soup, coarse dark bread, and some kind of unidentifiable cold meat. The coffee, to his surprise, was fairly decent. Or would any lousy mug of coffee taste fairly decent after what he and Eleanor had gone through last night?

On a hard wooden bench, Ilahi stuck at his side, noisily sucking his coffee while he waited for Joiner to finish. When Joiner set his mug down, the chunky Arab stood.

"We go."

They went. Back into the heat, across a wide stretch of rock-strewn sand toward the big central building. Joiner glanced into the glaring sky. Not a cloud. Could there be a surveillance satellite up there, its sensitive lenses trained on this odd encampment? Seeing an apparent oil exploration site and its crew. And no more than that?

As they neared the big central structure, the hammering Joiner had heard grew louder now with an undercurrent thrum of generators. Ilahi elbowed him toward a small door near the building's end, the east end, Joiner determined from the sun's early morning position. Ilahi yanked the door open, grabbed Joiner's shoulder and shoved him inside.

Though Joiner expected a workshop, he was stunned. He stood in a big, concrete-floored workshop that rose at least forty feet to a peaked roof. Carpenters banged away up there on wooden trusses, apparently reinforcing a building not designed for permanence. Along its walls stood the stocked shelves and tool cabinets of what appeared to be a fully-equipped machine shop. At this end, only dangling bare bulbs provided an eerie glow.

At the far end of the building, Joiner spotted a flatbed truck with a crane mounted on it. And... Good Lord! Were those a pair of military surface-to-air rockets flanking the crane?

But what really impressed him in this cavern filled its entire central length. From here at the east end, a pair of rails rose on metal framework to an elevation at least three stories high under the roof's peak. A fifty-degree slope, Joiner judged. Up there, the top third of the building's west end was open, providing additional light. Which, Joiner realized, was not its real purpose.

Though the launching rack made a breath-catching impact on him, what left Joiner's knees weak was the silvery forty-foot-long missile already mounted on the lower portion of the rack's length. The hatches of the engine compartment in its rear section were open, and Joiner could see several dozen white tips in the big honeycomb area. *Fuel rods! My God, they've got fuel rods!*

Pluto, the weapon from hell, the horror he himself had helped create three decades ago, was *here*, just five yards away. A strange nostalgia swept through him, touched with bitterness. He had been instrumental in developing Pluto from a maverick idea, helped design and build the airframe and static-test the engine. Then had come the shutdown order. Their bird had never flown.

Now here it was, well on its way to actual flight. Everything in this valley was dedicated to this clandestine launch of Pluto: the fake oil derricks, all the outbuildings, and especially this big hangar-like structure, sure to be sacrificed in the flaming blast of those booster rockets, down there by the truck. All this for one launch.

A purposely devastating launch. Joiner jolted back to the potential horror of this intricate engineering project. Up on scaffolds erected along both sides of the launching ramp, a half dozen workmen were already bolting the stubby wings in place.

A slender man in dark trousers and a white shirt stood near the foot of the launching rack. "You!" Ilahi shouted at him. "Come here."

In a deliberately slow amble toward them, the slim Arab seemed to Joiner a cut above the rest of the gang in here. The fineness of his olive features spoke of other than working-class heritage. Though clearly he was under Ilahi's control, he carried himself like a man in charge. Joiner saw something behind the exhaustion in the eyes of this clean-shaven man. Resentment, bitter and deep.

"You work with him," Ilahi told Joiner. With that, he walked out of the building.

Which was a surprise to Joiner. Were there no guards? All the rest of the men in here seemed to be workmen, not guards.

The slender man read his mind. "Where would we go?" His English was barely accented. Joiner expected a rueful smile. He saw only bitterness.

Where would *we* go? Was this man a prisoner, too? "Cornelius Joiner," the veteran scientist said, wondering whether to offer a handshake.

Now the young Arab—he appeared to be in his early forties—gave him a wan smile. "I am Dr. Muzaffer Ghavam." As if that were to mean something.

Ghavam? Then memory served. Sometime last year, before Saddam's forces were bombed blind and staggering, back when his nuclear capability was considered a major threat, Joiner remembered, that evening's SRAE program had featured Dr. Muzaffer Ghavam. Iraq's leading nuclear scientist. MIT-trained, for God's sake. Why was *he* in on this damned project?

"I have heard of you," Joiner said stiffly.

"You know why we are here?"

"Suppose you tell me, Ghavam."

A workman on the nearest scaffold called something in what Joiner assumed was Arabic. Ghavam shouted a reply then turned back to Joiner. "They do not care what we say to each other." He nodded at the missile on its launching ramp. "They care only that we rebuild Pluto."

"To launch capability."

Ghavam's eyes probed his. "Yes. Are you paid for this?"

Joiner bristled. "That is a damned insult! I was forced in here. My wife and I are consigned to a miserable hovel out there by *your* countrymen!"

He waited for an angry slap in the face, or even a punch sure to follow his outburst. But Ghavam's expression remained impassive.

"It is best we understand each other," the Iraqi said quietly. "I am here because they have taken my sister. They have sent me a part of her. They will kill her if I do not do as they want."

Was that true? But why would he lie?

"Why do they want you?" Ghavam asked.

"I was one of the primary developers of that monstrosity." He was unable to restrain the touch of pride in his voice. The reflex, of course, of an aging has-been now in the position of informing a younger…colleague?

"You helped build this cursed thing?"

Joiner nodded. "I see they have acquired what appear to be fuel rods. How in hell did that come about?"

"Unfortunately, the fuel rods accompanied me here."

"They were fabricated where?"

"In Iraq."

"In Iraq," Joiner echoed, with obvious disparagement.

"From your own specifications, Doctor. You are a doctor of science, are you not? My knowledge of the fuel rods was acquired from U.S. Atomic Energy Commission declassified documents."

"I see some rods in place, but sixty thousand were required."

Ghavam gestured toward the work counter. "Those boxes underneath."

"Uranium oxide and?" A little test.

"Beryllium oxide."

Joiner's arms prickled. He nodded toward the partially-completed cruise missile. "Is it possible?"

"Perhaps you should tell me."

Joiner leaned back against a work table. He wasn't sure he could trust his knees. "We built and tested the engine. It met propulsion requirements. We built the airframe. We installed the guidance system. But before we could conduct a flight test, the project was cancelled. So we don't know if it *is* possible, do we?"

"The engine did operate."

"On a test stand. My God, man, we had to lay twenty-five miles of pipe in the desert to store the compressed air for the test. The engine is a ramjet reactor. At launch, air enters the intake, heats, expands, and the reaction to the ejection of that expanded air drives the missile forward."

His outburst, Joiner realized, was just a lesson in elementary physics. But Ghavam had listened patiently.

"We need no such elaborate arrangement," the Iraqi pointed out. "You have already done the engine testing. The booster rockets are to accelerate the missile to the speed where rammed air reaches a pressure of 350 pounds psi. Then the reactor cuts in, and the boosters drop away. So your manuals describe it."

Joiner stared up at the launching rack and its almost finished missile. Whoever was behind this bizarre plan may have been carried away with its outrageous concept, but this Ghavam was a pragmatist who seemed to have done his homework.

"Boosters," Joiner said. "We never fabricated them."

Ghavan tilted his sleek head toward the far end of the building. "There, by the flatbed truck. Soviet ground-to-air missiles stripped of war heads and guidance units. Propellants only."

"Will they work as boosters?"

Ghavam shrugged. "The Pluto manuals offer no specifications for such stolen and converted rockets. One of our imponderables."

Drawn by an attraction he couldn't deny, Joiner pushed away from the worktable and walked toward the launching ramp and its silvery missile. Then he glanced back. "Imponderables, Dr. Ghavam? Perhaps you and I are the real imponderables."

"Oh, no, Dr. Joiner. They know what we will do. They have all the control. We have none."

16.

"Colonel Gammon."

She stood in the doorway of my VOQ room. Five-foot-ten in sandals, trim in a lemon-yellow blouse and flowered knee-length wrap-around skirt. Her golden hair swirled to her shoulders, carefully careless.

Her cool emerald eyes appraised me . "We meet again."

AFOSI Special Investigator Captain Laura Gorcy, deceptively gorgeous. She never burned in desert heat, nor chlled in winter's zeroes. Satin over steel.

"Laura." I stood and offered my hand. Her graceful fingers were cool and dry with a talon grip.

"So this time, it's lieutenant colonel," she said. "Two steps up from last time."

"Temporary rank. And for the mission, it'll be just Laura and Steve, gringo tourists. General Madden briefed you?"

"Of course. Now I'm going to brief you. Sit down."

This was the Gorcy I knew so well. I wondered if her ever-peckish attitude bristled from a lifetime of unwanted lustful attention. She put down her Tourister bag, slipped a folder out of it, planted her taut rear against the edge of the room's writing table, crossed her ankles, and opened the folder.

"First, your man with the facial scar. Despite his description from the truck rental company in Phoenix, neither Langley nor NSA at Fort Meade can place him in any known terrorist group. Not in Abu Nidal's organization. Not in the Arab Liberation Front. Not in Abu Abbas's Palestine Liberation Front. Not with the anti-Iranian Mujaheddin-E-Khalq, the Kurdish Workers Party, the PPK, nor the Islamic Jihad."

"How about Hizballah?"

"The Islamic Jihad *is* Hizballah," she said smugly. "Don't test me, Colonel. Now those are what he is not. But we think we know who and what he is."

I gave her a quick smile. "I'm sure you're going to let me in on it."

"The intelligence consensus pegs an unlovely cutthroat named Sayyid Bakhtiar. His psychological profile fits events to date. So sayeth Langley's office of Central Reference."

Oh boy, how she enjoyed this.

"What have we got on this guy?"

"Born in 1960 in Khash, Colonel."

"He's Iranian."

"Working-class parents. Sketchy schooling in Khash. A playground bully. Broke a teammate's arm in a soccer altercation. A taste for violence. In the 1978 anti-Shah riots SAVAK ripped his cheek open, hence the scar. After that, he was all for Khomeini. Joined Hizballah, but we have no detailed backgrounding on his activities during the Eight-Year-War with Iraq."

Jesus, I thought. She's beginning to sound like Bellingham.

"We know he was active in covert operations against Iraqi interests in Lebanon. He was involved in Hizballah activities in Beirut. That's where he earned the nickname 'Zul-Junnah.'"

"Meaning?"

"'Winged Wolf.' He's used it ever since." Laura dived back into her folder. "In 1987 he was seen in Baghdad just before an explosion at a military hospital."

"Nice fella, but how does he tie into what we're up against?"

"Just before the Gulf War, he mouthed off at a secret meeting of Hizballah hierarchy in Lebanon. He denounced Abbas, Nidal, and others."

I was getting parched listening to all this backgrounding. "Hey, you want some coffee?"

She shook her head. "Not so soon after an airline breakfast." And she plowed on. "Zul-Junnah has an independent streak. During and after the Gulf War, CIA field reports show him disgusted by the collapse of activities by Mideast terrorist organizations. Saddam promoted high expectations, but the known groups were—still are—moribund."

"So," I put in, "he's recruited his own dissident terrorists."

"Well, good thinking, Colonel. That is precisely what the CIA and NSA combined behavior profile for this guy has come up with." She looked up from her folder. "So that's the 'who.' Next: the 'what.'"

"The 'what' is the Pluto missile, so that takes us to the 'where.'"

"Which takes us to topography." From her folder, she pulled a map and spread it on the writing table. Mexico, large scale. Moving next to her, I caught the exhilarating scent of lilacs. God, she really was into our tourist cover mode.

"These" she indicated three red pencil dots "are the alleged Saudi oil exploration sites General Madden apprised you of yesterday. This one, about a hundred miles south of Big Bend National Park, has been in operation almost two years."

"Too long."

"Right. This next one between Navajoya and Rosario de Tezapaco has been in operation more than a year, and I think it's too close to Ciudad Obregón and its airport. No way could it hide the prep for a secret missile launch."

"Which leaves us with this one." I tapped the red dot northwest of Hermosillo. "Your map shows low hills between that site and the Gulf of California."

"It's been there only a couple months. But eastward sits the Sierra Madre chain, and across the gulf to the west, Baja California is one long, high ridge."

"Right, Captain. So if I were assigned to plot the launch track, I'd go north-northwest, right up the gulf. It's much flatter terrain—and on a bee line to LA with just those few low hills in the way. Los Angeles, then the open sea."

"Followed by General Madden's projected hundred-or-so degree turn eastward to bring it back over the U.S. mainland." She straightened. "Do you think there's a real chance they could pull it off?"

This was the first time I could recall her ever asking my opinion of anything. "Obviously they think so, and they've managed to bring in two well-qualified experts to help them do it."

She tapped the map with a slender, crimson-tipped forefinger. Perfume? Nail polish? Not parts of the Laura Gorcy I'd known. Neither were her colorful blouse and skirt nor the wedding ring. She was in disguise for the mission.

As was I in my orange hibiscus aloha shirt, khaki wash slacks, and a pair of gaudy Reeboks I'd picked up at a Tucson mall last night.

"Can't our super technology simply eliminate that thing with one well-placed blast?" she asked.

"Not in Mexico without time-eating diplomatic foreplay, and not with two American hostages on site. And there's another complication."

"The thing you said you'd tell me about."

"Yeah. Yesterday afternoon a suit from Langley named Bellingham paid me a visit in San Diego. He was busy as a dung beetle trying to roll up all of this in a neat bureaucratic bundle. Even had a name for it. Project Grapple, code for something he called a 'multi-faceted cope mode.'"

For the first time, Laura smiled. "You are kidding! Is he going to be a problem?"

"He's going to be in Hermosillo. Thinks he has at least a couple weeks of 'window,' as he put it. That may keep him out of our way. But he wants AFOSI out of the loop entirely. That might put him in our way."

"You've reported this to General Madden, of course."

"Right. But Madden was already aware of the CIA's 'fact-finding effort,' as he called it. We agreed this thing demands a far more active approach than that. If Bellingham contacts us, we cooperate, but we do not 'deflect' in any way. Madden's word."

She rolled her emerald eyes. "Just what we need, a little interagency tussle."

"It's bigger than that. There has been a meeting of the National Security Council at the White House. By noon tomorrow, a Lockheed ES-3A will be orbiting off the coast. And a Patriot anti-missile battery is being activated in Southern California."

Laura's delicate eyebrows arched. "Did the Council hold an emergency meeting or a regular meeting?"

"Very perceptive, Captain. It was an agenda item at their regular meeting."

"Sounds to me like they think the Pluto theft isn't a real threat. But just in case, they're ass-covering."

"There isn't a lot that can be done defensively. Ground radar won't pick up anything incoming as low as five hundred feet, even over water, until it's within thirty miles. So they're orbiting airborne radar. But even if that managed to blip Pluto a couple hundred miles out, what fighters do we have that could pull off a Mach 3 intercept? Our fastest, the F-15, pulls Mach 2.5."

"What about the Patriot anti-missile missiles?"

"The jury's still out on the Patriots, Laura."

"No time to waste, is there? What kind of vehicle have you rented?"

"Jeep Cherokee. Socially acceptable four-wheel-drive truck. You ready?"

She folded her map, slipped it back into her briefing file, and stuffed the file back in her Tourister.

"'Forth to the wilderness, the chosen start,'" she quoted. With a quick glance at me, she added, "John Masefield."

"I'm not sure he's who you want. How about: 'Hermosillo, population 200,000.' Frommer."

17.

Just after sunrise, "Mr. and Mrs. Steven Gammon" crossed the border between Nogales, USA, and Nogales, Mexico. I stopped our rented maroon Cherokee at the Mexican immigration office. Laura's briefing file included our tourist cards. A detached heavy-set official checked the paperwork then added another loop of red tape.

"You are driving, *senõr*. It is necessary for you to get a vehicle permit." He pointed toward an adjacent building. That done, we eased through the cluttered commercial section on Obregón Street. Then we sped out of Nogales, bound for Hermosillo, nearly 200 miles south.

"You going to tell me what happened between you and Lizabeth?" Laura pressed, as we raced into the Sonora Desert.

"No. How about some insight on your own marital adventures?"

"No."

"Any prospects since?

She stared straight ahead, then relented. "Only a tiresome flurry of fellow-officer come-ons."

"That's what you get for looking like a Dior model."

"My God, Colonel. You too?"

"Sorry. Must be the isolation out here."

"I'll stay isolated, thank you."

With that, she stared out her window like a schoolgirl in a snit. Minutes later, her head drooped. She fell asleep.

A little over an hour later, we passed through Santa Ana. Then we left modern civilization behind. In the next 110 miles, we zipped past two hamlets. To the west, rolling hills offered an expanse of saguaro cactus-studded wasteland. To the east hulked the soaring Sierra Madres.

Two hours into our southward grind, Laura suddenly snapped out of her snit-induced doze. And in a most unprofessional way. "So, c'mon, Colonel. What did happen with Lizabeth?" she blurted. "Last time we worked together, you were married, then not much later, you weren't."

Unexpectedly glad to have her back in this world, I relented. "A year ago, we split. We just didn't mesh. I was meat and potatoes. She was meringue."

"Style over substance."

I kept my eyes on the undulating pavement. "Hell, Laura, it was more than that. I was spending fifteen hours a day on my consulting business, except for a brief AFOSI assignment. I just wasn't there enough. She felt she was married to an absentee. So it ended."

"I'm sorry."

"Well, we parted friends if not lovers. She went back full-time to her winter Palm Beach circuit and summer season in Virginia horse country. Up in the Old Dominion, her horse balked. Lizabeth fractured a leg. Now she's laid up in Palm Beach contemplating the seascape.

"Ow, a busted leg. That's rough." Laura watched the arid scenery roll by. Then she said, "Despite all that, you were luckier than I was."

"I heard about that last guy. Hell of a thing."

"I did manage to brand him for life. Did you hear about that, too?"

"Word gets around." I chuckled. "My God. With an ice cream scoop!"

"His just desserts."

That was the only shot at humor I could recall her ever taking. I glanced at her. A tiny smile played on her peerless lips.

"Dumped him," she said, eyes straight ahead. "Took back my maiden — pardon the expression — name for the second time."

We zipped through another tiny settlement, oddly named Benjamin Hill. A little boy in a tattered shirt and oversize straw sombrero — and nothing else — held up a large live iguana.

"He wants to sell us a pet?"

"No, Laura. He wants to sell us lunch."

"Oh. You interested in a non-lizard lunch, Gammon?"

"In Hermosillo. The map shows nothing at all between here and there. And you should get used to calling me Steve. We're supposed to be a pair of married gringos."

"*Si*, Steve. You don't have to brief me. Next move: check into the Hotel America on Boulevard Francisco Eusebio Kino, which is Highway 15 in northeast Hermosillo. Our SSV contact is supposed to find us there."

"You don't sound like you have a whole lot of confidence in the Mexican FBI."

"Remains to be seen." She gazed out her window at the passing rock, sand and scrub. "This looks like southern Arizona."

"Same desert."

Silence. Then she said, "You realize if this rental decides to die out here, we could, too? There hasn't been a sign of a phone since Santa Ana. And hardly any traffic."

"Have faith in the *Angeles Verdes*."

"The what?"

"The Green Angels. I read about them last night in a travel guide. Governmental bilingual mechanic teams in green panel trucks. They patrol major Mexican highways twice a day looking for cars in trouble."

"Impressive, *darling*."

I glanced at her.

"Just practicing, Gam... Steve." Then she said, "Don't you feel undressed without a sidearm?"

"It's less chancy to come in unarmed as tourists. We'll depend on SSV materiel, if it comes to that."

"Right." She said not another word all the rest of the way to Hermosillo's outskirts where the highway swung into the city's encircling thoroughfare. To our surprise, the pavement widened to a boulevard flanked by graceful orange and laurel trees, their leaves rippling in the warm breeze. When we'd driven only a few blocks, the blue script on the Hotel America's red-and-white sign leaped from among the trees.

***

We had decided there was no need for a name cover on this assignment. Here "Gammon" was as anonymous as that of any tourist. I registered us as "M/M Steven Gammon, Ft. Myers, USA."

Our third-floor room overlooked the beautifully landscaped boulevard. "Too bad we're on such a tight schedule," I told her as the bellman pocketed his tip and shut the door behind him.

"Stay on track, Colonel," she said over her shoulder as she headed for the bathroom. She emerged, hair neatly brushed, pale lipstick refreshed. "You trying to starve me into submission? Won't work. I'm not mellow when I'm hollow."

"I've never seen you mellow, Captain; hollow or not."

"Right. Let's eat."

We returned to the lobby and found the nearly deserted coffee shop. Over burritos and coffee, I said, "Next stop?"

"The *aeropuerto*."

"I'm impressed. How did you figure that out?"

"Memory and applied reasoning. I remembered your hobby is flying a little puddle hopper—"

"Jumper. The correct cliché is 'puddle jumper.'"

"Hopper... jumper... Hermosillo has an airport. What would I do this afternoon if I held a pilot's license and wanted to get a quick look at something out in the desert? Ergo, it computed."

True to form, a self-satisfied jump ahead of me.

"Wait for me in the lobby," I told her. "I'm going back up to get the binocs."

She tapped her beach bag of a purse. "Ahead of you again. Dear." And she strode out in front of me to the parking area, trim in charcoal slacks and snowy white blouse. Hair rippling in the light breeze.

The airport lay several miles west of the city. The runways were ample, but air traffic was desultory. At the main terminal, a single Mexicana DC-9, with its nose-to-tail yellow stripe, unloaded its passengers onto the ramp. Across the field, four military helicopters—American Hueys with Mexican markings—sat droopy-bladed in front of an open hangar. The general aviation operations building stood apart from the terminal. I pulled the Cherokee into a vacant slot near its entrance.

A healthy tip cut through some of the paperwork and won us an oft-folded area chart. The portly manager of operations personally walked us through the stifling heat of the tarmac to a faded red-and-white high-wing monoplane with tricycle gear. Each wheel was enclosed in a multi-dented, streamlined "pant."

I made a walk-around inspection and checked the fuel level. As we belted ourselves in the front two of the four seats, Laura threw me a scowl. "Did you happen to notice the paint on the nose? Looks like it's been sandpapered."

"Probably from flying in rain. The propeller blades are abraded, too. I'm more concerned about the small dents in the leading edge of the left wing. But I don't think that'll affect flight characteristics much."

"God. What is this thing?"

"A Cessna 177 Cardinal with a hundred-fifty-horse Lycoming engine. Cruises at nearly a hundred-fifty. Or should have, when it was new."

"Which was when?"

"In the 1960s."

"It's damned near as old as I am."

"Let's hope it's as durable, Captain." I turned the key. The old engine coughed out a blue smoke-swirl. The propeller flipped over grudgingly, then decided to get with it. The nose lifted a couple inches. I eased the control yoke forward. The plane settled back down to begin the long taxi to the downwind end of the east-west runway.

I tried the radio. Dead. The windsock on the operations building roof told me the light westerly breeze still held.

At the runway's east end, I checked for incoming traffic. Hit the brakes and revved the engine. Slight piston slap, but otherwise the Lycoming sounded smooth enough for a near thirty-year-old engine. We took off into the lowering sun, a relief as cool air flooded through the window vents.

To our right, the 3,000-foot peak of Cerro Cuevas jutted from the desert floor. Past the rampart of jagged mountains west of the city, the terrain flattened into a series of lower ridges that rolled on toward the Gulf of California..

I banked the Cessna northwest. Fifteen minutes later, I shouted over the engine's racket, "From what I saw on your satellite info, it should be just ahead, on your side."

She was already scanning with the binocs. We flew on. Late afternoon updrafts buffeted the little Cessna. Shadows lengthened across the uneven desert floor. Maybe we were too late in the day.

"There!" Laura pointed down at an area about forty-five degrees to our right. "Between those two ridges."

I nudged rudder and wheel to bring the blunt nose more northwesterly and throttled back. We sank slowly in a long power glide.

"I don't want to alert anyone down there," I told her. "I'll hold this heading. We'll have to see whatever we can in a fly-by a good five or so miles away." At 2,500 feet, I leveled the plane and edged power back to normal cruise.

As we passed south of whatever she'd spotted, Laura kept the binoculars glued downward. I couldn't see it at all. Then it was behind us.

"Think that was it?" I shouted in her ear."

"It correlates with the overhead imaging photos."

"See anything we don't already know about?"

"I saw what could be sentry posts on the ridge overlooking the access road."

"How many?"

"Looked like one man on each shoulder of the access road cut. No sign of gun emplacements. I couldn't make out whether they're carrying hand-held weapons."

"We'll fly straight on for ten minutes, then come back on a reciprocal course. I hope twenty minutes between their possibly spotting us twice could give them the impression we were heading elsewhere."

On our return leg, I again held the Cessna off to the south. Now the area in question was on my side. And it looked like the enlarged satellite pix of the site in question: a big central building in a haphazard scatter of smaller buildings and three oil derricks down there. I borrowed the glasses. On the cliffs flanking the access road, I made out the probable sentries Laura had seen. That access road... Where did it originate? I peered past her and banked the plane slightly. There it was, a remote lane winding southeastward to intersect a wider roadway that itself met the desolate lower portion of the Nogales-Hermosillo highway.

I peered back at the construction site, now falling behind us. And I saw what I was hoping for. I settled back and headed us toward the distant twinkle of Hermosillo's early evening lights.

"You look pleased with yourself," Laura said. "Except for those two guards, I don't know any more now than I did when I studied the satellite photos back at Bolling."

She had missed it, but I'd noted it could be possible to drive within almost a quarter-mile of the valley entrance without being spotted by the sentries.

18.

This damned big barn is an eerie place, Joiner thought. A huge, hastily constructed wooden shell, its towering slab sides groaned even in a moderate breeze. Only this wedge-shaped metal framework that supports the launching rails looks as if it had been built with an eye toward durability. The place is a creaky echo chamber, and it always smells of dust and the acrid bite of acetylene welding.

Yesterday, his loading of fuel rods was interrupted by his commandeered attention to the just-installed vertical stabilizer and the horizontal stabilizer on Pluto's aft end. The problem lay in the intricate push-rod connections of the guidance control unit to that tail assembly. Joiner managed to straighten out the mess, but it ate up the entire morning.

Just before dark, he and Ghavam completed inserting the thousands of fuel rods into the reactor core. The precisely-packed clusters of ceramic tubes would remain inert until just after launch, when the seventy-two interspersed control rods would begin to spin. By the time the boosters dropped away, the nuclear furnace would generate some 2,000 degrees Fahrenheit.

Now, as he began his measurements for the booster rocket attachments, Joiner marveled anew at this impressive weapon. Can I and this young Iraqi actually accomplish what the U.S. Government had denied to its scientists? he wondered. Might Ghavam and I actually get this thing to fly? Not "might," damn it. We *can*...

One evening, in a surge of confidence, he had blurted to Eleanor, "I'm becoming convinced this thing can actually work."

"Corney! You *can't* want that!"

"My God, Eleanor, I'm doing this to save our lives. Surely you realize the threat we face. That scar-faced son-of-a-bitch says it flies or... You know what he's threatened to do."

He peered at her. "Eleanor...Look, kiddo. It flies. Then when it's out of sight, there are possibilities. And I'm the guy who knows how to set the guidance control."

Silence.

Why can't she appreciate what I and Ghavam have already been able to get done out in this God-forsaken valley? We're working in a world of dust, sand and heat. Each sweat-sticky day, I'm impressed by Ghavam's ability. The guy is something of a genius of improvisation with a remarkable ability to grasp the intricacies of a nuclear engine he's never before seen.

The next day, though, up on the rickety scaffolding to inspect the newly-welded booster rocket fittings, Ghavam had surprised him in another way. In a near whisper, he said, "I do not hate Americans."

What brought this on? "I hadn't assumed—"

"Do you hate Iraqis?"

"I hate *these* sons-of-bitches, whatever they are."

"They are mostly Irani. I know Zul-Junnah and Ilahi are."

"Zul who?"

"Sayyid Zul-Junnah, the Winged Wolf. Our friend with the scar. I recognize him from newspaper stories during the Eight-Year War."

"A terrorist?"

"A renegade terrorist, Doctor. Even more dangerous."

"And you, like me, are trapped into working for this amoral shit."

"We are working for whoever he is working for. I've never heard Zul-Junnah described as a rich man. So some persons or something with much resource is behind this complex and obviously well-financed project. I would never do this, but they hold my sister. They sent me her... nipple. They trapped me with a woman in Zahko. If I do not do as they say..."

He paused, then in better control, told Joiner, "We must give obvious attention to these mounting brackets, or that hulking puppet, Ilahi, will report us."

That evening Joiner told Eleanor, "Apparently we and my 'colleague' out there are in the hands of a freelance terrorist. One with quite an organization behind him. We are in one lousy position here, and I..."

He was dismayed at her appearance, hunkered on the edge of her cot, hair in disarray, face slack.

He forced enthusiasm. "You're a real soldier, kiddo. And somehow, we'll get out of this mess."

"Oh, Corney! I'm so filthy and...and just plain bored."

Bored? She faced the very real possibility of rape, even death, and she was *bored?*

Perhaps, though, her boredom was easier to contend with than a new spasm of terror every time the shack door was thrown open. Had she consciously adopted this abject outlook as a means of coping? Had her mind begun to...begun to—

"Corney, dear," she said earnestly, "You do what you have to."

What I have to do... God. How do I cope with nth-degree anxiety?

Late today, he and Ghavam had worked in relative isolation at the far end of the northern building, attaching newly machined fittings to the pair of booster rockets on the floor.

The nearest worker was well out of earshot. The Iraqi moved closer to Joiner. "I suspect my sister is already dead."

Joiner stared at him. "If you suspect that, why are you still...? Then he was struck by the impression Ghavam had reached a moment of crucial decision.

"If I am wrong and we launch the missile and she is released, I could not return to Iraq. There is the matter of those blackmail tapes made in Zakho when I worked on the fuel rods. They believe they have control of me in that way so when I return, even if Maha survives and they release her, they will insist I help develop Saddam's nuclear capabilities. But I will never go back there. If they do not kill me here, I will try to return to America."

"Are you telling me," Joiner asked in a near whisper, "you would not care if Pluto doesn't get off the ground?"

"Zul-Junnah has told me he must have the missile fly over Los Angeles then turn to leave its trail of radiation over more American cities. That is how you are to program its guidance system."

"Considering the northwest orientation of the launching ramp, I've already guessed as much. I'm expected to do that without maps of any kind? Without coordinate references?"

"Detailed charts are available in one of the workbench drawers when you need them, but..." Ghavam gave Joiner a hard look. "Can your conscience truly let such a thing happen?"

They fell silent as one of the workmen carried a pair of gas cans past them, then out a nearby exit door, apparently to refuel a stuttering generator out there.

"Might it be possible," Ghavam wondered as the exit door closed, "to abort the launch?"

Abort the launch... Joiner stared down the length of the building to Pluto's gleaming fuselage and stubby wings poised on the lower portion of the launching incline. The "Flying Crowbar," they had called it back in the hot days of the Cold War.

"If it were only myself..." Joiner's words hung in the building's dead air. Another emotion had just forced its way into his churning thoughts. That meeting back at Bolling had made his heart beat faster. After all these years since, might the pioneering missile actually fly? No. Unworthy thought... Yet here, when he had walked into this building, and each day since, the sight of Pluto thrilled him.

The years dropped away. He remembered the day thirty years ago. He stood in the control bunker at Jackass Flats, trembling in anticipation of the engine's first static test. When it rumbled, then howled into life, his heart soared. And now, in this makeshift machine shop, he had the chance to prove out all those years of research, of dedication to Pluto, excluding back then, almost everything else in his life. God help him, he wanted to see Pluto *fly!*

He edged closer to Ghavam, his voice low. "I've already planned the flight path, Muzaffer. Pluto launches successfully. It flies northwest. Then, well out of sight, it plunges into the upper reach of the Gulf of California. That will" Joiner fell silent. The man fueling the generator had slipped back into the building. He walked past them blank-faced.

"I don't think he was close enough to—"

"And does he understand English? And the import of what you were saying?" Ghavam shrugged.

Twenty minutes later, Zul Junnah burst through the main entrance door. Footsteps echoing on the cement floor, he strode straight for them.

"Duktoor Joiner. Duktoor Ghavam. You hear me good. If missile does not launch, *you*" he pointed at Joiner, "and your wife, and *you*, Ghavam, and your sister all *die*. If missile falls after launch, then, too, all *die*."

He glared at them, swung around, pounded back to the main entrance and slammed the door behind him.

When Joiner struggled to speak without his voice shaking, he said, "So now what do we do?"

Ghavam's eyes met his. "Pray," the Iraqi said.

As they left the building in late afternoon, Joiner heard the hum of a distant engine. He shaded his eyes and peered south. Well beyond the valley's southwest ridge, a small red and white light plane at medium altitude headed east.

"Sight-seers," Joiner muttered. "Without a damned care in the world."

19.

T he hotel's supper service did not get into full swing until after 8:00 p.m., Mexican style. Though Laura and I spent more than an hour being obvious in the shops off the lobby, there was no sign of our SSV contact.

Now from our corner table, she surveyed the dining room then scowled at me. "Look at the time we're blowing, waiting around for this guy."

After the tense drive down here, our "sight-seeing" flight this afternoon had been a pleasant relief. The Cessna's engine noise held conversation to essentials. Here in the dining room, our cover called for appearing as a happily married couple on holiday. But Laura was still way up on her high horse.

A waitress waited. "*Pollo con arroz* for my wife," I told our gaily -skirted attendant. "And I'll have the *carne de...* I pointed at the menu. "The pork chops,"

"*Ah, si. Carne de cerdo.*" She trotted kitchenward.

We sat in silence awhile, then Laura said, "How about a little brainstorming while we're camped here on our duffs? Now we know the general layout of that set-up out there. We know they've got two sentry posts flanking the valley entrance. And I saw that a vehicle can get within about a quarter-mile of the place without being seen, if it doesn't kick up a dust plume."

She hadn't missed noticing that, after all.

"So," she pressed on, "how can you—"

Our dinners arrived. We fell silent as the dark-haired waitress set them down. Stepped back. *"Bon appétit,"* she chirped with a mischievous little grin.

As she flounced away, I ignored my plate and asked Laura, "'How can I *what?"*

"How can you be happy sitting here munching pork?"

"Eat your chicken."

"I'm serious, Steve. Joiner and his wife must be going through hell out there. And that damned missile might take off any minute."

"The problem is, Laura, we aren't certain the Joiners are there at all. Hell, we aren't even sure the missile is there. Those are two suppositions we have to confirm before any counter action is taken."

Holding her fork aloft, she glared at me. "You sound like a...like a damned lieutenant colonel." Then she shrugged and stabbed the chicken breast. "Yeah, you're right."

"And?"

"That's all. You're right. I hate it, but you are. Inactivity always bugs me."

I couldn't help laughing. "We've just driven through nearly four hundred miles of desert, flown a near-antique Cessna across miles of wilderness, reconned what may be the biggest threat to the U.S. since the Cuban Missile Crisis. Also, we are about to go upstairs to spend the night together, and you say you're disintegrating from inactivity. What more do you want?"

"Tell you what I don't want. That's for you to forget we are no more than two AFOSI agents carrying out an assignment, and that's all we're doing."

"You brought it up, I didn't."

"No, you brought it up." She dabbed her lips with her napkin. "With that reference to a night together."

"Let's eat up and get out of here."

***

When I unlocked the door to our room, the hair on the back of my neck rippled. We had turned out the lights, but now they were on. Then I relaxed. Had to be the maid. They made a big deal in hotels about turning down the beds.

But the guy sitting in the chair by the corner table was no maid. Olive-skinned, black hair neatly trimmed. Dark eyes luminous with either fervor or…bemusement? I couldn't tell which. In his hand, our uninvited visitor held not a gun, but an unlit cigar.

He stood, neatly attired in crisply-pressed gray with a maroon tie. Medium height. Late thirties.

"I trust you will excuse the intrusion, *Señor, Señora,* but it seemed the best way to contact you unobserved. The maid provided the key. I am Julio Arriaga, Hermosillo office of the SSV. Much like a field office of your FBI."

"ID, please," I demanded.

"ID? Ah, *identidad.*" From his breast pocket, he produced a black leather folder and flipped it open."

I took a look. "Don't you want ours?"

"No need. I have been given your *fotografías.*"

Arriaga settled back in his chair. "Shall we all relax?" With a wave of his cigar, he indicated the remaining two chairs.

Laura pointed at the cigar. "You light that thing," she warned, "and you are out of here."

The SSV agent chuckled. "I never light this 'thing,' *Señora.* It is a crutch. I gave up smoking one year ago." He turned to me. "Now let us get to this story most *fantástico* that has been told to me personally by the *Director de SSV* in Mexico City. A rocket launch installation in the Sonora Desert?"

"A cruise missile, Arriaga, nuclear-powered." I sketched the details of what we suspected and what we had confirmed to date.

"I am told you rented an airplane today. You flew over this place? *Audacia, Señor, audacia.*"

"*Audacia?*"

"Daring," Laura translated, though I was questioning word choice. Already got the meaning.

"We flew some miles south of the site, not over it," I told him. "I doubt we were noticed from the ground." I leaned forward in my chair. "I think the time for sitting around and talking is over, Arriaga."

"I am told the radioactive missile, if it truly exists, could soon fly over Baja California and perhaps the U.S. So said our director, who was briefed by your intelligence people."

"The way I see it, Arriaga, our immediate problem is to get out there on the ground, close enough to confirm two suppositions. One: the Pluto missile actually is out there. And, two: whether the Joiners are on site. If the missile is there, and the Joiners are not, then it's a matter of taking the missile out by the best means possible to—"

"We have such means, *Coronel*."

"As have we, *Señor*."

"But, *amigo*, this is Mexican territory. Mexicans will do this thing."

"I assume our people have called your people for permission for possible action." I pondered a moment. "We have the capability, Arriaga. Your assets are—"

"You are aware of our Northern Border Response Force? We have leased twenty-U.S. Army Huey helicopters."

"Like those we saw at the airport?"

"*Si*. They are part of the force based here in Hermosillo. Their purpose is to attack drug smugglers at transfer points in Northern Mexico. Each helicopter carries four armed troopers. Unless there are anti-aircraft weapons out there at the suspected launch site, our helicopter assault will—"

I shook my head. "If Joiner and his wife are out there, Arriaga, and get killed by a Mexican helicopter assault, then you will have a problem of international proportions on your hands. Another ball of wax, entirely."

"Ball of wax?"

"*Bala de cera*," Laura offered. "Hell, Arriaga, *una problema diferente*."

"*Gracias, Señora*." He turned back to me. "Tonight, you may find a visit to one of our *cantinas* to be of unusual interest. The *Cantina Culebra Roja*."

"The Red Snake Canteen." Laura gave me a dismissive glance. Damned smart-ass.

"It is the place visited almost every night by Gaspar Diaz."

He threw me with that one. "Who the hell is Gaspar Diaz?"

"He was the foreman of the Mexican workers who built that site in the desert. SSV agents have tried three times to get him to talk. The third questioner was, I am sorry to say, inept. And now Diaz distrusts friendly Mexicans." Arriaga smiled benignly. I have been waiting for just this chance. A seemingly *ingenuo*—"

I glanced at Laura.

"Naïve," she translated.

"*Si*, a 'naïve,' but clever *gringo*. A, shall we say, friendly and *generoso* person Diaz wants to impress. You see my plan?" The SSV agent looked at his watch. "We must leave."

Laura and I rose with him, but he frowned at her. "My respect, *Señora,* but we are going where a woman of your...station would not be welcome."

"Agent Arriaga," Laura said icily, "I am a captain in the United States Air Force on assignment. I go where I have to go. Also, the colonel's Spanish isn't worth a lead peso."

They stared at each other. Arriaga blinked. And shrugged. "On your own responsibility, *Señora Capitan.* Come, I have an auto."

He had a Chevy, born-again from a Hertz clearance sale. The remains of the yellow and black bumper sticker still read -*RTZ.* Using this battered vehicle was not a bad move, I realized, as Arriaga drove us into a truly lousy part of town. The narrow street was splashed with garish neon signage, and the whole length of it smelled of cooking grease and decay. A scatter of scruffy-looking locals ambled along dirt sidewalks. Definitely not a standard tourist beat.

Which I mentioned to Arriaga.

"That is so, but a few *touristas* do come here for the local flavor and, ah, charm. Among them tonight: you. There." He pointed at a drab cement-faced building wedged between taller structures that appeared to be run-down apartment houses. "There it is."

A coil of luminescent scarlet neon over the entrance passed for a Red Snake sign. But we didn't stop until our chauffeur pulled the Chevy around the next corner.

"I wouldn't park even this thing here," I told him. "There's not a single streetlight."

"I stay with the auto, *Coronel.* You and the *señora* must go in there without me. In that place, they can smell SSV."

"How do we find this Diaz guy?"

"He is a large man with one ear badly twisted. How do you say..?"

"Cauliflowered," Laura offered from the back seat.

"Ah, cauliflower. And be generous with drinks. The *touristas* are sometimes resented, but not when they buy. I wait for you here."

When we stepped out on the hard-packed earth sidewalk, I felt we were dangerously exposed by the raw neighborhood and by the situation.

As we worked our way through a straggle of drunken locals, I asked Captain Laura, "How do you like this so far?"

"Rough area. Man with a cauliflower ear, for God's sake, and Arriaga stays in the car. So far, it reeks of a set-up. That's how it strikes me."

"Roger that." I maneuvered us past a knot of teenagers clustered around a shabby dirt bike. "Except that it's so damned obvious."

"I can go along with that. If Zul-Junnah has gotten to the SSV, I'd expect something more subtle."

We pushed through the *cantina's* swinging louvered doors. And we were assailed by the discordant output of guitars in the smoke-obscured far end of the place. My nose recoiled at the near-gagging smell of cigarettes, stale beer, old urine and new sweat. The clientele was almost entirely male, labor variety, with a woman only here and there. This looked a bad place for a *gringo* and especially not healthy at all for his *gringa*.

20.

Laura's comparatively classy appearance in the Red Snake provoked a sudden lull in the jabber among the scatter of tables and at the bar along the left wall of the stuffy little boozery. As we walked on in, the silence gave way to a rising fanfare of whistles and obviously ribald comment. Every nerve twanging, I swept the smoke-choked place for big men, as Gaspar Diaz had been described Among the generally smaller local clientele, I spotted six. With Laura close beside me, we strolled most of the cantina's length before we found an empty table near a scruffy guitar trio.

When we plunked down, several men at the bar stared over their shoulders in obvious amusement. One of them, a squat guy with a ragged red mustache, slid off his stool and wobbled over, his beer bottle waving perilously. On my rickety chair, I tensed. Surprise was the vital half of any fight.

"Eh, *Señor, Señora,* you wait for *el camarero,* you wait a long time!" He broke into raucous laughter and reeled back to the bar.

"What was that all about?"

Laura gave me a quirky smile. "It's self-service."

"Oh. What can I get you?"

"Something in a bottle, and make sure you see the bartender take off a virgin cap."

At the beer-splattered bar, I edged into a space and returned with two Coronas.

"I personally witnessed the uncapping," I assured her.

She took a sip and nodded toward the bar. "Check the hulk just past the guy you elbowed in there next to. Wait 'til he turns this way. There. See his ear?"

"I'll be damned. Could be our boy."

"Now the trick is to get him over here."

"That's no trick. What's the word for 'sorry'?"

"*Perdón.* What are you up to?"

"Keep your eyes on your colonel."

I stood, carrying the bottle of Corona, and strode toward the bar. Halfway there, I tripped, stumbled forward, and crashed into the man with the mangled ear. Beer sloshed over the big guy's shoulder.

"Oh, God, fella, I'm sorry!" I whipped out a handkerchief and dabbed at his sodden shirt.

The guitar plinks and vocal gabble died. In the silence, the burly workman swung around, his walnut-hued face stiff with anger.

"*Perdón, perdón!* Hey!" I shouted at the barman as I slapped a U.S. twenty-dollar bill on the spattered bar, "a drink for my *amigo* here." I banged down another twenty. "Drinks for all these fine, uh, *hombres!*"

A chorus of appreciation gusted from the crowd. I stuck out my hand. "A mistake. You understand? You speak American?"

"*Si. Poco.*"

Laura's call rose above the resuming raggedy music and bar chatter. "*Venga aquí!*"

The big laborer jabbed his thumb at his chest. "Me?" he asked in disbelief.

Laura smiled, nodded, and pointed to an empty chair at our table. The man grinned, shrugged, and ambled over there with me in trail.

"Laura Gammon," she said. She reached out. He hesitated, then took her hand.

"And you?" she asked.

"Gaspar," he rumbled with a long bemused look at her.

"Gaspar *quien?*"

"Diaz. Gaspar Diaz."

We had the right man.

"Sit, Gaspar. Tell us what work you do," she pressed, with a smile.

"Construcción."

"A carpenter?"

"No, no. Big *construcción.*" He set down his bottle of Carta Blanca and held out his hands, wide apart. "Big."

"I'm in the oil business," I said. "Texas oil. *Comprende?*"

"Ah, *si*. Texas oil."

At that point, one of the more inebriated celebrants at the bar apparently noticed how well Gaspar was getting on with us gringos. As big and muscled as Gaspar, he wobbled toward us, eyes on Laura. *"Bonita,"* he slurred. *"Bonita Señorita."* And he reached out to touch her hair.

Gaspar and I yelled at him and shoved back our chairs. I saw the next five seconds as a blur. She kicked the guy's legs out from under him and double-fisted the back of his neck as he crumpled to the floor.

Silence. Then a huge cheer. I gathered she had just felled one of the Red Snake's most obnoxious clients.

She watched him lurch to his feet and hobble back to the bar. Then she turned to me. "You were saying, darling...?"

"Uh huh." My God, she'd done that without leaving her chair... What the hell *had* I been talking about? Oh, yeah. "You ever work in the oil business, Gaspar?"

Diaz frowned, and Laura translated that for him.

"Ah, *si*. We build one out in the Sonora. Big place."

"Many buildings?" I pressed.

"Si, many."

"What is the largest building you have worked on?"

Laura translated. Diaz scowled in concentration, then answered in a burst of Spanish.

"Hotel Buena Vista in Mexico City," she told me. "After the earthquake."

"No, no. Tell him I mean buildings in the oil business."

She translated that, and Diaz's deep-set eyes above purple pouches took on an interested glitter.

"La Barraca," he said.

"Barracks?" Laura shrugged. "Where? Out there in the desert?"

"Si. Grande barraca. Big, big."

"Ask him how many men slept in that building."

She fired Spanish at him, and he looked stunned as he answered.

"He says he doesn't know. When only the walls and roof were finished, he and his crew were fired. The roof was hard to do, he says, because it was high, and there was no second floor."

"No second floor? Ask him about that."

She turned back to Diaz, translated then told me, "He says no, no second floor. He and his crew put up only the building's shell. Then all the Mexicans were paid and trucked out of there."

"*Lac barraca, Señor,*" Diaz put in, "*muy débil. Poco sólido.*"

"It's what?"

"Flimsy, Steve."

"*Señora...*" Diaz said tentatively...Then he burst into what sounded like earnest pleading.

"He says he and his men didn't want to build something halfway, then leave it. That's not their way. For you, they would do finished work."

I gave Diaz a reassuring nod and smile. "I'm sure you do good work. How can I get in touch with you?"

Laura translated and Diaz offered a phone number. I made a show of writing it on the back of a card from my wallet. "*Muchas gracias,*" I said. And he walked back to the bar.

We finished our beers, then I stood. "Come on, Laura, let's get out of here."

We walked out then hurried along the packed-earth sidewalk, back toward where I hoped Arriaga's Chevy still waited for us.

"Diaz and his crew weren't building any barracks," I said as we strode past a group of suggestively whistling teenagers clustered around a dirt bike. "They were building a stage set. I'd bet a year's pay that big barn conceals a launching ramp."

"But we aren't sure, Steve. And we have to be."

"Yeah, that we do."

The Chevy still crouched in the side street's deep shadows. "Mission accomplished?" Arriaga asked like a schoolboy participating in a Halloween prank.

I buckled my seat belt. Laura sank into the back seat with a sigh.

"*¿Problema?*" Arriaga asked her.

"Only for a barfly with a new limp," she said.

"*¿Que?*"

"We found Diaz," I told him. "The Mexican laborers built what they think is an oil exploration site with a big two-story barracks. Got the walls up and the roof on, Diaz said. Then before they could build the second floor, they were sent packing."

"A two-story building with no second floor?" Arriaga fired up his old Chevy, and we headed back toward bright lights.

"Could be cover for a launching rack," I said. "But we've got to be sure. You don't want to flatten the place then find out you've made a helicopter assault on a storage barn."

"So how"

"By going in there."

"And how do you plan to do that, *amigo?*"

"I'll think of something." I was purposely vague. I already knew what I was going to do.

"Need I point out, *Coronel*, that if what your intelligence services believe is out there truly does exist, it is a Mexican problem."

"Mexico is not projected as the cruise missile's probable target, Arriaga." Were we sliding into a jurisdictional dispute over this?

He nodded. "But Mexico is where the *problema* exists. You realize, of course, *un lio de mil demonios* that will—"

"The what?"

"'A hell of a mess,'" Laura muttered from the rear seat in a tone that told me she didn't like being relegated back there.

"*Si,* a mess." Arriaga agreed. "You realize, of course, the hell that would result if the missile does launch from here? Our three heads, *Coronel* and *Capitan*, would surely roll together down this fine Boulevard Augustin de Vildosola."

We rode in silence for a block, then I said, "I'd feel a lot better about all this if you would supply us with personal armament. I believe that is part of our interservice agreement."

Arriaga nodded, without enthusiasm.

"Something maybe with at least a fourteen-shot magazine."

"I do not like what I hear. But, as you say, it is part of the agreement."

"And hold off the helicopter assault, You hear me? Hold it off until we verify what's out there."

"And how long will that take, *amigo?*"

"Give us forty-eight hours."

Arriaga shook his head slowly. "*Audacia,*" he muttered.

"Damned right. When can you get the armament to us?"

"Tomorrow morning. In your room at nine." The Mexican agent swung the wheel, and we rolled into the hotel driveway.

I reached for the door release and felt Arriga's fingers close around my left wrist. "There is much at stake, *Coronel*. We all three know that. You have your forty-eight hours. Forty-eight only. Then we attack."

I pulled free. "You crafty bastard, you've been planning to attack all along, haven't you?"

"*Coronel,* if the missile is launched against the United States from Mexican soil, we will be held accountable. Such will be far worse than the loss of an American life or two in stopping it. *Comprende?*"

"Yes, I do. Let's hope the joint intelligence window estimate is accurate."

***

"He has a point," Laura said, as we walked into our room. No surprise visitor this time.

We were alone, and again I felt the oddness of our situation. A married couple cover between colonel and captain, two AFOSI agents with a still rough teamwork approach to what was growing into an international crisis.

"I'm not one hundred percent sold on Arriaga, nor on Mexican helicopter force efficiency, Laura. And I'm not sold at all on the CIA's 'several-weeks-window' estimate before a possible launch."

"This whole situation is made up of imponderables." She dropped her handbag on the bed nearest the windows. Then she swung around to face me. "We have to go out there, don't we?"

"*I* do."

"Damn it, Colonel! We are a *team*. General Madden himself selected me to be part of it. Why else do you think I'm here?"

"Window dressing?" I grinned. Anger flamed her cheeks.

"*That,* Colonel, is totally uncalled for!" She grabbed her suitcase and stalked into the bathroom, shutting the door with an in-my-face thud.

Maybe I'd handled her implied sidelining with less than diplomacy, but God knew what I would run into tomorrow out in the Sonora..

She emerged blank-faced in her green-striped pajamas and didn't say a damned word to me. When I came out of the bathroom, the room was dark. I tripped over my own luggage, then fumbled to my solitary bed. I lay there, staring up at the ceiling as my eyes adjusted to the gloom — the room's and my own.

I could tell by her rapid breathing she wasn't asleep. Then her voice came out of the darkness, low and purposeful. "Do you have any idea what my duty assignment has been for the past eight months?"

"No."

"You haven't even asked."

"It isn't my business."

"It is now. For the past month, I haven't been at my personnel evaluations assignment in D.C. I've been at Hurlburt Field in the Florida Panhandle on detached service to AFSOC."

"Special Operations Command."

"That's correct. As an instructor. I teach Air Force women how to survive, and, if necessary, how to kill."

Jesus! No wonder that smartass drunk in the Red Snake found himself crawling on the floor.

"That's what qualifies me to go with you tomorrow."

While I pondered an answer, she added, "Since your last AFOSI assignment, Colonel, what have you been doing? Desk work for your consultant firm. I'm more qualified to be out there than you are."

I choked down a reflex snap at her gall. She had a point. I mulled, then I said, "Late tomorrow, when it's dark enough to do it without being seen by the sentries... *We* will find out what the hell is going on out there."

"Thank you, Colonel."

"Good night, Captain."

"Good night, Steve." A few seconds later: "No sleep walking, please."

After the day we'd just had? I didn't think I could. And if I could?

"I wouldn't dare," I said.

21.

When Gaspar Diaz returned to the bar, he knew exactly who would want to know why the *Americanos* had called him to their table. And here he was, nosy Juan Reynosa, the nineteen-year-old kid at his elbow before Gaspar could order another bottle.

"So what did they want, Gaspar? Why would those two *gringos* buy a drink for you? Tell me, old man. I'm bursting to know."

So Diaz told him, almost word-for-word, relishing the attention even of this juvenile bar-fly. And as he gabbed away, he saw the two at their table push back their chairs and walk out.

"*Adiós, amigo*" said young Juan Reynosa, and he turned toward the door.

Diaz gave him a hard look. "I tell you all that the big *Americano* asks me about, and my chance to work for him, and all you say is *adiós?*"

"Hard day," Juan grumped. "It catches up with me."

"So early?" Diaz gave Juan a yellow-toothed grin. "The young cannot keep up with the old? Or does an eager *señorita* wait?"

Juan grinned. "You are right, old man."

"About not keeping up, or about keeping *it* up?"

A burst of laughter rolled down the bar. Juan clapped Diaz on the shoulder. "See you *mañana*."

***

Juan had to get out of here before the two *Americanos* were lost in the darkness or got into an automobile. He pushed through the swinging doors, peered right then left. *Si!* There they were, walking fast. He rushed to his parked dirt bike. "Get back," he told the kids clustered around it. He ran his eyes over the travel-worn Kawasaki, gave the oldest a few *pesos*. "You did well. *Gracias.*"

He straddled the bike. The engine sputtered to life, and with the bike's light off, he rode slowly along the street, well behind the striding *Americano* couple. When they turned into a side street and walked out of sight. He stopped, uncertain...

Then he heard doors slam and saw the glow of headlights. He held his breath.

An automobile pulled into the main street. To his relief, the car turned away from him. He powered up his idling bike and trailed them a half block behind, his headlight off.

The scar-faced *Árabe jefe* at the desert drilling site could pay extra tonight. Maybe more than he pays me every two weeks for driving out there with the van load of food and whatever comes to his Hermosillo post office box.

"And extra money," the big scarred *jefe* promised, "for what you might hear of this place. But if you ever lie to me to make money, you will not leave this valley alive."

With that warning always in his mind, Juan watched news on his ancient TV, scoured the papers, then bumped into big-mouth Gaspar Diaz, who had worked out there. Diaz babbled a lot of words, but none of value. Until tonight. The *Americanos* had encouraged Diaz to talk about the construction work there, and that was all they talked about. Surely the *jefe* would find that worth money.

As he followed the Chevy's taillights into the Boulevard Rosales, Juan tingled in anticipation. The scarred *jefe* will be even more generous when I tell him of the two *Americanos* themselves.

He smiled to himself. Revenge, in a way. I do not love people in the north. Before the *Americano* chemical factory came to our town on the border near Nogales, there had been little work. But we had clean air and water. Then the factory came. Lots of jobs, but the air stank and the water was poison. When my goat would not drink from the canal behind our house, I kissed everyone goodbye, walked to the dusty main road and begged a ride on a Pemex truck to Hermosillo. All because of *Americanos*.

Working for the grocery wholesaler does not pay much. But I get to drive the Mitsubishi delivery truck. Luck brought me the bi-weekly deliveries out in the Sonora. And from the top man out there comes the monthly *cohecho,* the money to keep my eyes and ears open for anything that could interest the *jefe.* This extra money got me this dirt bike, battered but it runs.

The Chevy drove straight up Rosales to where it became the Boulevard Rodriguez, then around its eastward sweep where the name changed again. Now Juan guided the Kawasaki along the Boulevard Francisco Eusebio Kino in a plusher part of town.

He glued his eyes to the Chevy four cars ahead, but easy enough to track if he pulled close to the curb or shifted to the centerline.

Then a panel truck pushed past and edged back into line. Juan veered to the right edge of the lane. And he slapped the handlebar. I've lost them.

He scanned the boulevard. Where did they go? The Chevy must have turned off and... Yes! There it is! Pulling up to the entrance of the Hotel America.

He slowed, turned off the boulevard and guided the puttering dirt bike to a parking slot at the near end of the building. He shut off the engine, dismounted, and waited in the shadows. In a few minutes, the Chevy pulled away, and the two *Americanos* walked into the lobby.

Juan hurried to the entrance, strolled in and watched them enter an elevator. Then he walked to the registration counter.

"*Buenos noches, señorita.*" She was a pretty one, this dark little desk clerk "The two *Americanos* who just came in. What are their names?"

She gave him a long look, eyes taking in his rumpled jacket. "I did not notice them." Her Spanish was not of the hills, like his. And she eyed him with distaste.

"Those two *Americanos* who..."

"We have many of them here..."

"The tall man, the tall yellow-haired woman?"

"What about them?"

With luck, he hoped for their room number. The *jefe* might be especially generous to know that.

"I have a message for them."

"Leave it with me, and I will see that it reaches them."

He was pushing too hard. He could see that in her eyes. Better get out of here before this becomes something she might report.

"Forget it. *Buenos noches.*" He hurried back into the night..

In the parking lot, he wondered: now what? In the *cantina* bar, the two *blancos* had pumped Diaz about the drilling site. That was exactly what he should report. But ride into the desert at night? A damned frightening idea. He had made the trip many times in the grocery van, but that was in daylight.

Yet the *Árabe* had told him to bring any news like this *inmediatamente*. Easy for him to order, Juan thought. It will be a long, dark ride. But I can tell him what the two *Americanos* look like, what they asked of Diaz and where they are staying.

What talks louder? Fear of the ride? Fear of the *Árabe jefe?* Neither. Money talks loudest. What I have to tell him will surely inspire a—what is the word? Uh…Bonus.

Juan threw his leg over the Kawasaki's saddle and started the engine. Sixty kilometers to ride. In the nighttime desert.

On Hermosillo's outskirts, he found a gas station with a small store inside. He filled the bike's tank, checked the oil, then walked into the store. He ordered and drank the largest Coca Cola they had, bought four candy bars and two bottles of water. Outside, he stuffed the candy into his jacket pocket and stored one of the plastic bottles in each of the bike's saddlebags.

Now he was ready. He fired up the engine, swung out of the station, bent low and gunned the bike north on Highway 16.

22.

By the time Juan Reynosa reached the westward turn-off into the most remote part of he desert, the rushing night air had chilled him to the bone. Even watching his odometer, he almost whipped past the entrance to the obscure trail. Just in time, he spotted the skeleton of the dead seguaro cactus that stood at the turn-off. In his headlight's beam, its naked vertical ribs flashed white as a cluster of bones.

Now for the worst part of this night ride. He hunched in the saddle and guided the bike into the turn-off. Months ago, the trail had been rammed through the wilderness by trucks carrying the oil exploration materials. Juan knew it by daylight, but in this darkness he was a blind man feeling his way.

For a half kilometer, he pushed through sandy scrub. Then he hit a familiar washboard of rock. He stood to let the bike jounce and buck under his knees. His arms shared the shocks.

Four kilometers in, he lost the trail. The machine's front wheel dove into deep sand. The bike stopped dead. Juan hurtled over the handlebar to sprawl flat. *Dios!* A snapped bone out here where only he traveled could mean death when the sun came up.

He wobbled to his feet. His shoulder twinged, but nothing seemed broken.

In the starlit gloom, he pulled the bike upright and walked it back. He swung back aboard. The engine roared to life.

Through an hour of bone-bruising jounces, he cut through or rounded the ends of ridge after ridge. He prayed the next...or the next...or the next would resolve itself into the notched ridgeline that formed the construction site's southwestern rim. In the delivery truck, this ride never seemed so endless.

At last he spotted the familiar gray V cut in the black ridgeline ahead. As he gunned the bike toward it, a pair of brilliant beams shot down from the powerful lights held by the two sentries up there.

"¡El jefe!" he shouted. Your, uh, *rayyis!*" He'd heard them call him that. He stared up at them, hoping for recognition. "I am Juan!" This in English, the language he shared with these foreign men out here. But only some of them.

He heard the two up there calling back and forth in their tongue he did not understand. The man high above him on the right motioned Juan through the cut.

The rock walls rolled past on both sides. Then he hit the brakes hard.

Just inside the entrance, a squatty man with huge shoulders stood in the middle of the entrance lane, one hand upraised, the other cradling a machine gun.

A hard prod in his back whirled him around. Another guard, this one with a forked beard, stood behind him, jabbing his side with a machine gun muzzle.

"Get off," Big-Shoulders ordered in accented English.. "Move to light." The gun nudged Juan forward into the glare of the bike's headlight.

"Ah. Grocery boy," Fork-Beard said.

"I have a message. For the *jefe,* the big man."

The two of them conferred in their talk that sounded to him like senseless gabble. Then Big-Shoulders motioned Juan forward. The second guard moved with him. Sandwiched between these two with machine guns, he was herded on the bike at idle to the construction trailer. Yes, this was where he always did business with the scar-faced *jefe.*

One of the men tapped on the door as if he knew he had to do it but was afraid to. This prompted an angry shout inside. Juan recognized the *jefe's* voice. He was not happy to be awakened; that was certain.

Inside, a lantern threw a weak glow through the window next to the door. The *jefe* threw the door open. In trousers but no shirt, he shot a hard look at the two guards and rapped out something. Then the *jefe* glared at Juan. In English, he said, "You! Come in here."

Juan stepped in alone. The *jefe* shut the door behind him. "What takes you here at night?" He pulled on a shirt and buckled his belt.

Juan felt the cold wash of panic. When he paid out front for deliveries, the big *jefe* was like a businessman. But now, in this shadowed office trailer well after midnight, the *Árabe jefe's* power seemed fearfully magnified.

"You said you will pay me to tell you," Juan's voice cracked, "to tell you what I hear in the city." He cleared his throat. And he poured out what he had seen and heard in the *Cantina Cuebra Rosa*. In not-so-familiar *Ingles,* his words tumbled over each other. He took a deep breath. "...I saw them go into the Hotel America."

The *Árabe* stood silent through all this. Then he said, "This man was tall with dark hair?"

Juan nodded.

The *jefe* opened a drawer beneath the work table and pulled out some *fotografías.*

"Is he the man in these pictures?"

At this moment, Juan realized the *jefe* was truly powerful. In the *fotografías* he saw the same man who had talked with Gaspar Diaz in the *Cuebra Rosa.*

"*Si, Jefe!* This is him!" He looked up at the big *Árabe.* "Same man."

The *jefe's* dark eyes glinted. Then he dug into his pants pocket, pulled out a wad of *peso* notes. He peeled off several and thrust them at Juan. "You have done well. Go back to the city."

Stuffing the bills in his pocket, Juan back-stepped to the door. "*Muchas gracias, Jefe.*"

From the doorway, the big *jefe* called something to the two guards. They marched Juan back to his dirt bike. He swung aboard. Now for the long bone-bending return to Hermosillo. But two good things: the *cohecho* money and the *Árabe* boss did not ask him to watch the *Americano* couple any more.

As he started the engine, he shuddered. When he identified the man in the *fotografía,* Juan had felt a coldness come from the *jefe.* A chill. Like death hovering.

***

When the two guards returned, Zul-Junnah pointed at the bearded one. "You, back to the valley entrance. And you," he ordered the other, "bring Ilahi here from the launch building."

Everything has gone well, he thought. Until out of the night comes the Mexican boy.

Curse the persistent American! Chicago was a long way distant, and the Air Force man's visit to the flatbed driver's wife should have been a dead end. But now this same man's appearance in Hermosillo is impossible to be coincidence. Only a fool would believe that he, and the woman with him, were here on vacation. No vacation would include their seeking out Gaspar Diaz.

For the first time since he had begun to build this project, Sayyid Zul-Junnah felt a threat.

Ilahi rapped on the trailer door.

Zul-Junnah shook off the cold wave of uneasiness coursing through him. "Come!"

The muscle-bound foreman edged into the trailer. "What is it? What's happened?"

Zul-Junnah noted Ilahi's frowsy appearance. "You are to watch the work out there, not sleep!"

"I sat down for mere minutes. All of us out there, we are asleep on our feet."

Zul-Junnah's eyes were hard as onyx. "How near launch is the missile?"

"One day. Or two."

"It must be ready in one more day. Do you understand me? One more day only."

Ilahi scowled. "Why"

"You will see that it is done. Or you will not leave this place. Do you understand *that?*"

Beneath his sunburn, Ilahi blanched. "One day. *Aywa!*"

"Do it." Zul-Junnah pulled a jacket off the chair in a corner of the office. "I am going into the city."

"*Now? Tonight?* What calls you there tonight?"

Zul-Junnah slapped the photos on the work table. "This man was in Chicago with the wife of our truck driver. Now this Air Force man is in Hermosillo. And he must be stopped."

"By you alone? Is such rashness wise?"

The question nettled him. "Who are you to judge what is wise?"

All my life, Zul-Junnah thought, I am told to be deliberate and far-thinking. Yet those who were so, where are they now? The Iranian Army I served is in shambles after the "deliberate and far-thinking" war. The "deliberate and far-thinking" Hizballah is mired in hesitation after its failure to do anything after the desert war.

Now the humbling blow against The Great Satan crouches over there in the launch building. Ready to trail radiation, fear and panic across decadent America. Vengeance is about to fall upon The Great Satan. One day more, and I will launch the fateful stroke. Only one matter remains: This cursed man in the photograph. Only I, Sayyid Zul-Junnah, can do what must be done: *Stop* this man in the photograph.

"Bring the Bronco here," he ordered Ilahi. Be sure it is filled with *banzeen.*"

"It is already outside the door."

"The work is to be finished a day from this dawn!" Zul-Junnah thundered. He took his Helwan pistol from the table drawer. "You fail at peril to your life, Ilahi 'The *Divine.*'"

***

Ilahi winced at the sarcastic twist given his name. In the lantern glow from the doorway, he watched the Winged Wolf climb into the dusty Bronco. The engine roared, the lights flashed on, and the car bounded away toward the valley exit.

Ilahi stared until the Bronco's taillights disappeared into the notch in the ridge. And he finally admitted to himself: In Zul-Junnah's eyes, I saw the obsession of a fanatic who can bring this whole project—all of us—to disaster.

23.

This early morning in the restaurant of the Hotel America, Zul-Junnah knew the Committee of Three would be furious at his appearing here, in Hermosillo. But who else could carry out this mission? Ilahi? An idiot. No one else out there in the desert could do what I, the Winged Wolf, must do this day.

He sipped his cup of watery Western coffee, head down between sips, eyes on the English language newspaper bought in the lobby, a newspaper he pretended to read.

Where is the American colonel and the obtrusive woman with him? I have photographs of him, none of her. And no photographs have ever been taken of me...except by the SAVAK when I was arrested during the revolt against the Shah. But that was more than ten years ago, before the scar, before the mustache. I was young then, and inexperienced, when I did things myself. Khomeini had not rushed to the front to lead his troops in the Eight-Year War. And the American victor of Desert Storm, Schwartzkopf, won that war from an underground bunker. My presence is what makes this project a success. Had I not been there to organize, direct and act, the stupid truck driver from Chicago surely would have botched our theft of the missile in that Arizona bone yard. And the abduction of the American scientist and his wife would not have gone so smoothly, had I sent two of my "oil field" workers and not myself.

So why now, in this crowded restaurant, do I feel—and detest—an apprehension I cannot ignore? The American will come here for breakfast; he and the woman. Why the woman? The tall colonel with the broken nose would not bring his wife here for a vacation while he... No, the woman must be part of this. Perhaps as cover. To the casual eyes, two tourists. But not to me.

Where are they? Since dawn, Zul-Junnah had lingered in his remote corner sipping, peering, faking interest in the damned English language newspaper. But they did not appear.

Had they walked through the only corner of the lobby he could not see? Left through a side door? Never entered the lobby at all? Remained in bed for early morning passion and room service?

Then: huge relief. Here they are. The tall, clean-shaven American colonel in the photographs. Now in dark slacks and a flowered shirt. The woman, also tall, with hair as yellow as lemon rind. In dark slacks and a yellow top. Dressed as a vacation couple. But they are no vacation couple.

They headed straight for his secluded corner. He bent low over his paper. Then they slid into a booth five crowded spaces distant. The colonel with his back to Zul-Junnah's corner.

They ordered, talked little. Was it possible all the planning, all the effort—the construction of the site, the theft of the missile, the delivery of the boosters, the making of the fuel rods, the blackmail to bring Ghavam here, the taking of the Joiners—was it possible all of this could come crashing down because of these two Americans sitting not fifteen paces distant, quietly eating eggs and toast?

In one more day—Zul-Junnah's heart raced—one more day, and the missile will take to the sky. I, Sayyid Bakhtiar Zul-Junnah of Kash, will be known in the circles that count, known as the most imaginative and daring of all enemies of The Great Satan. And my father and mother, murdered with American-made and American-supplied bullets, will be avenged.

Immediately after the launch of the missile, I and my men and the Iraqi scientist Ghavam will evaporate from the desert site. By the time the U.S. and Mexican authorities can put all the pieces together, they will find only the wind whistling through an abandoned oil site where no oil drill ever entered the sand. And they will find the old American scientist and his wife. Dead.

My men, I trust to keep their mouths shut even under torture. And the Iraqi nuclear expert? The Committee of Three wants Ghavam returned to

Baghdad. Their concern, not mine. I will return to Iran—and glory. The only remaining obstacle sits right here. The cursed American who made the Chicago-Arizona connection. Incredible, but here he is, and he must be stopped. Too bad about the woman, but the American colonel is a threat I must eliminate. This day.

The colonel and his woman finished their breakfast and were leaving. Zul-Junnah waited until they signed the bill and walked into the lobby. He picked up his own bill and followed. By the time the cashier handed him his change, the American couple had disappeared. His brain whirled. Had they already left the hotel?

No, there they are. At the elevator, with its door closing behind them. Most aggravating. I need them outside, out in the city where I can do what has to be done, then fade into the confusion sure to follow. I cannot kill them here in the lobby. Perhaps in their room? The numbers above the elevator would tell him the floor. But the room number? If I ask, security will surely be notified. He sank into one of the lobby's wicker chairs. Waiting.

Nothing of particular interest this sunlit morning. Tourists wandered about, grouped at the entrance to board tour busses, or pushed out to the parking area for their rented automobiles. Their chatter and ceaseless milling made Zul-Junnah drowsy. After the jolting sunrise drive here in the hard-sprung Bronco, and now this, he would welcome a—what did the Mexes call it? Ah, a *siesta*. A long one.

Then came the only incident of any note. The arrival of a local in a coat and tie. What made him stand out, aside from his more formal attire among these casual tourists, was what he carried under his left arm. A package wrapped in white paper and tied with a red ribbon. A gift for a wife? A mistress? Or perhaps for a 9:00 a.m. appointment with a hotel whore.

***

No-frills Gorcy checked her Timex. "Two minutes after nine. Where—"

We heard a quiet tap on the door. I peered through the security peephole then turned the deadbolt and swung the door open for Arriaga. The SSV agent stepped in like a guest arriving for dinner carrying an oversized hostess present.

I eyed the bright red ribbon. "Damned late for Christmas, Arriaga."

"Gifts from the SSV." He gave us a tight smile. "This seemed a not so noticeable way to carry such objects."

Or a touch of Latin wryness, I thought. He pulled the ribbon loose and tore off the paper. From the cardboard carton, he lifted a Styrofoam pad. Nestled beneath it were a binocular, two sheathed knives, and a pair of semi-automatic pistols with two extra loaded magazines.

"Nice gift," I said.

"Glocks. Seventeen-shot Model 17s," Laura said over my shoulder. She picked up one of them, ejected the magazine. "Fully-loaded." She slid the magazine back in. "Hungarian-made," she added.

"Seized weapons from a drug bust," Arriaga said. "Thought the knives might be of use also. And that." He pointed at the bulky field glasses.

"Night-vision binocs," I said. Then not to be outdone, I added: "Israeli-made."

Arriaga stepped to the window and idly peered out. "All of this is not to say I approve of what I know you have in mind."

"We're working without a script on this one, Arriaga. And I'm afraid you and your people are forcing the issue." I hefted one of the Glocks. "We thought we'd have several days to work whatever contacts you might be able to provide here in Hermosillo. But with the one day deadline you've given us before your attack on the site out there, we're finding ourselves on a damned short string.

"With luck, you could find yourselves doing nothing at all," the SSV man pointed out. "Each of the helicopters will carry four well-trained *policia* of our Northern Border Response Force. A landing force of sixteen, all trained to expect and respond to anything. And there will be a back-up force of fourteen entering by truck at the same time."

"By truck? They'll be sitting ducks for small arms fire from the ridge." I fought down my surge of exasperation. "Have your people done any recon out there? Do they know how many men Zul-Junnah has?"

"We have been given copies of U.S. satellite *fotografias* that show not more than two dozen men. And only a few civilian vehicles. There is no sign of heavy weapons, *Coronel*. And you, yourself, have impressed on me the need for fast response in this matter."

"But not for half-assed response."

Arriaga raised eyebrows at Laura.

"*Media nalga*," she said. "An expression."

"The plan," Arriaga bristled, "is far from 'half-assed!' Each step will follow the Response Force's standard procedure for a major drug raid."

"These aren't drug runners." I nodded at the carton on the table. "I don't see any communications equipment in there."

"Communications equipment?"

"Some way we can let your people know whether the Joiners are out there."

Arriaga shrugged. "It would make no difference. Our attack goes as planned."

"That's pretty damned cold-blooded."

"Much more is at risk than the possibility of such—how do you say?—collateral loss. The honor of Mexico is at risk. If we fail, *Presidente* Salinas will have all our heads. "But," he added with a little smile, "you do have until dawn tomorrow to do whatever you can."

"*Dawn?*" I exploded. "First you told us forty-eight hours. Then a day. Now we're down to *tomorrow morning?*"

"My apologies, but the timing has been taken from my hands."

"Damn it!" Laura wasn't happy about all this, either. "At least tell your Response Force we will be out there."

Arriaga offered her a little bow. "They are already aware of that, *Señora*. But you know as well as I that in uncertain light in the heat of possible combat, and with you and the *Coronel* not in uniform... I advise both of you to be extremely careful."

He threw us a quick smile, walked to the door, then turned back. "*¡Buen viaje!*" And he left.

Laura broke the uneasy silence. "Notice how much his English improved as he got down to brass tacks?"

My stomach churned. "This started as an on-the-ground recon assignment with a wildly optimistic thought we might somehow disable or destroy the missile. That's gone by the boards. Now it's a rescue mission. But with the SSV in the act, there goes our hope for more time to get the Joiners out of there before all hell breaks loose."

"Yep, and their battle plan that sounds like it's cobbled together in too much of a hurry."

I handed her one of the semi-automatics and an extra magazine. "Wear this some place where the general public won't spot it. And we'll both want to change into dark tops."

"What about the knives?"

"Stick one in your handbag. We'll pick up some adhesive tape on the way out." I hiked up the tail of my Hawaiian shirt and slid the Glock under my belt at the small of my back. Slipped the extra magazine and the other knife into a pocket. Then I rooted in my suitcase, pulled out a black turtleneck sweater and wrapped it around the binoc.

Laura, already clutching a navy blue jacket under her arm, peered at me. "What are you staring at?"

"Your glowing blond hair. Could be a beacon out there, even in the dim starlight."

She gave me the kind of look you give a hopeless child, dipped into her handbag and pulled out a knitted black watch cap.

"How long have you had that?"

"Since my briefing in D.C. before I got on the plane for Phoenix."

"Well, good thinking, Captain." Actually remarkable thinking. This woman is an expert at her craft. And at one-upmanship.

I unfolded the large scale road map I'd picked up yesterday in the hotel gift shop. "Looks like about thirty miles from here to the turn-off from the Hermosillo-Santa Ana highway. Then fifteen or so miles west through rough desert on that lane we saw from the Cessna. With luck, figure two hours feeling our way without lights. Another hour to hike from where we'll have to leave the vehicle. Assume the notch in the ridge is guarded, we'll have to climb the ridge. All that's three hours at the outside, assuming no major glitches. Gets dark here between seven and eight. So to get up on the ridge after full darkness, we leave Hermosillo at sunset."

"We'll want to gas up the Cherokee," Laura added. "Get some bottles of water, and we'd better have something to eat. Gonna be a long time-killing day then a long night."

"All that is priority one," I agreed. "Let's get moving."

24.

In his corner of the Hotel America's lobby, Zul-Junnah drummed his fingers on the chair's upholstered arms. I sit here in an exposed position, but I see no other way. The American must be stopped.

He struggled for an attitude of calm. Watched a mountain of a woman in a ruffled white blouse and orange slacks plop into a nearby chair and fan herself with a travel folder. Fortunate, Zul-Junnah realized. This lobby of infidels will watch her now.

A young man in a gray business suit strode in, asked something at the desk then grabbed a phone. Zul-Junnah studied this one closely. An American businessman waiting for someone?

Another man, this one in ridiculous, knee-length shorts. Surely a tourist…Zul Junnah's eyes slid from him to the sound of an elevator door clanking open. Only a family with two young children.

Then Zul-Junnah's fingers stopped drumming. Behind the family, the American colonel and the yellow-haired woman stepped from the elevator.

Zul-Junnah immersed himself in his newspaper. Let them cross the lobby and go outside. Then I will follow.

Eyh da? What's this? That well-dressed businessman pushes away from the counter and strides up to the colonel and his woman.. Saying what? The noise of the children fills the lobby. I can only sit and watch.

Then the woman hurries into a lobby shop. Minutes later, she steps back out, stuffing a small bag into the large bag she carries. Then she, the colonel and the businessman walk together to the front exit and disappear toward the parking lot.

Zul-Junnah stood, left his newspaper in the chair and hurried to the entrance. Outside, all three climb into an American-made maroon auto, much like Zul-Junnah's own. The colonel sits behind the wheel with the woman beside him. The over-dressed man leans forward from the back seat. Who is he? Do I kill all three?

***

In the Cherokee's driver seat, I twisted around to face an increasingly adamant Bureaucrat Bellingham. "When did you arrive on the scene?"

"Late last night, Colonel. We're at the Motel El Encanto two blocks west of here. We're setting up the command center there. Then the next step — "

"Hold it right there," I broke in. "What's this 'command center' business?"

"Orders of the DDO."

"The Deputy Director of Operations himself?"

"That's my understanding, Colonel."

"Coordinated, of course, with General Madden?" Laura put in.

"This is now a CIA operation," the field agent told her.

"You didn't answer her question, Bellingham."

"Who the hell *is* she, Gammon?"

"AFOSI Agent Gorcy. Captain Gorcy."

"God," Bellingham sighed. "There are two of you now."

I let that pass and asked him again, "*Are* you coordinating with General Madden?"

"I'm not at the DDO's level, Colonel. I'm the principal agent on site. My responsibility is to organize the command center at the El Encanto, initiate the indigenous intelligence cycle, and conduct elicitation interviews as opportunities arise."

"Jesus H. Christ," I muttered. "How long will all that take?"

"No more than six days. A week at the outside."

"And in your view, what are Agent Gorcy and I supposed to do while you initiate and elicit?"

"Cooperate."

"Cooperate!" I bit down on surging anger.

Bellingham shrugged. "You've done your work, and we thank you. Now the Air Force can step aside. All we ask is that you observe strict COMSEC."

That tore it. "Listen to me, Bellingham!" I bristled. "You can futz around with proper proceduring all you want. But you do not blow in here all set for a leisurely week in the tropics and tell us how to run our assignment. Your time scale."

"My time scale came through our Mexico City station chief, but it was set in *Washington*," Bellingham shot back, as if that decision, 2000 miles away, had come directly from God.

"I don't give a rat's ass where it was set! This thing could be about to blow up in our collective faces. We can't afford the luxury of your command center bullcrap."

In the rearview mirror, Bellingham glared at me. "I have my case directive, Colonel."

"And we have ours."

"And I'm telling you CIA supersedes AFOSI."

"Where, Mr. Bellingham, did you get that information?" Laura's voice was frigid as dry ice.

"Goddammit!" Bellingham exploded. "I'm going to do precisely what I've been told to do, and do it how I've been told to do it! You two are advised to comply."

I twisted around to give him a tight smile. "You do exactly that, Bellingham. When it's all over and Los Angeles is cut in half by a band of radioactivity, you can go back to Washington and tell them your paperwork was right. Now, if you don't mind, Captain Gorcy and I have some items that require attention."

"Such as?" Bellingham demanded.

"Such as finding some gas for this vehicle. It's about dry."

"Then what?"

"Then we're going sightseeing. Wouldn't it be a shame to come all the way down here and see nothing but the Hotel America?"

Bellingham's flat eyes probed mine and apparently found nothing there to warrant further discussion. He opened the rear door and stepped out.

Then he leaned back in. He looked like an angry assistant professor who had just run up against his first rebellious student. "You could be heading into very deep shit, Colonel."

"You asked for cooperation, Bellingham. We will give you that by staying entirely out of your way. That's a promise. You Roger that?"

"Spare me the airplane talk." He slammed the door and stomped to a rented white Pontiac Fiero parked near the entrance drive.

Laura watched him lurch away then turned to me. "I love it when you talk like that, Colonel. I notice you didn't mention the Response Force's attack schedule."

"Well, now, he didn't ask, did he? You didn't mention it, either."

"Because I'm a good soldier. I don't take the initiative unless my colonel requests I do so... Or if I think my colonel is screwing up."

"You think I might be?

"Not so far."

"Yeah, we're both good soldiers. But only to a point." I started the Cherokee and twisted around to back out of the space. "I like Arriaga's plan of action a hell of a lot better than Bellingham's. The SSV is pushing this thing, and they're right to push it. For all we know, those bastards out there might be ready to fly that damned thing."

I wormed the Cherokee into the traffic stream on Boulevard Francisco Eusebio Kino.

"This is turning into one hell of a situation, Laura. The SSV has commandeered the Northern Border Response Force to attack a suspected Arab oil drilling site where AFOSI believes a missile is being set for launch by a kidnapped American scientist."

"Now the CIA arrives on the scene to set up long-range intelligence gathering, and they want a clear field. You'd think they would check in with the SSV."

"Maybe Bellingham will find that somewhere in his procedure manual." I steered our civilized truck around a slow-moving bus. "You haven't asked what we're going to do about all this now."

She shrugged. "I know what we're going to do."

"And that is — ah, there's what I'm looking for. A Pemex station."

"What we're going to do," she said, as we pulled up to the pump island, "is exactly what we planned to do before Bellingham showed up. We are going to rescue the Joiners before they get killed in the SSV's blitzkreig. That's what our mission has boiled down to."

***

Zul-Junnah followed the Cherokee from the hotel parking lot. He kept at least two vehicles between them in the boulevard's noisy, exhaust-ridden congestion. When the Americans stopped at a *banzeen* station, he pulled into a side street. He made a U-turn then parked where he could watch the colonel and the woman through street-side plantings.

When the Americans drove out of the Pemex station, he cut back into traffic and held his pace several cars behind.

A few blocks later, they stopped at a grocery store. He rolled on past, then pulled into a small parking area fronting a strip of offices.

Minutes later, the colonel and the woman emerged carrying two plastic containers. Water. For a trip into the desert.

How much do they know? Does it matter? When they turn off the Boulevard into Highway 16, I will trail them on that less traveled road, and when we are far enough from the city…

But they do not turn at the Highway 16 intersection. The maroon Cherokee drives past. Then some blocks further south, they turn west at Obregon, idle along for a few blocks then park at the edge of an open square. What means this?

Plaza de Zaragoza, Zul-Junnah read on a nearby sign as he pulled into a space several vehicles distant. From the Bronco, he watched the two Americans amble into the broad plaza. On the west side of the square stood a cathedral, its shadow beginning to creep into the open plaza. Opposite this extravagance to the god of non-believers, can that be a palace, he wondered. A palace open to tourists and locals who seem dressed as office workers? Or an ornate office building, wasting the people's money.

From his vehicle. Zul-Junnah watched the colonel and the woman wander into the cathedral. Twenty minutes later, they emerged, crossed the square and paused to admire the murals along the front of the palace. Then they walked out of the plaza to a small restaurant a half-block distant. A restaurant! They are doing no more here than…what is that despicable expression? Killing time!

How long can I trail them without being noticed? I follow like a flea on a dog. A flea that must bite. The woman is of no consequence. The Americans made big of their women in the Gulf War, but that was propaganda. Women count little in war, and this is war. I need the colonel in the isolated open where I can pull out this Helwan pistol. Then fire a 9-millimeter slug into his head.

More than an hour later, the Americans walked out of the restaurant and back to their Cherokee. They drove out of the parking area toward the Boulevard.

Zul-Junnah pulled out to trail them a half-block distant. What? That warning crawl on the back of my neck. What do I miss here? In the rearview mirror only an ancient station wagon, its back seat loaded with *tifl.* Children. Behind the station wagon, I see only the white roof of another car. And behind that, no traffic. But my neck still prickles.

When the colonel turned into the Boulevard Rosales, Zul-Junnah was caught by the red light. By the time it showed green, and he joined the northbound traffic, the Cherokee was a quarter-mile ahead. He accelerated to catch up.

Now the old station wagon turns off. In the rearview mirror, I see the white car has drifted close. Close enough to know I'm being followed by the businessman who talked to the colonel in the parking lot!

He must have pulled out of the lot. Waited to follow the colonel. Then he saw me trailing the colonel. Now the businessman trails us both. I am in a procession I do not understand.

There is no way I can kill the colonel and get back to launch the missile. Not with this white car following us every block we drive.

Mushkila! A problem. One I must solve in the next few minutes.

25.

W hen the Cherokee turned off Boulevard Rosales onto Boulevard Transversal West, Zul-Junnah followed. And felt a twinge of alarm. The white car driven by the man from the lobby had swung off the Boulevard to stay behind him.

In the city's western outskirts, Zul-Junnah trailed the Cherokee north into the Periferico, the ring road around the city. Is the American indeed sight-seeing? he wondered. Or has he spotted my trailing Bronco and now is trying to pull free?

In widely spaced tandem, the Americans' Cherokee then Zul-Junnah's Bronco then the white car rolled north on the ring road. Traffic on this by-pass of the central city included many trucks, and now Zul-Junnah noticed in his side mirror that one had pulled close behind the white car. An impatient semi pulling a huge trailer.

Opportunity! But the timing had to be precise. Zul-Junnah eased pressure on his accelerator. The white car slowed, and the semi edged even closer behind until it was only a few feet from the car's rear bumper. Then Zul-Junnah slammed on his brakes. Smoke erupted from the white car's tires as its panicked driver hit his own brakes. Then Zul-Junnah heard the semi's tires screech as the truck driver stood on his brakes.

Too late. The rig's towering radiator plowed into the white car.

Now Zul-Junnah rammed down the accelerator, raced clear. In his rearview mirror, he saw a spurt of flame. The semi's impact must have ruptured the white car's fuel tank and jammed the car's doors. He could see the driver banging around in there as the semi driver jumped from his cab and raced toward the wreck.

His rearview mirror's image of the disaster was erased by a curve in the roadway, but not his elation. Now he could do what he came here to do.

But on the highway beyond the curve—in the long stretch ahead—he saw no maroon Cherokee.

***

I kept one eye on our rearview mirror and gunned the Cherokee up the ring road.

"I think we've lost the son-of-a-bitch."

Laura gave me a puzzled look. "Who?"

"The guy in the blue Bronco who's been on our tail since we left the Plaza. Maybe even before that."

"The way you've been jack-rabbiting the last couple of miles, I thought something was amiss."

"You didn't say anything."

"Figured you knew what you were doing."

I glanced at her. An unexpected, oblique compliment.

"Looks like flooring it after that last curve did it." I checked the mirror again. "Don't see him, so here's our chance."

I veered off the ring road into a cross street. In seconds, we were out of sight from the highway. "With luck, he'll keep racing along Periferico trying to catch up with us."

"Who do you think it is?"

"Coupla possibilities" I swung around a slow-moving car. "The CIA may not trust us and wants to keep tabs on what we're doing. Or in spite of Arriaga's scenario, the SSV has the same mind-set."

"Or the people out there in the desert have somebody in town," she offered.

"How would they connect a pair of American tourists with their project?"

"A leak?"

"Doubt it," I said. "Anyway, now we're—what the hell is that?"

Through the streetside trees, I spotted a column of black smoke climbing into the hazy afternoon.

I'd pulled off the main road just after it made a right turn from north to east. Now we drove leisurely southward on a suburban street. That put the source of the smoke possibly on the stretch of Periferico we had driven northward just minutes ago.

I nodded at the roiling black column. "With luck, maybe our tail is blocked on the ring road by an accident."

When we reached the intersection at Boulevard Transversal, we still had hours to kill. Going back to the hotel was risky. The blue Bronco could be lurking in the parking lot, hoping we'd roll in.

"Tea time," I announced, and pulled into a small roadside restaurant. I parked in the rear of the building out of sight from passing traffic.

"Think they might by some remote chance have iced coffee?" She was almost drowned out by the siren of an ambulance howling past on the boulevard. As we walked into the restaurant, another emergency vehicle wailed by.

***

At that moment a few blocks west, Zul-Junnah turned into the Boulevard Transversal, then headed out of the city and back toward the launch site, cursing himself. I got rid of the white car but lost the trail of the Americans. When I slowed to set up the crash, the colonel must have turned into a side street. Now they have disappeared.

Better to return to the desert site than to waste more effort here. He guided the Bronco toward the Hermosillo-Santa Ana Highway. Their dark clothes could be a warning. I will double the guard tonight. Any man caught sleeping will have his eyes pierced with wire. And to Ilahi, the sternest warning of all. Ilahi the Divine will make certain the launch will take place at first light tomorrow or his bones will remain in this land of infidels.

***

At the launch site, Cornelius Joiner was absorbed in his calculations. With access to a computer, Cornelius Joiner thought, all this would be far more accurate. Specific data on the two booster rockets would resolve several imponderable factors. But I have neither computer nor data on the jury-rigged booster rockets. Forced, as I told Ghavam, to "wing it." The big question: will these make-shift boosters provide enough thrust and duration to accelerate the missile fast enough for the impact air to initiate nuclear ramjet propulsion?

No computer. So I sit on this damned packing crate with a sheet of scrawled brown paper in my lap. Behind me, a clumsy worker swears as his fumbled tool clangs off a launching ramp brace and hits the floor. That's the biggest problem here. Dubious competence of the inexperienced labor crew. Young Ghavam knows what he's doing. But this rag-tag bunch of Iranians, or whatever they are, is a supervisor's nightmare.

The booster rockets are in place, secured by much-modified brackets. No way to incorporate explosive bolts into the assemblies. Pluto's bolts were discarded long ago, and the great scar-faced mastermind overseeing this project either assumed such bolts would be in the crates, or the man has no idea what explosives bolts are or what they're for.

So after their solid fuel is expended, the booster rocket casings will stay attached as wind-resistant dead weights. Pluto will begin to slow down. If the nuclear engine hasn't already been activated, that could...

"Doctor?" Ghavam's voice at his elbow startled him. "It is time to make the final adjustments to the ignition circuits."

The Iraqi's tone sounded curiously flat for a man who almost single-handedly accomplished the feat of restoring and refueling the 30-year-old nuclear engine. And the ignition circuits were Joiner's responsibility, not Ghavam's.

As if reading Joiner's mind, Ghavam amended, "I will assist you."

"I can handle it."

"I will assist you," Ghavam repeated, his eyes on Joiner's.

On the scaffolding, isolated from the work crew, the Iraqi bent close to Joiner over the ignition circuit access panel.

"We must make the decision," Ghavam said quietly.

Joiner deftly spliced two leads and wrapped the connection in black tape. "The decision?"

"The obvious one. Do we program the missile not to turn when it is at sea? Do we permit it to fly out of sight then dive into the Mexican hills? Do we even allow it to launch? There are a dozen ways we can—"

Joiner felt his heart pound. "Any of these outcomes and my wife... your sister..."

Ghavam's voice was soft, but it penetrated Joiner to the bone. "Your concern is not for your wife, is it?"

"What the hell are you trying to say!" Controlling an unexpected jitter in his fingers, Joiner spliced another wire into the master firing circuit. Every one of these connections should be soldered and well-insulated..

But in these hard field conditions... and with this conscience-stricken Iraqi at my elbow.

But the man is right. I've given myself over to this intoxicating opportunity to show all the hours of sweat I poured into this bird four decades ago can prove valid. Pluto can rise from the ashes of its political death and roar aloft...Spewing radiation.

Do I want that?

Ghavam wants to kill it right here. Out of the question! Or have me program a fatal plunge after Pluto passes out of visual range. He's willing to chance his sister's fate.

Or does he assume Zul-Junnah is bluffing?

"Cornelius," Ghavam said quietly. "You must listen to me. We cannot allow this calamity to progress."

Words. Joiner spliced another lead into the firing circuit.. I *need* to see this bird soar aloft. *Need* to prove a nuclear ram jet engine can be activated in flight.

The door in the east side of the building burst open. Ilahi pushed in, carrying a carton. "You eat!" he called to the two scientists on the launching ramp. "Eat quick, then finish work. Launch in morning. We need to make building ready. How much longer you work?"

Ghavam looked at Joiner. "My part is finished."

"Two more hours, maybe three," Joiner called down to the big Iranian.

"Eat now." He placed the food carton on the workbench.

Eat now, Joiner thought, for tomorrow we...what?

26.

We killed the afternoon with a tension-filled drive south, down fifty miles of the Hermosillo-Guaymas highway. I hoped this also would be a deceptive move, should the blue Bronco somehow have picked up our trail again. But the isolated stretch of highway remained empty of the Bronco and just about anything else on wheels.

As the sun sank below the western horizon, I swung us around and we headed back, rolled through Hermosillo, then turned north. A couple miles later, Laura broke into my mental jumble of facts and suppositions.

"Hard to believe how far out of hand this whole assignment has gotten."

"Just because the Mexicans are going to attack the place at dawn, and if the Joiners are there, they could be killed, and if the SSV attack fails, the damned missile could still be sitting there ready to go? Call that out of hand?"

"I call it impending disaster of maximum magnitude. And we're heading right into the middle of it."

"Now you know what 'expendable' feels like."

In the dashboard glow, she stared at me. "You serious?"

"But not suicidal. We haven't been ordered to get the Joiners out of there. We were intended to gather intelligence, like the CIA's genius is doing. But thanks to Arriaga, we know that's gone by the boards. All we can do now is try to get the Joiners out before everything goes to hell."

I concentrated on our strip of paved highway arrowing through a blackness of sand, rock and cactus. A glance at the odometer told me we'd driven almost thirty miles from Hermosillo's northern outskirts. The narrow westbound access lane we had spotted from the Cessna should be coming up .

And there it was. A sandy turn-off with only a saguaro cactus skeleton as a marker, bone white in our headlights. I slowed. We bumped off the pavement. I killed the headlights and we sat there with the engine idling.

"What?" Laura's voice was a near-whisper.

"Coupla minutes for the eyes to adjust."

When I could vaguely make out the lane's dim contrast to the flanking tangle of brush and rock, I nudged our Cherokee into a muttering creep on the sand and gravel lane. We wound past ridges and dipped through low areas. Tough driving in the meager light of stars half hidden by a hazy overcast.

Forty minutes into our eye-straining desert creep, I spotted an open area off the lane. I pulled into it. Stopped. Switched off the engine.

"This should leave room for Arriaga's truck convoy. We walk from here."

"About a third of a mile, I'd say, from what I saw on our recon flight."

There sure as hell was nothing pleasant about our hike along gravelly sand in near-total darkness. Seemed like we were doomed to plod the whole damned night away before we...

Laura grabbed my arm. "That rise about a quarter-mile ahead. I think that's it."

I unwound the strap of the Israeli night-vision binoculars, hung them around my neck, flipped on the switch and focused.

Captain Gorcy had cat's eyes. Through the dual lenses, the ridge appeared as an undulating greenish mass against the darker sky. A U-shaped break in the dancing dots of the ridgeline marked the pass into the site. And on each shoulder of the cut, the ambient-light-enhancing binocs picked up small figures. Four men up there, two on each side. A doubling of the guard? Not a good omen.

Laura rooted in her handbag, handed me a flat tin. "Black shoe polish. Best I could do."

"You really come prepared."

"I told you, I teach this stuff."

I'd already threaded my belt through the sheath slits of the remaining knife and strapped it on. I checked my Glock semi-auto and shoved it back in my waistband. Then I dabbed the waxy, harsh-smelling polish on my face and hands.

In her somber garb, Laura was almost invisible, her shoe-polished face dark as mine, as she reached into her handbag again. "You got any idea how hard it is to find women's pants with pockets?" Her Glock went in one side; the knife in the other.

"You set?"

"Check," she said, and tossed the handbag back in the Cherokee.

I raised the glasses again to the ridge. In glowing green, neither pair of guards showed any sign of agitation. Then I noticed a pinpoint of light at ground level on this side of the ridge. I levelled the night glasses.

"There's a guy standing just outside the cut, smoking a cigarette. Looks like he's got a rifle. We're sure not going to stroll in that way. You good for a climb?"

"Ready when you are."

"Here we go," I said, thanking God for my morning exercise regimen back in Florida.

We stepped off the narrow lane and picked our way as silently as possible to the foot of the ridge. Pebbles crunched. Cactus spines speared through my sweater and shirt. I slipped on sand-covered rocks. Barely caught myself. Behind me, I heard Laura having difficulties of her own, but, cat-like, she managed to be a lot quieter about it.

When I judged we'd reached a point some hundred yards short of the cut and its flanking sentries, I stopped. Laura padded up behind me. "Now for the hard part," I whispered.

We began the long climb up the ridge's southwest face. About a thirty-degree slope, I judged. In daylight, with no worry about noise, this wouldn't have been a tough climb. But now, in the desert's silence, I knew the sound of even one tumbling stone could alert the sentries.

Halfway up the slope, we heard a faint burst of laughter. We froze.

"That tells us how well sound carries out here," I whispered.

The stony slope still radiated daytime heat. We picked our way higher through warm cloying air that smelled of dust and some spicy shrub. Through the climb, Laura stuck never more than ten feet behind me. I could hear her cautious foot placements and her hard breathing.

As I grasped a rocky knob, I heard something scrape against stone. Scales? A night-hunting lizard? A snake? God knew what was out here with us in this alien darkness.

I squinted upslope. The crest of the ridge loomed black against deep gray sky. Another twenty feet to go. Laura crept up beside me.

"You okay?" I whispered.

"All right so far," she whispered back.

We reached the crest and lay panting in a saddle of sandstone between low outcrops. Good cover for the moment. The ridge's long, rocky spine stretched southeast behind us and northwest ahead, with armed sentries up there. The pair on this side of the cut, two more beyond. And that guy on the ground at the valley entrance.

I swung the night glasses down, into the scatter of dim lights that marked the false oil drilling site. Off to my left, on the other side of the entrance cut, I spotted a greenish rectangle. A construction trailer with its metal sides reflecting what little light there was from the scatter of lights down there?

Numerous small buildings were scattered along this side of the valley. Had to be worker shacks and storage. The stovepipe of a larger frame building off to the right told me that was probably the mess building. A single bulb glowed over its entrance.

I heard the drone of generators. Out in the middle of the valley, I made out the outlines of several oil derricks. Nothing green. I was sure they'd never burped up even a cup of oil.

About 300 yards straight out lay the site's largest structure by far. The two-story "barracks" Gaspar Diaz had told us about at the Red Snake bar. The night glasses picked up a bright green rectangle at the base of the building—a major-sized generator humming away. If AFOSI-CIA-SSV suspicions and assumptions were accurate, the Pluto missile had to be in there.

I handed the binoculars to Laura. "What do you think?"

She swept the area slowly. "Headquarters trailer there on the left, past the cut. Worker facilities down here and to our right. If the missile is here, it's got to be in that big central building."

"Problem is, which one of those shacks could the Joiners be in?"

"The only activity is in that big barn. I'd say they're working like beavers in there... Wait a minute." She adjusted the focus. "Foot traffic." She handed me the glasses.

I saw green figures converging on the central building.

"What do you think is going on?" she wondered.

We heard the faint rapping of…hammers? Then a tiny flare of brilliant green appeared at the building's southeast end. "What the hell?"

"What is it, Steve?"

"Looks like they're tearing out the end of the building." Then it hit me. "Jesus, Laura! I think they're getting ready to launch!"

"Aren't they opening the wrong end?"

"Not if the missile is in there on its launching ramp pointing northwest. The take-off blast would blow out the other end of the building, maybe bring down the whole thing before the missile gets away. So they're clearing out that end."

"You're sure it's aimed northwest."

"Yeah. I doubt they're going through all this to send the thing over South America."

"Northwest," she agreed. "Over Los Angeles."

"So the other end must be already open, or they'll have at it next. It'll take them awhile to clear away all that siding. Enough time, I hope, to find the Joiners and get them out of here."

"But how can we tell which shed they're in?"

"That's the hard part."

I refocused on what I was now certain was the launch building. One crew kept banging away. Another bunch began to install wooden braces along the building's sides.

"These damned things are tough on the eyes." I handed her the binocs.

A moment later, she handed them back. "Check that shack down there on the right. The one a couple hundred feet from what looks like the mess building."

"See something?"

"I see some green. All the other shacks have gone-black. But that one has some light showing through cracks. Somebody could be in there. The Joiners?"

"Or just Eleanor Joiner. Assume they've got the doc hard at work out there."

The rocky ground under me was rough on the elbows. I shifted position and put the glasses on the shed Laura pointed out.

"I'm going down there."

"*We're* going down there."

"No. We don't need both of us exposed."

I expected a protest, but she was silent. I gave her a see-ya tap on the shoulder that meant stay fast...or reassurance. Or both. I slipped across the last few feet of our vantage point and began my nerve-twanging descent.

Easing down the ridge with as little noise as possible was harder than the climb up. Near the bottom, on a sand-covered flat rock, my feet shot out from under me. I crashed down backward. Smacked my left elbow on the rock. My forearm went numb to my fingertips.

I grabbed the battered elbow with my right hand. Wet... With blood.

27.

I'd never had a broken arm, so I didn't know how one would feel. At the moment, I felt nothing. The arm was numb. If I'd busted it, I was no longer an asset, but a liability, and Laura would be pretty much on her own.

Ah. Some feeling in my fingers... Wrist. I flexed the arm. No major damage. A torn sweater and a skinned elbow. The bleeding was a sticky ooze.

I edged through a tumble of stones to the valley's sandy floor. No concern now about making noise, not with all that hammering and wood stripping out there. A third of the southeast end's siding was torn off. Pale light from inside spilled across the sand toward me.

But I was still in darkness. Down there to my right, a bulb glowed over the door of what we'd assumed was the mess building. A black building. In the bulb's feeble light, I could see the shack was tarpapered. And I was struck with a possibility.

To my left stood the shack we had I.D.'d as potentially the Joiners'. I reached behind me. Pulled the Glock out of my waistband. Cocked it. I felt better with a pistol at the ready, but I hoped to hell I wouldn't have to use it. The reaction to a shot could trap me down here.

I eased along the foot of the ridge toward what we decided was the Joiners' shack. Halfway there I froze. I heard a soft footstep somewhere close. Held my breath and squinted into the blackness. Nothing.

With the shack between me and the central building, I cut away from the ridge and headed for it, hoping the sentries up there couldn't spot me. Made it without any noticeable stir up on the ridge.

Dull orange glowed through chinks in the slapped-up siding. I put an eye to one of them. In the glow of an oil lamp, her hair awry, her blue dress runpled, an elderly woman hunched on one of the two cots. She picked at some gray slop in a cardboard carton beside her.

I edged around the corner. The door was locked on the outside by a barrel bolt. I slid the bolt aside and slipped in, six feet of black-faced stranger with pistol at the ready.

"Mrs. Joiner?"

She jumped up.

"Colonel Steve Gammon," I said. "U.S. Air Force. Here to get you and your husband out."

"You're not—" Her voice broke. "Not with them?"

"No."

"Oh, thank God. Thank God!"

"Where's Dr. Joiner?"

"They're keeping him in that big barn out there. I'm so worried. Can you... can you...?"

"First we'll get you out of here." I leaned over the oil lamp. Blew it out. The shack went pitch black. I took her hand. Eased the door open. Peered into the night. Listened. Generators. The endless hammering. I grabbed her arm. We rushed along the side of the shack, headed for the ridge. I heard her ragged gasps. "Sorry," I whispered, "but we—"

Behind us, I'd heard the unmistakable click of a weapon being cocked. I swung around to see a vague shape loom up behind us.

"*Yuaf!*" a man's voice grated in the near darkness, I saw him raise what he was carrying. I aimed the Glock.

"*Don't fire!*" Laura's voice.

I heard a thud, and I heard him fall.

"A Glock makes a really good club," Laura said.

"I thought I told you to stay up—"

"I didn't interpret it as an order, Colonel." She was silhouetted against the central building's weak glow. "He had a gun aimed straight at you."

I let out a long gust. "Thank God for your interpretation. And your cat's eyes. Mrs. Joiner, go with Captain Gorcy to the foot of the ridge. I'll take care of our friend, then we'll regroup."

The two women rushed off.

Had Laura knocked this guy senseless or killed him? I took his rifle, a Kalashnikov AK-47 with a curved 30-round magazine. Found a fully loaded magazine in his pocket. Slung the AK-47's strap over my shoulder. Grabbed the guy's arms, dragged him into the shack and left him there I shut the door behind me and slid the outside bolt home. Then I hurried to the foot of the ridge.

I took Laura aside and kept my voice low. "Three objectives now, Captain. Get Eleanor out of here. Likewise, Dr. Joiner, if that's at all doable. Then disrupt things, hoping to hell that promised Response Force hits at daybreak."

Crouching close beside me, Laura nodded. The night was cool, but I was sweating.

"Colonel," Eleanor said, "where are the rest of your men?"

"Captain Gorcy and I are it until the Mexican police arrive at dawn." I hope.

"I assume you know what they're doing out there," I said.

"Yes, and I think they're almost ready to launch it. That's all he talks about. It's his brainchild. And I'm afraid Cornelius *wants* to see it launched! Thirty years ago, he put everything he had into it. Then it was canceled. He's never forgiven the government for abandoning what he calls his 'gift to science.'"

Not good. "You've got to get out of here. Captain Gorcy will take you clear of the sentries up there, then help you with the climb."

"Can't you get Cornelius away from those people? Away from this terrible place?"

I patted her arm. "We'll do what we can. First we get you out of here, Mrs. Joiner."

"Then what?" Laura whispered.

"Get her to the Cherokee, and put her in it." I handed her the key. "Then come back up the ridge where we started this."

"That's a lot of climbing and walking."

"Too much for you, Captain?"

"There is the cut, Colonel. We could—"

"With that guy patrolling it and four sentries overlooking it? That's five guns. No strolling out that way."

I watched them fade into the darkness. Only one possibility now: delay the launch and hope the promised SSV force gets here. The question: will the crew keep working out there or rush to save their mess building?

With the assault weapon at the ready, I made my way along the foot of the ridge, picking up some of what I needed for the risky plan I was cobbling together. Now I could see into the end of the big central shed. The missile was in there, all right. Its fuselage on a sloped rack, its stubby wings and tail assembly gleaming in the work lights. I made out two cylinders flanking the fuselage. Booster rockets. Where in hell had these people managed to get those?

The weak glow of the outside bulb felt like a spotlight as I rushed across the space between the ridge and the mess building. I crouched between garbage cans. Listened. All I heard was the thrum of a generator on the other side. Refrigeration, probably. I heard no sign of anybody moving around in there.

I slung the Kalashnikov's strap over my shoulder. Made a little pile of the bits of dried leaves and twigs I'd scooped up along the foot of the ridge. Then I had a further inspiration. I lifted the lid of the nearest garbage can. Held my breath against the sour smell. And reached in. Found a mound of greasy paper plates and pulled out a handful.

At the bottom of the tarpaper sheeting, I found a seam and worked the corners loose. Bent them outwards. Put my little collection of dry debris below them and topped all that with the greasy paper plates.

I'd long ago given up cigarettes, but I found uses for the lighter I still carried. I thumbed a flame. The dry stuff caught, then the greasy plates. My little spurt of arson licked the loose tarpaper edges. The sheathing softened. A stab of flame crept up the seam.

With my knife blade, I loosened the sheets higher up. The flames brightened. The bottom edge of the bone-dry plywood panel beneath began to char. A ripple of flame licked its bottom edge.

I faded into the darkness at the foot of the ridge and clawed partway up the slope until I found a rock big enough to hide behind. Out in the valley, hammering and the squeal of pried wood went on.

I looked down at the mess shack. Once the fire took hold, I'd have to wing it in the confusion sure to follow. We'd gotten Eleanor out of here, but in the launch building, Dr. Joiner was beyond reach.

From here, the fire I'd set was no more than a disappointing twinkle. It could be seen only by someone along the ridge. I'd get nowhere with a hidden flicker. I needed —

The little blaze brightened. Or was that wishful thinking? Then it shot an orange spear up the siding to curl under the roof overhang. If construction was loose enough, the fire should be working its way under the eaves into the ceiling. In the motionless night air, smoke began to pool behind the building and ooze along the foot of the ridge.

With a muffled thump, flame burst from the roof to twist twenty feet into the night.

Shouts erupted from the launch shed. Their burning kitchen was a lot more important than their tedious wrecking job. Like ants racing to control an emergency in their hill, they swarmed toward the fire.

Near the foot of the ridge past the cut, I heard the door of the construction trailer open so fast it slammed against the trailer's side. In the glow of the fire, a tall man leaped out the trailer door, yelling. As he raced toward the growing fire, I saw the scar along his right cheek.

Zul-Junnah.

28.

N
ow Joiner and Ghavam were alone in the launch building, except for the bulky Ilahi, of course. Our watch dog, Joiner thought. Absent only to fetch our occasional meals. There he is, up on the launching rack's scaffolding with Ghavam, peering through the inspection hatch into the booster rockets' electrical circuits. Checking complex wiring in ignorance, pretending to know what he's doing up there. Or maybe thinking he can discourage Ghavam from attempting sabotage.

Joiner had begun to watch Ghavam as closely as Ilahi did, with the difference, of course, that Joiner knew what to watch for. It is Ghavam who can spoil the flight, or even the launch. Rob me, after all these years, of vindication, of my last chance to launch the world's first nuclear-powered missile to fly!

Could Ghavam actually... But Ilahi has hung over our shoulders every second either of us has been up there. And he's double-checking Ghavam now.

No bombs aboard. In effect, this will be an extended "test flight." The much ballyhooed radioactive trail in its wake? Theoretical, but that's what killed the project.

I was never convinced...

"Ready for the lead wire," Ghavam called down.

The final step. At last.

Joiner picked up the coil of insulated wire near the end of the launching rack, slung it over his shoulder and labored up the scaffolding to hand it to Ghavam.

The somewhat demeaning delivery completed, Joiner backed down the shaky scaffolding ladder. Winded, he leaned against the worktable to catch his breath. Some moments later, Ghavam joined him, set down the wire coil, and wiped his hands on cotton waste.

"It's connected," he said, his face expressionless.

"Ilahi stayed up there. And the hatch is still open. What's he doing?"

"He is what you Americans call a 'Nervous Nellie.' Making, or faking, a final check of everything."

"How can he? He's only a stupid Iraqi, a guard."

Ghavam gave Joiner a hard look. Then controlled himself. "He is Iranian."

"That doesn't make him any more of a rocket technician." All this was giving Joiner an uncomfortable sensation in his chest. "Can you tell me what he expects to see in there?" he fumed.

Apparently satisfied by what he had seen, or not seen, or pretended to see, Ilahi secured the hatch, climbed ponderously down the scaffolding, lumbered to them, and gabbled something in Arabic.

Ghavam nodded. "We're to wait for Zul-Junnah's signal to string the ignition wire outside. Along with this." He pointed at the small cylindrical device on the floor next to the coiled wire. "Hand-held blasting machine."

Flames still flared where some dumb cook had set fire to the mess shack. A ragged bucket brigade passed containers of surely precious water from the site's deeply dug well. But the building was surely a total loss.

Silhouetted against the flames, the distant figure of Zul-Junnah rushed back and forth, screaming at his men.

Then he pulled out his pistol and shot one of them. The workman dropped his pail, threw his arms wide and crashed down backwards.

"My God!" Joiner gasped. "He just shot one of his own men."

"Make them come here," Ilahi rumbled in his meager English.

The workers dropped their buckets and cans and rushed back toward the launch building. Behind them strode the menacing figure of Zul-Junnah, pistol held high.

The work force swarmed around the launch building. Hammering began again on the reinforcement of the sides. Zul-Junnah stormed up to Joiner, Ghavam and Ilahi. After a rapid-fire Arabic exchange, Ilahi turned toward the two scientists.

"He say, when is ready?"

"Now!" Joiner burst out. "Tell him we are ready as soon as the scaffolding is cleared."

***

Behind my rock partway up the ridge, I checked my watch. The fire had delayed the launch building's bracing work not quite an hour, less than I'd hoped. Zul-Junnah's ruthlessness had restored discipline too quickly.

Apparently it crossed his mind the blaze might have been purposely set. I watched him call out a half dozen of his work force. They trotted off into the darkness and rushed back armed with assault rifles. And they carried armloads more of them, which they stacked near the launch structure. Then in a widespread line halfway between the building and my ridge, the six armed guys took up guard positions.

Not good.

Crouched behind my rock, I could hear Zul-Junnah's shouts as he strode back and forth out there. He was as desperate to get the launch ready as I was to abort it.

With the sidewalls braced, the crew hurried into the shaky structure. I heard banging in there. The launch rack's scaffolding was coming down.

Once that was done, nothing else looked to be in the way of a launch, though I thought one good wind blast could knock down what was left of the rickety building. Unfortunately, the night air, heavy with the stink of burned wood and carbonized tar, stayed lifeless. As the mess shack fire dwindled to embers, the valley faded back into gloom, penetrated only by the work lights at the launch building.

Time was not passing fast enough. Our chances of recovering Dr. Joiner before the dawn arrival of an SSV assault force were nil. And judging by the progress out there, the damned Pluto might fly out before dawn's light.

My legs cramped. I shifted position and stretched... Ouch! By now, Laura must have taken Eleanor to the Cherokee. I'd told her to come back to the ridge because I knew she would anyway. But now I was having second thoughts about...

What the hell are they doing now? Evacuating the launch building.

A chill arrowed straight down my back. The Response Force attack was more than an hour away, but these bastards look like they're ready to launch!

What the hell can I do? Run out there with the Kalashnikov blasting? Hope I could charge close enough and have enough rounds left—to do what? Rake the missile with automatic rifle fire? I'll never get that far. Those armed guys will cut me down in the first ten seconds.

A stand-off.

And desperation.

A burst of AK-47 rounds from this distance could penetrate the launch building with enough force to damage the missile. If I hit it at all. A last resort? Hell, a futility tantrum. I've got to find a better way...

From the launch building's open end, three men emerged. I raised my binoculars, but the pulsating green faces were unrecognizable. Two large blobs flanking a slimmer one. Joiner?

I lowered the glasses and strained my eyes. With the building's glow behind them, I could see the man in the middle—Joiner, I was almost certain—walked backwards. Backwards?

And he carried something. It hit me. Joiner was laying wire from the launch building. Forced to, by the men on each side? Or was Eleanor right? Was he obsessed with seeing his mothballed brainchild come to life and fly?

Halfway to the ridge, the three stopped. Closer now. In the binoculars' green gleam, I made out Joiner. Guessed the other two were Ghavam and whoever was supervising the two scientists. Another man trotted toward them and pushed one of the three away. What was that all about? Then it hit me. The fourth guy was Zul-Junnah, eager for his moment of glory.

If I could pick off Zul Junnah...Still too far away for an accurate shot.

The big terrorist turned toward his nearby and now-idling work crew. Gestured and shouted something. Two of them trotted off to the construction trailer. In a couple minutes, two pairs of headlight beams split the gloom. A pick-up truck and, here it was, that blue Bronco. The two vehicles rolled to midfield where Zul-Junnah directed their positions. He was building a makeshift bunker. A shield against a blast, should something go wrong in the launch.

Leaving the Bronco's headlights on, the two drivers rejoined the scatter of workers. Zul-Junnah stayed with Joiner, Ghavam and the other guy. In glare from the Bronco, I could see Joiner hooking his wire to something on the ground. A small twist-type blasting machine.

We'd gotten Eleanor Joiner out. Cornelius Joiner was out of our reach. The missile was about to be fired. Dawn, the time for the promised SSV attack, was less than an hour away. But now it looked like the missile could be launched in seconds.

I watched Joiner finish his hook-up. Zul-Junnah motioned to him, and Joiner handed the blasting machine to the terrorist.

God! In a sudden sweat, I rammed the Kalashnikov to my shoulder. Zul-Junnah, Ghavam and Joiner stood close together. A sniper's rifle could have picked off Zul-Junnah, but a sub-machinegun burst from the Kalashnikov could hit all three.

I had to do something to delay…delay…

I thumbed the AK's select-fire button. Aimed the assault rifle above Zul-Junnah's head to allow for bullet drop. And squeezed off a single shot. I heard the distant clunk of the bullet hitting the Bronco as Zul-Junnah threw himself flat. For his size, he had damned quick reflexes, but the slug probably hit the metal before he hit the ground. I'd aimed too high. An unlucky shot with a lucky aftermath of confusing echoes from across the valley. Wild shooting broke out all around the site. A couple slugs spanged into my shielding rock and whined off in ricochets. Probably some wildly firing shooter's dumb luck, but too damned close. When Zul-Junnah roared out a cease fire, I scrambled out of there and clawed uphill. Fast. Thankful now, for the obstructing darkness.

Near the top of the ridge, I took a quick look back. What I saw made my knees buckle.

Amid all the wild firing, Zul-Junnah dropped the blasting machine. Cornelius Joiner picked it up. He crouched beside the Bronco. And he gave the machine's handle a hard twist.

29.

In disbelief, Joiner stared at the launch building. Nothing. He looked down at the blasting machine. Hadn't he hooked it up properly? The thing was simplicity itself, a mini-generator with two connections for the dual lead wire.

He twisted the T-shaped handle again. Nothing. And again. The machine was designed to fire blasting caps, but he was sure wiring it into the missile's system would close the relay and jolt the electrical components into operation. Another jury-rigged set-up, but hadn't he worked it out carefully? Why the hell hadn't the blasting machine generated the current to start the onboard systems?

He'd heard the single gunshot in the darkness and the slug's *thunk* into the Bronco. Saw the big bastard dive into the sand. Heard the scattered return fire as he grabbed the fallen blasting machine and gave its handle hard twists.

Not a sound from Pluto.

Zul-Junnah scrambled to his feet, spitting orders. Then he drew his pistol, aimed it at Ghavam's head. "You!" He waved the gun at Joiner and Ghavam. "Get back in there. See what is wrong. Ilahi, you go with them."

They hurried back to the launch building, Ilahi repositioned the access ladder against the launching ramp scaffold. Joiner grabbed a screwdriver from the worktable, shoved Ghavam aside and labored up. He leaned across the nose of the portside booster rocket, uncoupled the fasteners of the circuit inspection panel and raised the cover.

The red arming wire had come loose from its connection to the terminal bank. What? He had personally affixed this wire as the final step in arming the booster rockets.

He bent closer. The wire's end was frayed. This connection hasn't worked loose. It has been pulled loose! He felt a hot wash of anger. Who the hell tampered with *my* project? Purposely crippled it?

Ghavam? No, the last one up here had been that dolt of a guard, Ilahi. But, Joiner thought, I watched him while he pretended to check the... My God, the saboteur has to be *Ilahi!*

Joiner reconnected the arming wire. Slapped together like everything else in this God-forsaken desert site. But now Pluto, at long last, was on the brink of actual launch.

Zul-Junnah strode into the building's open end. "What is the delay?" he shouted, his pistol threatening both of them.

"A break in the firing circuit," Joiner called down. "Already repaired." He stepped down the ladder. Our big Iranian guard had me totally confused, he thought. Ilahi herded Ghavam and me day and night, imprisoned us in here to complete the work on Pluto. Even followed us back and forth to the latrine. Toted in our meals during the all-nighters... Now he sabotages the missile? Because of his miserable treatment by Zul-Junnah?

"Ready to fire?" Zul-Junnah demanded as Ilahi carried the ladder clear. Joiner nodded.

"Then we go back to the trucks and *launch!*" Zul-Junnah turned toward the building's open end.

With no warning, Ilahi grabbed a heavy wrench from the workbench and slashed it down. At the last second, Zul-Junnah ducked forward. The wrench slammed him between his shoulder blades. The Winged Wolf stumbled, fell to his knees. Then he pitched himself flat, rolled, and raised his pistol to meet the onrushing Ilahi.

The big guard launched himself in a desperate dive for the gun. Zul-Junnah threw himself sideways. The Helwan barked twice. Ilahi crashed down where Zul-Junnah had just rolled clear. The Iranian was dead when he hit.

Joiner and Ghavam stared at each other, frozen.

"Move!" Zul-Junnah shouted.

***

Partway up the dark ridge, I worked my way from sparse cover to sparse cover, never stopping more than a few seconds to fire a single shot into the valley. I crouched behind a tumble of rocks to discard the AK-47's empty clip and slap in the reserve magazine. I hoped my shoot-and-move technique gave the illusion of several people up here firing down into the launch site. Return fire sang off the boulders around me. I'd given up any lingering thought of trying to rescue Joiner. Now I was desperately playing pest, praying I could delay the launch. Hoping to hell an SSV force was on the way.

At last, the sky began to brighten.

Ricochets of return fire lessened. I angled off to my left, picked through a scatter of stones and flattened behind a jagged outcrop. Fired again.

Not far above me, I heard the rapid *dud-a-dud* of the access sentries' assault rifles. Nervous reaction, firing at nothing. Good. That would increase the confusion.

I saw Zul-Junnah and the two scientists rush out of the launch building toward their makeshift bunker behind the two vehicles. I fired a half-dozen shots over them into the launch building. Fat chance of hitting something vital. The wild response fire thrashed the hillside around me. I felt a sharp impact on my right ankle. Probed with my fingers. No wound, only a lingering ache. Rock fragment, kicked up by incoming fire.

As the undisciplined fusillade subsided, I moved again, this time toward the ridge's crest.

The armed workmen nearest my ridge moved backward as they realized how exposed they were. I banged a shot downslope to help them along. They fell back among the small structures that dotted the valley on both sides of the launch area.

Then I thought I heard... Wishful thinking again? No, not this time. I did hear it: the distant thudding of rotor blades. Thank God!

Into the southeast end of the valley roared four Bell UH-1 Huey helicopters. One split from the line-abreast formation to begin a long swing north, obviously intending to loop around the site, then put its troopers down northwest of the launch building. The other three choppers sank toward the open area a quarter-mile southeast of the launch shed.

Above me, up on the shoulder of the cut, a flash. In a flat trajectory, a fireball streaked from the ridge, raced across the valley, veered left, then tore straight for the northbound helicopter.

The chopper stood on its rotor tips in a wild, evasive turn. But it didn't have a chance. The missile slammed in and blossomed into a bright orange ball. Seconds later, the earsplitting *Bang!* jarred the ridge.

I scrambled upward and almost crashed into someone crouched near the crest.

"My God, Steve! A Stinger missile!"

Laura.

"Launched by the sentries up here. Where's Mrs. Joiner?"

"In the Cherokee. I thought you needed some help."

"Damned good thinking. We've got to put these sentry posts out of action. This near one first. You take the left side of the ridge. I'll take the valley side. Work just below the crest. Give me about a minute, then we'll hit it from both sides."

She disappeared into the gloom. I dropped ten feet below the crest and picked my way toward the sentries as fast as I could make it. Over the helicopters' racket, I heard frantic firing. As the three remaining choppers settled on the valley floor, more workers swarmed around the stacked rifles near the launch building.

I checked the sentries on the other side of the cut. One of them suddenly stood, another bulky Stinger launcher at his shoulder. He swung it toward the landing choppers.

Caution to the winds! I aimed the Kalashnikov across the cut and triggered a quick burst. The sentry fell back. The Stinger assembly jerked skyward. And fired. Riding a tail of flame, the missile streaked straight up. It began to spiral aimlessly, its heat-seeker finding no target. High above the valley, it flamed out.

Inches from my knees, bullets whined off a boulder. A few yards above me, I saw the sentries on this side silhouetted against the gray sky. One lifted another Stinger. The other looked my way. I threw myself flat, but there was no adequate cover here. A flashlight beam lanced down.

I heard two quick pops. The light went out. Both silhouettes crumpled out of sight.

Laura and her Glock.

I scrambled up to the rock-ringed sentry post. Sudden firing from the other emplacement ricocheted off the edge of this little emplacement. When it slackened, Laura crawled up from the ridge's southwest side. I tossed her the Kalashnikov.

"Do something about that guy over there! I got the first one." I climbed over the two bodies and dropped into the shallow sentry post.

"I thought I saw one of these two pick up another—"

"Yeah, another Stinger. You just saved a chopper, Captain."

***

Zul-Junnah watched the three remaining helicopters settle. Their doors flew open. The blue-uniforms rushed out and set up a skirmish line. There were only twelve now, not regular police thrown together in an emergency attack force. Their uniforms and precise tactics told him they were trained for emergency operations. And his armed workers nearest the helicopter force began to fall back

He flailed his arms at the milling workers. *"Idiots!"* he shouted. *"Fight or be executed!"*

Scattered fire from the rapidly back-pedaling workers dropped one of the SSV men. The others fell prone, firing back with precision.

"The detonator!" he screamed at Ghavam, who had grabbed the machine from Joiner. Now the Iraqi scientist fumbled with it. Zul-Junnah yanked the thing from Ghavam. Shouldered him aside. One of the wires had been loosened. That was what the man was doing. In fury, Zul-Junnah jerked up his pistol and fired as Ghavam and Joiner dived around the front of the Bronco.

Zul-Junnah jammed the pistol back in his waistband. With shaking fingers, he looped the loosened wire back in place and tightened the retaining nut.. Then he faced the launch building and gave the T-handle a hard twist.

***

Crouched in the sentry post up on the ridge, I heard a rumble. A plume of white smoke boiled out of the launch building's open southeast end. A spear of brilliant flame shot through the smoke. A roar shook the ridge.

Jesus H. Christ! They've actually managed to fire the thing!

30.

Prone on the sand behind the Bronco, Cornelius Joiner rose to his shaking knees. Sharp pain stabbed his chest. He must have hit something when he crashed down. That meant nothing now. The lashed-up booster system *worked*, by God! Calculations: correct. Thrust: adequate... Or was it?

Pluto did not leap skyward. It rose out of the shed nose-high, airborne, but riding the boosters' thrust, its stubby wings not yet biting the air fast enough for aerodynamic lift.

Yet, he quickly noted, it would clear the hills to the northwest. Once past those, it should accelerate to true flying speed with ramjet capability before the booster fuel was expended.

Despite its sloppy initial seconds, a thumbs-up launch.

His stab of pain now extended down his left arm. A wave of heat seared his cheeks. The launch shed had caught fire. Its dry frame and siding dissolved in a churning pyre of flame.

***

As the missile thundered out of the shed, the ridge shook under my feet. My heart sank.

Laura and I had come so close, so damned close. But now nothing could —

The remaining Stinger! I grabbed the bulky thirty-three-pound launcher with its pre-installed heat-seeker missile. Pulled it out of the sentry's dead hands. I'd had familiarization training on this thing, but I'd never fired one.

The dead sentry had already removed the cover from the tube's muzzle. I shouldered the grip assembly. And I tripped the safety switch.

I stood to aim the launcher. Shots from the opposite sentry zipped past my left ear. Just two before Laura's Kalashnikov cut that off.

Riding its tail of flame, Pluto howled out of the valley, struggling for altitude. One chance to stop that thing. I aimed the launcher. Pluto, now almost a mile distant, still flew awkwardly nose-high, riding the booster's thrust.

A loud beep told me the Stinger's target seeker had locked on. I depressed the trigger.

The ejector charge fired. The little missile shot from the tube. Twenty-five feet out, its dual-thrust solid-fuel rocket cut in. On a spear of flame, the Stinger raced up the valley. Straight for struggling Pluto.

A blinding flash shattered the gray dawn. Seconds later, the sound and shock wave hit the ridge. Debris rained out of the roiling smoke cloud. I felt a surge of elation. We had killed the damned thing.

I pulled my eyes from the distant smoke smudge and peered down at the valley floor. Only Joiner and Ghavam lay prone out there by just one shielding truck. As the firing from the troopers picked up, I saw Ghavam roll under the truck. But Joiner lay still.

Zul-Junnah and his Bronco had disappeared.

"My God." Laura stared at the rolling smoke cloud that marked the end of Pluto.

I touched her shoulder. "There's still work to do, Captain. Zul-Junnah—"

"There he is!" She pointed toward the cut's exit. The Bronco bounced out of the valley and swung into the access lane. Then it skidded to a halt.

What the hell was he doing?

Now it careened backward off the lane and disappeared into a deep swale.

Then I got it. A stakebody truck loaded with armed men jounced into view. Had to be the SSV's late arriving ground support. Zul-Junnah must have caught a glimpse of it just as he pulled onto the lane.

The truck rolled past our Cherokee parked off the lane some 200 feet beyond Zul-Junnah's hidden Bronco.

"Clever bastard," Laura said. "Once the truck rolls past him, he's gone."

"Not if we get down there fast enough."

I grabbed one of the fallen assault rifles and we plunged off the ridge toward the access road. No need for stealth now, but this was no easy descent. More of a controlled tumble over broken stone, around big rocks, through cactus stands. When we were halfway down, a second truck roared past. As we raced onto the lane, a third rumbled into sight.

We couldn't see the Bronco from here, and I assumed Zul-Junnah couldn't see us. We dashed across the lane and, in seconds, knelt at the edge of the concealing swale. Down there, Zul-Junnah hunched over the steering wheel of his idling Bronco, staring at the lane thirty yards in front of him.

As the last truck rolled by, I heard the Bronco's engine race. We rushed in. The Bronco began to move. I banged the assault rifle's muzzle on the driver's window.

"It's over, Zul-Junnah!" I shouted. "Get out with your hands where we can see them."

He whirled toward me, eyes glaring. He threw the Bronco into gear. And it leaped forward.

The assault rifle bucked as I fired every cartridge left in its magazine. The Bronco ploughed through erupting sand, reached the end of the swale and veered hard right. In a burst of black fragments, both right side tires blew. The little truck tilted at a crazy angle, pitched over and crashed down on its right side.

We raced along the swale as the driver's door opened upwards. Zul-Junnah's head and shoulders pushed out.

Her Glock centered on Zul-Junnah's forehead., Laura shouted, "Get your damned hands UP!"

The big terrorist glared at her. Then he spat on the door jamb. "A *woman!*" he said.

***

With Eleanor safely in the hospital, we parked the Cherokee in the hotel's lot. As we crossed the lobby to the elevator, we had to be a startling sight. Still smeared with shoe polish blackening. Clothing torn and grubby. All that mattered now was a shower and sleep.

"No need for any more pretense," I said in the elevator. "If you'd rather I get a room of my own..."

She slumped against the elevator's side. "We're both too tired for logistical niceties, Steve. Let it ride."

"I'm glad Arriaga arranged prompt medical attention for Eleanor Joiner."

"And put off debriefing until tomorrow. I feel like I'm walking on foam rubber."

In our room, I said, "Go shower. I've got to phone in our prelim report."

The connection was made surprisingly fast, with General Madden himself on the phone. "Damned good work, Steve. I mean it."

"I haven't told you what happened yet."

"Already got two prelims. One from the CIA, which is missing a man."

"Bellingham." That confirmed what I'd suspected from that column of smoke during our drive out of Hermosillo.

"Correct. The other is from the Mexican SSV. I'll have the sergeant read it to you for an accuracy check."

I was too tired to fend that off. The sergeant had a sweet, clear voice. She had the facts straight, which was commendable for a PIO non-com who hadn't been within 2,000 miles of the action. Both Joiner and Ghavam were portrayed as working under the duress of death threats to relatives. I had no objection to that. Ghavam would be promptly repatriated. Joiner had been found deceased at the site. Heart attack suspected.

Zul-Junnah faced a Mexican trial with a predictable outcome.

As I hung up, Laura emerged from the bathroom wrapped in her terry cloth robe, her hair damp.

"Got to thinking in there, Steve. You suppose Joiner programmed that thing for the flight path Zul-Junnah planned? Or did he set it to dive into the Pacific after he proved it could fly?"

"We'll never know how Joiner programmed it, Laura. We can think whatever we want to think."

"I'd like to stop thinking about today. But I'll never be able to." She handed me a jar. "Try this on the shoe polish. It'll help get it off."

In the shower, I worked on the damned stuff for fifteen minutes until I decided I was too tired to worry about its persistence along my hairline. I dried off, stumbled into my pajama bottoms and stepped into our semi-dark room. At 2:30 p.m., Hermosillo was sun-soaked, and she had closed the drapes. In her robe, she sat on the edge of her bed.

"G'night...morning...day," I muttered. And fell into my bed.

Silence. Then: "I'll never forget I killed people out there today."

"Part of the job. Get some sleep."

"I'm too wound up to sleep. I might never sleep...I need therapy, Steve."

"Therapy?"

"Yeah. *Physical* therapy."

I felt the mattress depress. "Wrong bed, Captain."

"No, it's not."

"You sure?"

She slipped in beside me, still swathed in her robe.

"You okay?"

"No, I'm not okay. I've never killed anyone before."

I reached for her, drew her close. After awhile, the trembling subsided and she slept. I slept, too.

Sometime in the early evening, I woke up with her nestling close, warm and soft against my chest. Now the robe was on the floor. Waning sunlight edged the closed drapes with gold. In the room's hazy glow, I kissed her softly. "You okay now?"

"I'm going to be, Steve," she whispered. She slipped her hands behind my head and kissed me, not at all softly.

"There is a point of no return, Laura."

"I've already passed it," she breathed. "Oh, God, how long has it been since I've been with a man who isn't a bastard!"

She was passive and yielding. Then she was steamy and urgent, teeth on my earlobe, an armful of wild need until she sighed contentedly. Then whispered, "It's your turn, Colonel."

"This," I murmured, "could be habit-forming."

She grinned up at me, and her bright green eyes softened. "I wouldn't mind," she whispered. "I wouldn't mind at all."

Author's Note

In the late 1950s, the U.S. Air Force let contracts for a project officially known as SLAM: Supersonic Low-Altitude Missile. It would be powered by a nuclear ramjet engine, would fly at three times the speed of sound on a pre-set, long-range course to drop up to a dozen hydrogen bombs on a series of separate targets.

Its revolutionary engine, code named "Pluto," was developed by the University of California's Lawrence Radiation Laboratory, Livermore, California. Two versions of the ramjet engine were built and tested. A third design, powered by ceramic fuel elements fabricated by the Coors Porcelain Company — now the brewers of Coors beer — and supplied with piped-in compressed air, ran on a test stand at Jackass Flats, Nevada, for five minutes at full power. The world's first successful nuclear ramjet engine, it produced more than 35,000 pounds of thrust.

In July 1964, after seven and a half years of development and 260,000,000 pre-inflation dollars, Project Pluto (the engine's code name had become the code name for the entire project) was canceled. The advent of accurate intercontinental ballistic missiles had superseded the low-altitude Pluto. Its practicality was already in question.

To reach enemy targets, it would have had to cross friendly territory releasing a trail of radioactivity and an ear-shattering 150-decibel howl.

Though the airframe was never built, the Pluto in the story is not entirely fiction. Dr. Cornelius Joiner and all other characters are indeed products of imagination.

For assistance in his research of Project Pluto, the author thanks the archivists at the University of California Lawrence Livermore National Laboratory, operated by the University of California under contract to the United States Department of Energy.

Acknowledgment

My thanks to the Sanibel Writers, especially Carole Greene, for their interest and editorial suggestions — most taken; some "under advisement."

Other Books by William Hallstead

We hope you have enjoyed William Hallstead's *Pursuit of the Weapon From Hell*. Mr. Hallstead has become a prolific story-teller and this is his fourth title published by BluewaterPress, LLC. May we suggest you try his other novels published by BluewaterPress LLC? We think you would enjoy his other stories as well as this one.

Germany's use of the great Zeppelins in World War I marked the very first time aerial strategic bombing took place in the world. It was a terrible way to wage war. For the British, it was horrible on the ground underneath the behemoths dropping their bombs.

For the Germans flying the great airships, survival became a daily question. Using this historical time as a backdrop, William Hallstead penned a novel of action, adventure, intrigue, love, and espionage.

Another fantastic novel from the mind of storyteller Bill Hallstead is his tale of Rod Montgomery in *Hard Days in Paradise*.

Elrod "Rod" Montgomery (please don't call him Elrod), a Philadelphia private investigator, had thought a visit from the IRS to inspect his home office would be his only major headache that fateful day, until he received a call from a Florida Public Defender.

Apparently, his ex-partner, Stanley McKance, who disappeared with all $20,000 of the partnership's money two years previously, was alive and well in a South Florida jail — charged with murder. Irene Hutchins, Esq. was calling to enlist the aid of Stan's old "buddy" in proving that he didn't do it.

Currently, Mr. Hallstead is hard at work on the next Rod Montgomery mystery.

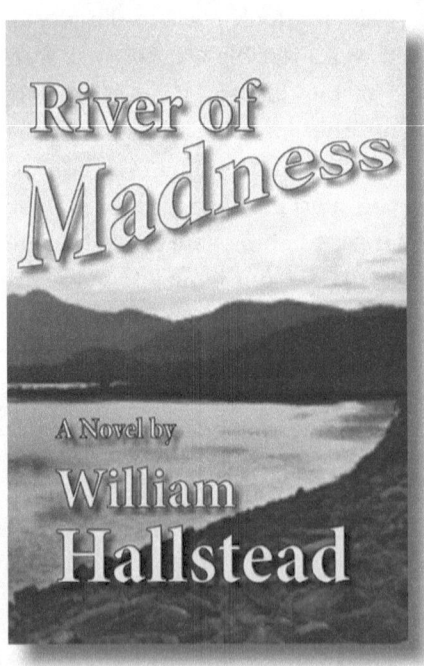

Emmett Durkin stands on the 20-foot-high embankment overlooking the Amazon's Trombetas River. He accepted a science posting in South America thinking he and his new wife, Felicia, would enjoy a two-year period of "unhurried scientific study" cataloging marine specimens for the Foundation.

Then, Theodore Rebner, screw-up nephew of the Foundation's chairman, Oliver Rebner, showed up somewhat unexpectedly. What follows is a contentious period of conflict between Durkin and Rebner that soon spills over into the lives of the others at Station Four.

Check out all of our other titles online at

http://www.bluewaterpress.com

www.ingramcontent.com/pod-product-compliance
Lightning Source LLC
Chambersburg PA
CBHW020841260626
47169CB00003B/1085